DEATH

Before

Dawn

The SEAL STRIKE Series

Book One

By

M. L. Strong

DEDICATION

This book is dedicated to my Grandson Landon. May he learn, love, laugh, and follow an interesting and stimulating path.

ISBN: 978-0-9994810-9-7

Prologue

The rain sliced at sharp angles toward the ground, mixing easily with the young man's tears. His hand, trembling ever so slightly, wiped away the tears. His eyes, a striking deep blue, were red and puffy. Unlike the others assembled all around, he didn't mind the chill and the rain. Matthew Barrett had been raised to ignore trivial distractions. His father had always required a constant state of Spartan discipline, a code of personal conduct that stood as law in Matt's small world.

Matt was oblivious to the presence of the other attendees. He was focused, instead, on the dark muddy hole containing the sharp outline of his father's casket. He stood numbly, struggling to mask his rage and frustration from the people standing all around him at the sober gathering.

The deep baritone of the Episcopalian minister's voice faded in and out. The rhythm of the storm attempted in vain to intrude on his eloquent message of faith and hope as it rose and fell in perfect modulated intensity.

A ceremonial Marine honor guard, complete with shiny chrome-covered rifles, polished dress shoes covered in wet leaves and grass, and bright brass fittings blinking through the down pour, stood ramrod straight to one side of the mourning family. The young Marines, eyes locked forward, awaited their cue to execute the traditional tribute, a gun salute to a fallen brother-in-arms.

Those young Marines had never met the legend, Colonel Arthur Barrett, United States Marine Corps, and it didn't matter—not to them. For in the great tradition of the Corps, any Marine—all Marines—were Marines for life and deserving of their respect. But this special Marine, they knew, deserved a little bit more.

Matt tore his red eyes away from the grave site to look at the friends, family, and guests. They were his devoted followers. A pitiful collection of idol worshipers; some close, most simply tourists seeking fame by association. They huddled together in a shapeless mass of umbrellas and oversized raincoats feigning sorrow.

Then, there was the family. It was clear to anyone taking inventory that Arthur Barrett had been the only success story in a long line of morons, failures, and fools. They'd always fed off of Matt's father in their own way, basking in his glory, deriving a small measure of local notoriety for themselves. He knew theses misfits would miss his father more than anyone.

The professional wax finish refused to allow the pounding raindrops the satisfaction of staying in one place on top of the dark coffin. The harder the rain fell the higher the raindrops bounced. Matt was mesmerized by the effect—hypnotized. Until the loud report of the honor guard's rifles startled him out of his trance.

His eyes snapped up to watch the Marine honor guard as it completed their well-practiced drill in complete silence and perfect unison. Arthur Barrett would not have found fault in their execution; he would have been proud.

Matt looked skyward, allowing the rain to pummel his upturned face as the Marines finished performing their ceremonial dance. With the last echoes of the rifle shots drifting away, a tall well-conditioned officer in his early fifties solemnly approached where his mother sat in a metal folding chair, too fatigued and anguished to stand. The officer halted and stood at attention in front of her for a moment before slowly bending at the waist and slowly stretching out his hands.

Grace reached up, too fast, and grabbed the offered triangle-shaped bundle, clutching it to her chest. The new military widow looked down at the deep blue field and bright white stars on the flag in her hands then gazed up, focusing on the three silver stars resting on each shoulder of the Marine general standing before her. Their flashing brilliance easily pierced the pouring rain. The General began to deliver the words heard by countless generations of patriotic mothers and wives.

"Mrs. Barrett, on behalf of the President of the United States and the men and women of the United States Marine Corps, a grateful nation presents you with this flag."

Matt rode home in silence, squeezed tightly in between his overfed cousin Ralph and his always over-perfumed Aunt Celia. The overall effect of sight and smell made him queasy. It took forever to travel the relatively short distance from the cemetery to his family home. When they finally pulled into the driveway of his modest home,

Matt didn't hesitate. He waited for his aunt to shimmy out of the car then jumped out of the rented limousine. Matt bounded up the porch steps two at a time, and yanked open the front door. Streaking through the foyer and into the narrow hallway of his two-story brick house, Matt turned a corner and pounded up the carpeted stairs.

Matt stepped inside his bedroom and slammed the door, safe at last in the peaceful safety of his rather cluttered sanctuary. In short order, the noise of guests arriving downstairs began to mix with the metallic clattering of folding chairs as Uncle Billy directed the catering staff.

Matt didn't care. He tossed his body in the air and twirled halfway around, landing on his bed in a jumble of legs and arms. Determined to ignore the noise and the people, Matt rolled on his back and took a deep breath. He exhaled slowly, letting his eyes wander across the ceiling. He felt guilty. He knew things were different but that wasn't it.

For a long time, Matt knew his father didn't love him. A strict and starched personality, his father didn't have time to love. His son was an object, a possession—nothing more. Just another family head to count. Matt didn't feel guilt for that reason. No, Matt felt guilty because his father's death cheated him of any chance at redemption. The old battle horse had robbed him of any opportunity to even up the score and maybe—just maybe—measure up to the Marine's high standards.

Arthur Barrett's heavy-handed badgering and strict rules of conduct had driven Matt to tears more times than he could count. His old man taunted him relentlessly. "Don't quit, Matt! Don't let anyone see you cry, Matt! Always be the best, Matt!" On, and on, and on. But no matter how hard he tried he was never able to pull it off. He couldn't rise to the level of his father's severe standards of performance. Of course, now, he never would.

He understood the full nature of his father's curse and hated him for it. Without his father alive, Matt would always be the weak son, the failed son. Death had conspired to place the prize beyond his reach. It wasn't fair! His eyes started to sting again.

Hearing a loud pounding, Matt swiveled his head in a tight arc toward the door. “Go away!” Matt shouted. “I don’t want to see anyone!”

“Matt?” The soft feminine voice seemed strangely out of place against the backdrop of noisy and unwanted guests downstairs. “Matt, honey, can you please open the door?”

Matt grudgingly swung his legs off the bed and shuffled to the door. He twisted the knob and eased the door open half-way.

Matt could see his mother’s outline in the dimly lit hallway. She seemed somehow smaller today and very much alone. Grace Barrett looked fondly at her only son. “Matt, please come downstairs, honey, show yourself. People have been asking for you!”

Matt stepped forward and hugged his mom. The hug was tighter and longer than he intended, but he felt stronger somehow when they gently pushed away from each other. Grace was the product of small-town America. Born and raised in Iowa, her early years were spent helping raise ten siblings. As the oldest, Grace continued to help in the family home until the day she met a handsome, freshly-minted Marine officer attending school in nearby Sioux City.

Arthur Barrett was ready to take on the world and Matt’s mom was swept up by the dashing first lieutenant. Grace needed a little prodding to persuade her to leave home and start her new life. Later in their marriage, when his father’s tours to Vietnam started to add up, Matt’s mom would draw on her childhood sense of duty to family and muster up the courage to cope.

The love had left the marriage years ago—even after Matt was born when she was in her late thirties the old man didn't change. In all those rough years his Mom would never think of leaving the colonel. She wasn't a quitter. He knew his mom would never say it, but she felt set free by his father's death. They were both free now.

"Okay, Mom," Matt said, smiling weakly.

"Let's go down and pretend to like everyone." Matt's mother smiled. She always said there was strength in his eyes. His eyes confirmed her faith in his judgement and his commitment to the family. His mother was also fond of noted how her son was so much like her husband.

He had the same all-American look. Wavy blond hair, crystal blue eyes, and an infectious grin that belied a keen intellect. Matt hated the comparison; he was different from his father. He suffered his setbacks with poise and humor. He was generous, and routinely protected his family and his friends. These were traits not associated with his late father.

Matt and his mother came down the stairs and entered the crowded parlor, walking hand in hand. Within seconds they were surrounded by teary-eyed well-wishers. Most of the guests had been stuffing their faces with a passion, acting as if the food was going to be taken away. The mixture of bad breath and the press of so many bodies made Matt ill. He didn't want their pity. And he didn't need their reassurances.

Matt shoved himself away from the crushing weight of the guests, moving toward what looked like the nearest point of escape. Cracking open a solid oak door, Matt slipped quickly into his father's study. It took a moment for his eyes to adjust to the dim interior of the room. He then recognized his terrible mistake.

Standing transfixed, Matt stood at attention, his eyes riveted to a small object across the room. It sat in a special place high on the mantle near the rest of the mementos collected by his father over the years. One thing was for certain: Arthur Barrett had been an achiever of the first order. The walls were covered with splendid plaques and fancy certificates, each by itself worthy of praise and awe. But eventually, any visitor to this—the most sacred place in the Barrett home—would see the object on the mantle, and stare.

The oak frame was noble in its simplicity. The military shadow box was a three-inch-deep rectangle lined in red felt on the inside to better show off the items contained there. The red signified that his father was a Marine veteran. Inside were displayed his father's accumulated military insignia and personal awards. The rectangular frame was topped by a triangular section that held an American flag. The soft red felt provided a startling contrast for the single most powerful object in Matt's young life.

The Congressional Medal of Honor seemed to pulse brightly as if possessing its own internal power source. Matt stared at the medal. The pale blue ribbon was designed to be worn around the neck. If you looked really close you could see little white swirls dancing along its length, twisting and twirling down until the two sections of cloth joined together with a ring made of solid gold.

Suspended below the ring was the medal itself. Crafted in twenty-four-carat gold, it was designed in keeping with the United States Navy's version of the nation's highest award for heroism and courage under fire. Yeah, the old man was a genuine war hero. Famous even. Turning with great difficulty, he walked to the large oak door and paused before opening it. Matt set his jaw in determination. Somehow, he had to find a way to beat his old man.

Chapter One

A thousand little pieces of broken beach shells worked their jagged edges into Matt's exposed flesh. This wasn't any fun at all, he thought, grimacing in pain. Since graduating from college, Matt's life in the United States Navy had been nothing short of a living hell.

The officer recruiter at the University of Nebraska never mentioned things could get this bad. Matt, like everybody else who volunteered for the elite SEAL teams, was sold a dream, a fantasy straight out of a Hollywood movie that was far from the reality of being a special warfare operator.

Seduced by images of heroic commandos defeating America's enemies after the attack on the Twin Towers using only their bare hands if necessary, Matt wanted the admiration and respect the Navy's special warriors received. Just being selected for SEAL training had been an honor.

He knew it was only one of a thousand steps he must make to compete with his old man. However, Matt was determined to make a name for himself in the SEALs. There were plenty of opportunities in the teams to see combat and maybe even pick up a few medals along the way! Matt knew exactly what he wanted, he had it all figured out.

"Damn it!" Matt muttered under his breath, his mind snapping back to the present. Every time he attempted to improve his situation and get more comfortable, the shift in body position only exposed a new patch of his skin to the mean little shells. Even when he tried to take a short catnap, the tiny slivers of shell continued to torment him like a sadistic alarm clock.

Close at hand, seven other dark shapes lay hidden, each suffering their own personal agony. Inland, a long thin beam of white light flitted back and forth, from the left flank of the beach to the right flank—like a lazy finger, tracing along the edge of the shoreline near Matt and his men. No one was aware of their presence, at least not yet. Timing a movement across this beach was going to be tricky. Matt doubted they'd get far before being detected.

Matt instinctively pressed himself to the ground to reduce his already small silhouette against the sand. The seekers high on the ridge were spending an extraordinary amount of time straining to pick out anything amiss on the beach below. That, in of itself, was strange. Normally guards were lazy, bored, and not committed to their task. These guards were alert and switched on.

Matt's target brief said little about fixed guard positions. He'd been informed the security along the beach was sporadic, roving vehicle patrols that stayed off the softer sand near the water. He studied the group above them on the berm line. These guys weren't in a hurry to go anywhere. The SOBs might even decide to pitch camp and really screw things up for Matt and his team, he thought angrily. He was certain of one thing: his SEALs couldn't advance inland toward their objective until the patrol moved on their merry way.

Matt stared at the luminescent face of his dive watch in frustration. He and his men were running out of time. "If the jerks don't move soon, I'm going to fire them up!" Matt whispered quietly to his men. He knew firing at the patrol wouldn't help matters, though. No matter how good it might feel to break the stalemate, it would only serve to alert the entire coastline and doom their mission.

Matt decided to drop the bullshit dialogue in his head. He and the other men needed to stay put and be patient, simple as that. They were trained to handle every kind of stress imaginable. This is exactly why they sent SEALs to do these jobs. They were especially selected and trained to suck it up. So, suck it up they would.

The minutes crawled by and eventually Matt's left leg fell completely asleep. Soon after that, he dozed off. He didn't see the enemy patrol depart the berm area. The sleeping Lieutenant Junior Grade missed this key event. The men around him had either fallen asleep from exhaustion or if awake, were waiting for Matt to give an order. Over the next hour, Matt drifted in and out of consciousness. His mind wandered freely, drifting as usual to the impact of his decision to join the Navy after college.

Part of the reason he joined was to avoid the post-college decision to grow up and do something productive with his life. His mother had reacted badly to the news when halfway through school Matt told her he'd joined the navy recruit officer training candidate program. Grace Barrett didn't see anything positive in her son's involvement with the military. She was even more concerned when Matt told her he'd requested assignment to the SEAL teams.

Matt never shared his mother's reservations. For him, it all seemed so natural. From the very beginning he knew in his heart he was doing the right thing. He was an athlete and at five foot eleven inches he was an impressive physical specimen. He told her she didn't need to worry—he'd sail right through the SEAL program. He'd excelled in many sports throughout high school and college. So, it was no surprise to those who knew him when he crushed the SEAL physical screening test on the first attempt.

The SEAL instructor administering the test sat Matt down and tried one last time to dissuade him by letting him know the odds of becoming a SEAL. Matt brushed off the warning that it wasn't about pushups and running, it was all about the mental aspects of the course that mattered. Matt listened politely then ignored the advice. He was convinced he was ready.

The SEAL teams routinely screened three to five thousand people a year. The hopeful candidates came from high schools, colleges, the United States Naval Academy, and even active duty sailors from the fleet. From this population, The Navy selected approximately seven hundred and twenty men a year for orders to the five-month-long Basic Underwater Demolition SEAL, or BUD/S course in Coronado, California.

As the son of a Medal of Honor recipient Matt's paperwork was destined to fly through the Navy bureaucracy, and by the time he graduated from college, Matt had his orders for BUD/S in hand. First, he had to attend the four-month-long officer candidate school—or OCS—in Newport, Rhode Island. The course was focused on naval engineering with a minimal focus on leadership and tactics. Matt was bored out of his mind but stuck with it, earning his commission as an ensign.

In the mid-1980s Congress created the United States Special Operations Command. This new entity was almost its own service, competing with the other services for funds and eventually for missions. Based in Tampa, Florida, USSOCOM as it was called, relied on the parent services to provide the candidates, through their respective recruiting capabilities, that eventually became students in the various Army, Navy, and Air Force special operations schools.

While awaiting final orders at OCS, Matt spent some time considering the daunting attrition statistics for the BUD/S course. The seven hundred and twenty students who arrived throughout the year were assigned to five or six 120-man classes. Traditionally only twenty original students from each class finished the six-month-long course. The eventual graduating group was comprised of a great number of rollbacks—students who started in one class and then for various reasons, were pulled out to recuperate or be retrained before being inserted in another class.

It had dawned on Matt as he read his new orders to BUD/S that he might be making a colossal mistake. He wanted to prove he was as good a man as his father but even his father didn't face the odds SEAL training represented. But it was too late. He'd made the choice to join the Navy, and not the Marine Corps, to become a SEAL--and that decision was behind him. Within days of receiving orders, Matt was on a plane bound for California.

A sharp, loud whistle jerked him awake, his body tensed up. He realized it was the people on the berm line making all the noise. He shook his head to clear the cobwebs, how long had he been asleep and why did he always dream about his decision to become a SEAL?

These jokers needed to move on! Matt tried to will the enemy to leave and as if in response, the security patrol, their voices barely audible above the wind, turned inland, moving briskly away from the SEALs' position. Matt smiled. He'd give it a minute or two then stand up to stretch. As usual, he was cold and wet, but the muscle cramps and numb body parts were combining to make this mission a special kind of shit sandwich.

The acronym SEAL stood for sea, air, and land. It implied the Navy's finest were capable of striking by sea or air while executing special operations missions against high-visibility targets ashore. The demands placed on men and equipment operating in this manner was unique. All eight of Matt's men continued to lie motionless for another five minutes, allowing the patrol to get beyond the range of small arms fire.

Matt was the first to move. With a series of deft hand movements, he signaled for the team to get up. He stood and stretched giving his men the non-verbal cue to do the same. Once he felt more limber, he signaled to move toward their objective, the high dominating just beyond the berm line ridge that separated them from the inland terrain. His only concern was where did the patrol go? Did they move along the beach or move inland toward the ridge?

Matt moved up to the berm and crouched down to observe the backshore. His men came up online and assumed their fields of fire. Nobody made a sound; they were cold but disciplined. Their job was to stay tight and keep their head on a swivel, looking for anything that threatened the small patrol. Their officer's job was to navigate to the target, execute the mission, and navigate back to the beach landing site so they could call in the boats offshore for pickup. If everyone did their part this mission would go smoothly. That's why they called it the "Teams."

Matt was satisfied the way was clear and he stood up crossing the berm line and descending slightly to the open terrain beyond. He signaled for the point man to assume his position up front and the team casually shifted from being on a line, shoulder to shoulder, to a new alignment in a single-file formation.

The point man wove back and forth in wide twenty-yard sweeps until he froze putting his left fist in the air. He unclenched his hand and waved forward indicating he wanted Matt to come up and talk. The point man had discovered the footpath their intelligence folks had told them would be there.

The serpentine path in front of them stretched for a hundred yards or more. The SEALs tried to maintain a separation of four to five yards between each man in the patrol. Proper spacing between operators was critical in a small group such as this. Get too close to each other and one burst of machine gun fire or a well-thrown hand grenade could take out half the team. Spread out too far, and the silent hand and arm signals would be too difficult to use in the dark. As always, there were risks and advantages to be weighed and it was Matt's responsibility to guess right.

The camouflaged figures each covered a pre-assigned side of the patrol, staggering their fields of fire—one man to the left, the next man to the right—sweeping their weapons back and forth in readiness. The key to this patrolling method was to move one's eyes in coordination with the movement of the weapon. Most problems would be detected visually. If you were sweeping correctly, no time would elapse between seeing a threat and pressing the trigger to deal with it. The group would patrol in this manner while covering both the left and right fields of fire until they reached their objective.

The point man was responsible for looking where they were going. He focused on threats both close to the patrol and farther out on their intended path. The rear security maintained coverage of the trail left behind by their passage. With the center of the formation looking evenly at both flanks, the process resulted in a 360-degree zone of observation and defense.

The patrol was easing into a natural rhythm. Each SEAL walked in single file stepping gingerly into the footsteps of the man in front. In this way, the point man determined the best path for the rest of the group, reducing the possibility of anyone else tripping a booby trap.

Matt kept tight control over his team as it glided across the rock-strewn coastal plain. From time to time, he couldn't help looking over his shoulder to see if the combat rubber raiding craft could be spotted where it sat hidden in the inky darkness offshore.

The barking of a dog up ahead froze the painted warriors in mid-step. The patrol waited to make sure the dog wasn't barking at them then continued ahead silently. The little island teemed with insects, rodents, and even small foxes—more than enough to justify the dog's behavior.

While they waited Matt took advantage of the break. He pulled the waterproof UHF radio out of a shallow side pouch on his equipment vest and pressed the rubber coated push-to-talk button. Hissing softly into the tiny microphone, Matt attempted to pass the mission's first event code word.

"TANGO TWO-NINE-ONE, this is TANGO TWO-NINE actual, code word PEBBLES, I say again, PEBBLES, over."

Three minutes went by without a response. In frustration, Matt checked his watch then attempted the call again. The radio's batteries were brand new and unused! Why wouldn't they answer?

He looked out to sea where he knew that beyond the natural sea barrier of the island's rocky shallows, there were two black combat rubber raiding craft, or CRRC, bobbed gently on the deep ocean swells. Were those goof balls asleep?

Matt went down onto one knee. His team mimicked his movement and each man slid a foot or two off the trail in the direction of their individual field of fire. Matt started to tear away the heavy layers of waterproof wrapping around the radio to expose the function dials. Maybe the frequency setting was wrong.

He located and then rotated the selector switch to the left, taking it off frequency then returned it to its original position. Matt's fourth attempt was interrupted by the CRRC commander's voice.

"TANGO TWO-NINE actual, this is TANGO ONE-ONE, say again your last. Over."

Matt waited impatiently until the call was completed before responding in a clear and hostile voice, "PEBBLES, PEBBLES, I say again! PEBBLES, over!"

"Roger, your last. Good luck. TANGO ONE, out!" The boat pool leader's voice was subdued.

Chapter Two

Matt shoved the UHF radio back in its pouch and snapped it shut. Those bastards had been asleep! He twisted around to face the lanky point man squatting next to him. "Let's get the show on the road, Duke. We're burning moonlight!"

Duke's slow nod of affirmation was lost in the darkness but his body language signaled acknowledgment of the order. The point man stood up casually, heading once again toward the high ridge above. The small team followed suit and crept silently up the steep embankment Duke reached the top of the ridge ten minutes later.

At the top of the ridge Matt moved forward until he was next to his point man. He could clearly see the hard-packed coastal road winding across their intended path like a lazy gray ribbon. It was wide enough for two vehicles but not illuminated in any way.

He glanced toward his left in the direction where the enemy beach patrol had departed. He thought he could see lights in the far-off distance that might be a vehicle or even flashlights. Matt estimated they were between two and three hundred yards away. They were no longer an issue.

Duke raised an open hand to signal to Matt and the others his intention to advance. Knees creaking and snapping in protest under the heavy combat loads, the team members rose up and continued their tense movement, following Duke once again in a file across the ridge.

Duke quickened the pace a little until he reached the seaward edge of the coastal road. He stopped at the gravel boundary and carefully sank down to his belly. Twisting back around with excruciating slowness, he used his hand

and made a slicing motion across his throat to signify to the rest of the team that a danger area blocked their path of intended travel. Duke added another hand signal resembling a peace sign. This designated the road crossing as a level-two threat.

The alert point man's signals indicated a situation that required very special handling. In accordance with the team's standard operating procedures—SOPs—each SEAL, in turn, passed Duke's signal back until the rear security acknowledged with a thumbs up. Matt allowed time for this silent communications process before passing his command to execute the proper tactical drill. The command was again repeated down the patrol.

The SEALs rapidly but quietly advanced to the road They stopped in front of Matt then peeled off left and right at the young officers indicated direction until the entire team was deployed around him in a defensive perimeter. The SEAL enlisted men were keenly aware they'd fallen behind the planned timetable. Each looked expectantly at their young officer to catch a hint of what he was going to do.

Matt squatted, balancing evenly on the balls of his feet while he weighed his options. Standard SEAL team operating procedures for a level two threat area called for placement of his most powerful weapons, M-240B machine guns in this case, on either flank of the road crossing, the big belt-fed guns effectively covering either approach in case of an attack as they became exposed during the road crossing.

With the men deployed, Duke began his movement across the road reinforced by a grenadier carrying an M-203 grenade launcher strapped under his M-4 rifle. Once across, the triangular formation formed by Duke and the grenadier at point and the two machine gunners on the flanks ensured the team could adequately deal with any worst-case contact scenarios. Matt's real problem was time—this maneuver was slow and methodical.

The SOPs didn't cover how to balance threat level against timeline considerations. This was a command decision, a matter of tactical judgment, and as the officer in charge, he was expected to figure it out himself. As the guys would say, that's why Matt was paid the big bucks. With the full weight of the decision on his shoulders, Matt began to feel his heart rate rise.

The dark night hid many mysteries for the young warriors. The wide-open terrain and dominating high ridge placed the SEALs in a terrible position. Matt saw Duke look back nervously from the opposite side of the road. Nobody was following him yet and he instinctively knew it wasn't a good idea to screw around exposed in the open and without adequate cover where they were. There wasn't even a bush to hide behind.

Duke took his time. Any minute Matt fully expected to hear the enemy patrol returning, tires crunching down the road to their left. Headlights illuminating the SEALs, half on one side, and half on the other side, of the gravel road, Duke spent ten minutes making sure the way forward was clear of threats. As he lay there, Matt's mind wandered to his record of poor leadership. Was he going to screw this up too?

His first test as a leader and as a frogman, BUD/S, was the crucible for all young men aspiring to be frogmen. The twenty-two weeks was now shorter than the twenty-six weeks that was traditionally associated with the ordeal.

After the attacks on September 11, 2001, several weeks were carved off the end of BUD/S and pushed forward into the next training experience, the four-month long SEAL Qualification course or SQT.

Matt's BUD/S class had filled the lodging facilities to capacity. A normal BUD/S class started with close to one hundred and twenty students. His class was an anomaly coming in at one 141 would-be frogmen. It was times like these, the stress of the mission and the dead time before the action began, that he found himself flashing back. He did so for two reasons. First, he couldn't believe he'd survived so much of what the instructors threw at them and second, he revisited every dumb mistake he'd made as an officer.

He'd been a lackluster performer on many fronts. The myth, perpetuated by recruiters, movies and other unclassified references, was that BUD/S was primarily a physical test of pain and endurance. Based on this assumption Matt should have been a star but the myths were wrong.

The BUD/S experience was a subtly designed torture session punctuated with classroom lectures to give the impression learning was the objective. In the first nine weeks or first phase of BUD/S, students were only taught skills that allowed the instructors to safely toss them into harm's way. In the pool, in the bay, and in the ocean.

Basic swimming, water survival, rubber boat operations, barracks inspections, personnel inspections, and physical fitness was the focus of first phase. After several weeks of near continuous activity, Matt's class found itself on the precipice of the infamous Hell Week event.

Hell Week ratcheted up the intensity of prior weeks, did not include instruction or lectures, and allowed for limited sleep periods—usually consisting of ten to twenty-minute cat naps. By Hell Week, Matt found himself gravitating to the second position of class leadership, right behind a seasoned fleet Lieutenant named Mike Seith.

Mike was a natural leader. He was older than most of the class at thirty years old, but he was an animal physically. His poise and calm demeanor radiated out in a way that soothed both the students and the instructors. Mike had a knack for saying or doing the right thing at the right time, avoiding much of the threatened punishment from the instructors as a result. Due to his stellar leadership, Matt's class had eighty-seven men survive long enough to begin Hell Week. The class's first loss at two in the morning of the first day of Hell Week was Mike.

Night rock portage was a violent and dangerous event practiced before Hell Week by the class who were broken up into seven-man boat crews. Each rubber boat was paddled out to sea and remained fifty yards off the Hotel Del Coronado rock jetty until signaled by the instructors to make their run.

Boat by boat, the instructors watched as the students were twirled around by the incoming waves and dumped unceremoniously into the dark churning water. That is, if they were lucky. A few boats were able enough to time the swells and the breaking waves to land on the rocks without incident. But once in a while, things went very wrong.

Matt didn't see Mike Seith get thrown into the rocks, he was still at sea awaiting the signal to paddle into shore. But once he'd landed successfully and was able to get his crew and boat over the rock pile and onto the sandy beach, he spotted Mike.

The class leader was being stabilized by a corpsman attached to the first phase staff. He was strapped down on an EMT board with his lower right leg jutting out at a weird angle. The military four-wheel drive ambulance was backing up slowly, its double backdoors already open and ready to receive the injured student. Just like that, Matt realized he was now the class leader.

Mike had been a great leader, but he'd been so good the rest of the senior students hadn't evolved their own leadership abilities. Matt was the fifth senior officer out of seven when his BUD/S class started. He'd glided through the first weeks of first phase, rarely called upon to exercise judgement of any kind. Then, in the last ten days leading up to Hell Week, he found himself one of three surviving officers. Naval tradition dictated that as senior man, he was responsible for the entire training class.

Matt made it through the famous gauntlet, experiencing fatigue and sleeplessness that made zombies of them all. He barely had enough energy and sense of purpose to make it through as an individual—there was nothing left for the men. They were on their own after Mike was hurt. The class paid the price for Matt's self-absorption. Of the eighty-seven who began Hell Week, only thirty-nine crossed the finish line late on Friday. Matt knew his weak leadership was a factor and so did the first phase instructors.

There were few opportunities to learn during the second phase of BUD/S. The second block of instruction dealt with basic SCUBA and advanced SCUBA apparatus as well as combat swimmer sneak attacks against enemy warships. It was far more technical and while the fitness became more and more challenging the academics and ability to operate underwater were of paramount importance. His class lost two more from academic failures and three men who couldn't pass the second most difficult event in BUD/S after Hell Week, pool competency.

Matt organized the other two officers into a study group to mentor and tutor the enlisted men in diving physics. He had some pride in knowing the academic attrition could have been far worse. His plan likely helped three of his classmates move on to third phase. Pool competency was a different matter.

The test was conducted in a training pool with underwater observation windows and safety divers positioned around the student. SEALs operated in dark, murky harbors and routinely maneuvered under and around commercial and military ships. It was imperative the commandos were comfortable in high risk situations such as a loss of air supply or becoming entangled. It was this fear and how each man managed that fear that made this evolution so difficult.

Matt's own experience was typical. He was waved over to the edge of the pool where he stood at parade rest, his hands clasped behind the small of his back just under the twin SCUBA tanks resting on his shoulders, suspended from rude canvas straps that bit into his skin. He was made to watch the student performing the test in front of him, but he wasn't able to see what the two instructors were doing to the SEAL candidate. The instructors were darting in and out, messing with the student's diving equipment and then moving away. The student's task was to remain calm and to assess each system failure as it was introduced. Slow, methodical gear checks tracing each piece until it was verified as working or confirmed it that it was not. No easy task as the face mask was taped up—the student was operating blind.

Each student was allowed two attempts at the first test. Failure on both meant academic probation or worse—a training officer board review. Students would receive additional instruction and, in a week or two, be retested. Failure meant dismissal from BUD/S. Matt watched the enlisted man, a young guy from Nebraska, thrash about and eventually pop to the surface. The two instructors surfaced next to him, one of them yanking off the face mask and the other pointing to the pool deck. "Saunders, fail! NEXT!"

Matt eased to the side of the pool and placed his mask in his hand. He held down the waist belt with one hand to stabilize the tanks and prevent them from rising up into the back of his head upon entry into the water. Once in the pool the instructors waved him over, directed him to place the regulator in his mouth, his mask on his face, and to submerge until he was kneeling on the pool bottom.

Matt acknowledged with an okay hand signal and followed the instructions. Once on the bottom, he waited. The attack lasted for five minutes. His regulator was removed, his tanks were shut off, his regulator hose was tied in a knot, his weight belt, which was holding him down was pulled off—it was crazy, insane—but Matt somehow felt calm during the entire ordeal. He passed.

When the nine weeks of diving phase was over, Matt had lost another five men. He was getting the hang of head counts and managing the instructors, but he was no Mike Seith. The standard operating policy for the course was to roll-in students from other classes who were injured or who had been allowed an academic amnesty. Matt's class stood at forty-four original members and five roll-ins as the third and final phase began.

Land Warfare phase is where BUD/S students began to learn their trade as future SEALs. The mind-fuck games and insane tests of inner strength and endurance were for the most part over Weapons, land navigation sing maps, compass and then GPS—along with small unit tactics—were all in the curriculum.

Most of the students looked at third phase as a break from the torture and near-continual sense of failure. They were wrong. Third phase was like pool competency times twenty. Handling demolitions and live weapons firing left no room for error. One critical misstep could cost a life. A few smaller gaffes and a student would be standing in front of the phase officer's board, his fate as a SEAL in doubt.

Matt did well as a squad leader and picked up some leadership tips from the instructors who were keenly interested in making the students better in every way. No one was trying to make them quit.

They were all physically and mentally tough. It was time to put their stamp on the young warriors before they moved on to SQT and graduation. Matt's mission pre-planning abilities shined while his leadership and decision making once conducting the mission, left something to be desired. It was a step-by-step process, the molding of a SEAL tactical leader. Raids, reconnaissance, constant practice evading or fighting the opposing forces—Matt loved third phase.

Chapter Three

Matt shook himself to clear his head. Daydreaming could get him and everybody who depended on him killed. Matt narrowed his focus on his point man. *Why is he taking so long?* He stared intently as the two-man point element went to ground on the far side of the road. Then, he saw his point man return to the road.

He lay down and waved at Matt. Matt nodded and signaled to the others that it was time to move across. Duke stayed where he was, looking back until he saw the rest of the team start to move. Only the whites of his eyes were visible on his painted war face.

"They're moving across!" he hissed at the grenadier next to him. Matt watched as the grenadier followed Duke as he adjusted his position by moving forward five yards, creating enough space for the rest of the arriving team members to set up a perimeter.

Matt couldn't see shit. The crunching of the patrol beginning to crossing the gravel road drown out any opportunity to hear movement in the darkness ahead. He blinked a few times and started his visual sweep once again. Then he froze. The distinctive metallic sound of a rifle's selector switch flipping to the automatic fire position echoed in the night. Matt's instincts screamed for him to do something! He simultaneously thumbed his weapon off safe and opened fire. "CONTACT FRONT!"

Caught in mid-stride on the gravel road, the other SEALs could not open fire forward without hitting their point element. Two team members, exposed on the road, thundered across and threw themselves onto the ground next to Duke and the grenadier. They immediately opened fire and began sweeping their weapons to the far left and right to cover all possible enemy positions.

Matt and the rear security were still lying on the beach side of the coastal road between two machine gunners covering the road in both directions when Duke shouted. He couldn't see past the pile of SEALs firing on the other side of the road, it was too dark. Nor could he and the men with him return fire without shooting into their fellow SEALs. Matt stared in disbelief at the dark huddle centered on Duke. Damn it! His guys were all clumped together. One round could hit multiple SEALs without trying. Matt jumped to his feet and yelled at the at the clustered SEALs.

"SPREAD OUT!"

He looked back at the two flank gunners still laying in position behind him. "Let's go, move up, move across!" Matt's words cut through the noise and spurred the men to action but before Matt could join the team on the opposite side of the road, he was knocked to the ground by a deafening explosion. Blazing red tracers angrily stitched across the night sky on both flanks and directly over the heads of the surprised SEALs. The intense fire was coming from a heavy machine gun well-positioned on a low hill directly to their front and slightly to the left.

Matt's team obeyed his commands. They spread out and the two flanking M-240B machine gunners crossed over and set up on the far left and right of the firing line. Matt crawled up to one side of Duke and the wounded grenadier. The SEALs kicked into high gear, returning deadly coordinated fire. Commands and questions were shouted by the men in cool, measured reaction to the enemy contact. Their training had taken over and the young men were on autopilot. This feeling of fear and exhilaration was what being a SEAL was all about.

Matt's numb mind struggled in slow motion to grasp what was being playing out all around him in all too-vivid detail. He was vaguely aware that his men were returning fire. Someone was administering aid to the grenadier. They were sustaining the volume of fire in measured bursts and reloading smoothly. His men were doing their job, he needed to snap out of his mental fog. Matt was aware that a real disaster was in the making if he didn't figure out how to get out of the mess he was in and fast!

Despite his men's initial reaction, the enemy had gained fire superiority and was in command of the fight, pounding them from well-prepared positions on higher ground. Matt was beginning to focus. He ran through his list of choices as he crawled up behind Duke. It was time to get a grip on the situation. Scanning the surrounding terrain, Matt spotted a dark gash in the ground thirty yards off to their right, a ravine deep enough to provide cover. He needed to get the guys out of the kill zone. If they could make it to the ravine, they stood a fighting chance of surviving.

On the berm line, Matt ducked to avoid a direct burst of tracers flying right over his head. He'd spotted a way out of the kill zone. He gave the order for the second squad to get up and execute a leapfrog movement to the ravine. However, his command was drowned out as two dark green military trucks roared out of the darkness on the team's exposed left flank.

Automatic weapons fire erupted from the vehicle as it careened down the gravel road toward the SEALs. Matt choked off his order and opened fire at the trucks. His men on the left flank automatically shifted their bodies around to engage the newcomers. The patrol now formed an L-shaped firing line. The SEALs were running out of time and ammunition!

The approaching trucks spun sideways and stopped close enough to spray road gravel on the trapped SEALs. Troops poured out, deploying to form a second firing line on the SEALs left flank. The troops immediately opened fire, placing the navy commandos in a deadly crossfire.

Matt's mind screamed in frustration. There was no way they could get to the ravine now. The only option left to them was to assault forward and try to silence the machine guns positioned on the hill. If those guns were taken out, the team might survive this action. They could control the high ground and stand a chance of fending off any follow-on attacks. Perhaps then, Matt hoped, he could fight a rear-guard action and move rapidly into the island's interior before looping around to the coast and extraction.

Once the SEALs broke contact, Matt would direct the CRRCs to shift to the Western beach to support his team's emergency exit. Matt jumped to his feet.

"ATTACK THE HILL, ATTACK THE DAMN HILL!"

The SEALs didn't need any more encouragement. The team understood his intent and jumped to their feet racing uphill toward the chattering guns on the rocky knoll above. In a series of short leapfrog movements, the SEALs started to close the distance to their new objective. Their well-conditioned legs pumped hard to keep up the rhythm of the assault drill. Matt continued to belt out commands in sharp clear tones, his earlier confusion all but forgotten. They were doing it!

His men realized collectively that they were better than the enemy. They knew how to fight, and how to win. Matt didn't have a doubt in his mind they would prevail. His attention was focused forward, so he didn't see the men pouring out of the two trucks that arrived behind him on the road.

The new arrivals joined their fellow soldiers and moved rapidly to strike the SEALs from behind. Although the force could have overtaken the commandos, they seemed curiously content to keep their distance while following them across the open plain as they continued to leapfrog the fire teams toward the machine gun position.

Matt was reveling in the glory of his assault. He glanced quickly at the second fire team as his team leapfrogged past their position. He'd never been prouder of his men. They were magnificent! Matt gave the order for his maneuvering fire team to hit the ground.

"EVERYBODY DOWN!", he shouted. As Matt hit the ground, he spotted a flicker of movement off to his right. The spider traps had been well hidden and placed perfectly to cover the slope leading up to the knoll.

Seven riflemen popped up and out of the ground from what had been flat empty terrain. The thin plywood covering their spider holes flipped back behind them. The enemy marksmen poured a withering fire into the right flank of Matt's tired men.

At the same time, the group following them from the road below threw themselves to the ground and began to select and shoot individual SEALs. The stunned and beleaguered team had been lured into a perfect three-sided killing zone! Matt was going to lose everyone.

The high piercing sound of the ceasefire whistle confused the young LTJG. His mind raced frantically to grasp its meaning. The answer came quickly enough in the shape of a bullhorn; it's rude bellowing intruding on the small arms noise.

"CEASE FIRE! CEASE FIRE! Clear, and safe all weapons!"

The defeated and thoroughly dead SEAL trainees did not hesitate to comply with the shouted command. Within seconds the once proud commando patrol was organized into two ranks of shivering twenty-year-old men.

The first instructor on the scene growled at Matt and the young officer immediately responded. He hit the ground in a classic push-up position. The rest of the SEAL trainees followed suit. They were required to do so because Matt was their officer in charge. When Matt was ordered to drop down for pushups, they entire class was required to drop.

"Ready?" Matt shouted.

"READY! Matt's fellow classmates yelled back in unison.

He pressed his body smoothly up and down while maintaining the count. He moved slowly enough for the group of SEAL trainees to keep pace. Once Matt finished the standard set of fifty pushups—normal punishment for fucking up in the third and last phase of BUD/S training—he sounded off.

"HOOYAH, instructor Jackson!"

When the angry instructor directed him to repeat the punishment, Matt knew it was going to be a long training debrief. The SEAL instructors who made up the various attacking "enemy" units wandered back to where the four-wheel drive trucks were parked.

Another instructor went to the shoreline to signal the student boat pool to come into the beach for the debriefing. Twenty minutes later, Matt and his fellow BUD/S trainees were still in the pushup position waiting for permission to stand up.

The sound of crunching boots alerted Matt. An instructor was coming up behind him. Matt was in great shape but after twenty minutes his whole body was shaking with the effort to stay in the prone position.

"RECOVER!"

The instructor's voice barked the command that allowed the trainees to leap to their feet. They immediately assumed the position of attention and waited for the next wave of games. By the third phase, they were all used to rolling with the mental and physical stress. It was tough but bearable. The instructor came around Matt's shoulder and stood in front of the LTJG.

"Didn't feel fair out there, did it, sir?" The "sir" was delivered with a hint of disgust implying the instructor only barely recognized Matt's status as a commissioned officer—just barely.

Matt turned his head slightly and looked directly into the instructor's eyes.

The instructor continued to taunt him. "You know this shit isn't supposed to be fair, sir, just realistic. If you can't pull it off here, in a simple and incredibly fucking safe training environment, then you sure as hell can't pull it off when the shit really hits the fan in combat!"

Matt lowered his head and stared at the ground below him for only a second then he looked up again at the instructor. His face went slack, going neutral. It was a trick they'd all learned over the past five months. *Never let the instructors see your feelings*. Always mask the pain and the humor. Especially the humor. Laughing at the wrong time could bring a world of hurt down on the entire class.

Matt watched as the instructor studied his emotionless face. Matt had gone zombie on him. Anything the instructor said now wouldn't result in a reaction of any kind. He waited for the inevitable harsh criticism. "It doesn't matter anyway, sir. You guys are so screwed up I personally think you should strip off those fancy ninja cammies and spend some time in the fleet where you might do some good. In fact, maybe you should spend some time in the cold surf zone so you have some quiet time to think about which type of ship you'd like to be assigned to when we kick your asses out of the program!"

Matt heard every scathing word, but he didn't care. They were hollow threats. There were only a few days left and the class had performed everything as well as possible. He heard the commotion near the trucks and voices he recognized. The instructors were directing Matt's boat crew too put the CRRC into the truck and then join the rest of the class.

The students in the boat crew were spared the pushups, but they struggled to load the rubber boats into one of the pickup trucks. When they finished, they jogged over to stand in formation with Matt and the others. The senior instructor had overheard the instructor's threat to send Matt and the trainees out into the surf zone and he checked his watch.

Matt and his classmates were cold—not hypothermic yet, but close. The senior instructor in charge of the exercise walked over to the group of shaking students. He gave a quick look toward the rest of the instructors and they dutifully drifted away. His demeanor was serious. The senior instructor now turned his attention to the class.

"We don't have time for more bullshit games! You gentlemen may have completed your last student mission in BUD/S training, but after graduation—in two days—you'll all be starting SEAL Qualification Training or SQT. So, you're not out of the woods yet."

Matt and the others had listened to variations of this same speech for several weeks, ever since arriving on San Clemente Island. The BUD/S course was like a concentration camp in a way. You came in and learned how to survive—you became mentally stronger and physically tougher or you went away. You learned how to deal with the instructors' personalities and learned the tricks that kept the class and yourself out of trouble. But this was an imaginary place, safety personnel everywhere, good food, medical surveillance, it wasn't real. It wasn't even close to being real.

"After SQT they'll ship you out to your first SEAL Team. BUD/S is tough gentlemen, but it's all fun and games compared to what comes next. Here we play nice-nice. You'll notice nobody died on this beach tonight, nobody saw their best friend's brains splattered all over their cammies after taking an enemy round. Fuck up here and you do pushups. Fuck up out there…" The senior instructor pointed toward the ocean for emphasis. "People come back in body bags!"

The senior instructor moved closer to Matt and locked eyes with the LTJG. "I can assure you lads of one thing. If you screw up in a real-world firefight like you screwed up tonight, you'll live the rest of your lives thinking about how you fucked things up and got your friends killed! Trust me, gentlemen, you don't want that on your conscience. It's a fate worse than death."

The senior instructor checked his watch and then ordered the students to get into the trucks for the ride back to the San Clemente Island training facility. The long, narrow island was covered in cactus and occupied mainly by a small breed of California fox.

The small Navy communications station was near the center of the island, but the BUD/S compound was on the northern tip, a multi-million-dollar playground for SEALs. Matt took a step toward the trucks but was held in check by a firm and calloused hand on his shoulder.

"Mr. Barrett, wasn't your old man a Marine officer?"

Matt nodded, going neutral inside. Going on automatic was a phrase that BUD/S students used to explain the state of mind they assumed when preparing for another endless round of being fucked with by the staff. Where the hell was this going?

"I also seem to recall he was awarded the big blue, is that true?"

Matt nodded a second time. Shit, he hated that topic. Even in college people seemed to find out about his father. Matt's dad was no less than a national hero.

The senior instructor looked hard at Matt. "Well, sir. after watching you operate out here, I've only got one question. Are you sure you weren't adopted?"

The other BUD/S instructors were still close enough to overhear the joke. Laughter echoed off the surrounding hills as the senior instructor walked away from Matt tossing out a command over his shoulder.

"Mr. Barrett. Get the stupid look off your face and join your classmates."

Matt turned and began to run to the trucks. He could still hear the laughter of the instructors echoing in his mind. Some heroic leader he turned out to be! No matter how hard he tried, he was unable to overcome the fact that he would never measure up to the old man. A man who'd successfully led men in combat—real combat.

His old man had been a pillar of leadership excellence. In contrast, Matt had barely passed the most basic leadership tests offered in the SEAL course. Although he knew tonight was only an exercise, he was painfully aware he wasn't cutting it as a leader.

Chapter Four

SQT was more challenging than BUD/S for different reasons. Matt was required to make more and more decisions, straying from the safety of pre-ordained SOPS, SEAL officers were expected to think on their feet. There were three officers in the SQT class, and they were all great athletes. That was the ante required just to be a SEAL. The differences in the enlisted and the officers began to show themselves as training became more advanced, especially in matters of judgment.

The polishing course was four months long. The instructors were more mentor than jailhouse guard and that made the students feel more like they were in the teams, but they were a long way from gaining that honor. SQT borrowed much of the more complicated and dangerous land warfare curriculum from the old BUD/S course which, for over forty years, was six months long. This change had allowed the community to ramp up learning and performance expectations and teach advanced skills often involving technology and outside mobility assets like aircraft and boats.

Matt did well in most categories of training and stacked up first in fitness and second in everything else among the officers. The mission planning was fascinating, so many moving parts and players to rely on to make it all a success. The students learned that SEALs may be badasses but they couldn't accomplish anything without a large supporting cast of intelligence assets, mobility platforms, firepower options, and specialists. Specialists like explosive ordnance disposal or EOD technicians, combat air traffic controllers, interpreters, and others, all gathered together in a mission team dedicated to delivering unique and often strategically critical outcomes.

Matt learned how to freefall, something he loved. Jumping out to fall thousands of feet, as a team or opening the square, multi-celled parachutes at high altitude to fly in formation toward the target. It was exhausting and exhilarating at the same time. SEALs used these skills in conjunction with air-dropped boats of different kinds or they simply used the air insertion methods to get ashore without detection. This skill set was a line, of sorts, with the class. There were men who were comfortable in the air and others that struggled. Eventually, they could only execute a plan that every SEAL could handle so being a slow learner wasn't seen as a stigma.

The time flew by quickly for Matt. Graduation from SQT was also a new tradition. In the nineteen sixties, seventies, eighties, and nineties BUD/S graduates went to U.S. Army jump school at Ft. Benning, Georgia, for three weeks of good old Army training. They would receive their lead jump wings after five jumps and then report to their respective SEAL Team. Once onboard, each SEAL Team conducted its own four-month finishing course. Later these separate attempts were consolidated at the group level, the staff responsible for all the SEALs and boat specialists on the east and the west coast.

SQT represented the last in a long evolution of training continuums. Consolidated under the SEAL admiral's staff in Coronado, SQT was more advanced, more expensive, and more supported than any of the earlier approaches had been. One other thing was different, too. For over forty years each SEAL Team commanding officer decided when and if a BUD/S graduate was ready to become a SEAL and wear the gold breast insignia referred to as the "trident". This final act of acceptance into the brotherhood of war was part of the SQT graduation ceremony.

He stood ramrod straight with the rest of his SQT class. The sun was starting to rise, and the California waves pounded the beach. There were others there also, friends and family, SQT staff, and senior SEAL officers. Each graduate was presented with a knife, the name of a fallen SEAL engraved on the blade. A reminder to each graduate that they were walking in the footsteps of brave men—men who'd haunt them if they let their brothers down in any way. Finally, each graduate was given the trident. They were now officially SEALs. But they all knew the real learning was about to begin.

Matt walked across the quarterdeck and waited for the sailor on the phone to finish his call. His orders after SQT sent him all the way across the street from the Coronado strand or beach where BUD/S, SEAL Advanced Training, and the teams were located to the amphibious base. Most of his class were being sent to schools en route to their commands. Matt was no exception. He was checking into the SEAL Delivery Vehicle or SDV School. Matt was going to learn how to fly mini-subs.

The sailor finished the call and reached out to take Matt's orders, a yellow, eight-inch by eleven-inch envelope packed with information about Matt. He read the set of orders taped to the outside of the package and then logged Matt's arrival into the school's log book. "Welcome aboard, sir! Class indoctrination briefings begin tomorrow morning at 0930. PT begins at 0730 so be here at 0700." The sailor handed the package back to Matt.

Matt looked around. "That's it?"

The sailor nodded. "Yes, sir. You can go back to the officer's quarters or do whatever you want to but be back here at 0700. They'll give the class a schedule for the entire course tomorrow so you can make personal plans as you see fit."

Matt raised his eyebrows. Personal plans? He'd been in a strict school environment for so long he forgot what real free time meant. SDV School was a slower paced program—no yelling and no pushups. Matt thanked the quarterdeck watch again and left. He was getting hungry.

Matt survived the PT session on the first day of SDV training and actually enjoyed their policy of running on your own after the group finished its fitness training. He took advantage by running out of the amphibious base and turning right toward Coronado Island. The Naval Amphibious Base was built on a manmade peninsula that jutted out into the San Diego Bay.

The BUD/S compound was on the opposite side of the highway. The SEAL Teams were also on that side. Coronado Island was to the north. Once isolated, it was connected to the south by the highway running up from Imperial Beach near the border with Mexico and to the east by the Coronado bridge, linking the island with the center of San Diego, California.

Matt reached the Hotel Del Coronado, looming magnificently on his left and turned to the right so he could run along the shore of Glorietta Bay, a small cove which was a part of the greater San Diego Bay. After a few miles he cut back into the center of the island, following one of the quiet streets running east and west and lined with homes inspired by Mexicana and Spanish culture.

Matt ran across the island until he popped out of the neighborhoods on the western side. There, right in front of him stretched the Pacific Ocean. He stopped and climbed up on the large boulders lining the sidewalk on the beach side of the street and looked up and down the long stretch of sand. To his right he could just make out a BUD/S training class on a run, instructors flanking their formation and the ambulance and safety truck trailing thirty yards behind.

To his left was the Hotel Del Coronado. The huge wooden structure made in the late nineteenth century dominated the island. The distinctive red roof always reminded him of landing on the rock jetty that lay just below the hotel during his Hell Week. He checked his watch; he needed to haul ass if he wanted to get to the first class on time. Fortunately, the run back to the Amphibious Base was all downhill.

SDV School was all about engineering, hydraulics, and electrical systems. The students were taught the history of manned submersibles going all the way back to ancient Greek attempts to sink enemy ships using air bladders and breathing hoses.

They went over the evolution of the submersible as a machine-propelled platform, a device that didn't require human muscles to generate power. The history of the American Civil War and both World Wars focused on design success and, more often, failures. This only took a day to accomplish. The rest of the SDV coursework dove into the modern age of manned mini-submarines and how they operated.

The SDV was battery-powered and capable of moderate speed and mission duration. The maximum limits were classified, and the students were taught the working values for the purpose of learning to operate the vehicles. The cockpit was festooned with advanced mission support technology.

Much like a tactical aircraft, the SDV was capable of navigating on instruments—no visual navigation was required. The data systems and communications tools were extraordinary. They had to be. Launching off a Navy submarine at night, executing a mission in enemy waters, and returning safely, was a high-risk endeavor. Matt loved the challenges it presented.

As the weeks progressed and the Basic SDV program neared completion, Matt relaxed and took stock of his life so far. He'd dated in college enough to know what he liked and disliked about women but never connected with anyone special. He was too focused, too driven to allow a love life to interfere with his bigger plan. He'd arrived, at least he was a SEAL and soon he'd be a qualified SDV pilot and navigator. Maybe it was time to think about other things.

Dawn – Alexandria, Egypt

Mahmoud el-Bandar stretched. He loved the early morning. The way the sun's rays illuminated the city, painting all the bland, white structures in a mixture of blue, orange, and red light. He took this time of day to meditate and inventory his failings for he was a man who believed in humility—and humility began with admitting one was human.

He wore his jet-black hair long, bound in the back so it wouldn't fall into his face. He adjusted the tie in the back and pulled a few stray hairs to the side of his face. He was conscious of the grey that was creeping in; too little to give him the appearance of wisdom, but enough to mark him as an aging man nearing the middle of his life.

He'd been raised in this city by the Mediterranean. A boy, one of seven siblings, who spent every waking hour until the age of eleven helping to scrape out a living from the chaos of Egypt's poverty-stricken economy. He and his brothers and sisters all contributed. The class system in Egypt was simple to understand. A few at the top were wealthy, most due to connections outside of the country—trade and global commerce helped them line their pockets every time a product entered by air or sea.

Then there was the merchant class, a hardscrabble population of business owners who ruled their immediate environment like tough mafiosos. If you wanted a job, a loan, anything, you went to them. Finally, there was the poor. The vast majority of Egyptians were of this class. They were the workers, the day laborers. Too poor to set aside wealth and too weak to protect it if they did manage to save some money.

It was that class that Bandar called brother, sister. It was that lower class, the poor, that would fuel his dream and eventually form the army he needed to achieve his vision. He was tall and thin but stronger than he looked. The years as a boy working to make bricks in the hot sun had hardened him in many ways. His nights studying the Koran with the imams opened his mind and in time provided him with a purpose in life.

When he was a young man, he made the decision to keep his birth name but changed his family name when he was called to jihad. El-Bandar was a place not far from his home near Alexandria. But it also meant the harbor. A safe place in a storm. He liked the image it represented; his quest was a path to safety and security in a new Egypt, a new beginning.

Bandar finished his routine of stretching and meditating. He was ready to eat his morning meal, then prayer, then on to business. His days were full but when he'd started the movement in his home two years earlier, he'd had nothing but time, and an idea. It began with himself, a few friends, and three cousins.

He had a simple message and they trusted him, believed in his intellect and piety. The hardest part, in the beginning, was taking the first step. Violence was a new means of persuasion for him but it was the only message governments and corporations listened to with any respect.

He ate alone and in silence allowing the sounds of the city waking up, penetrating into his modest apartment, through an open window. He had time. He could pause, accelerate or stop. The end game was foreordained so it didn't really matter. The way was clear and inevitable. The speed of change wasn't his concern. He paced his attacks to minimize exposure while he steadily built up his city-wide intelligence collection capabilities. Good information made for better targets. He needed to practice patience.

Chapter Five

Matt graduated on time from the basic SDV course. He considered swinging home on his way to Seal Delivery Vehicle Team Two in Virginia Beach, Virginia but thought better of it. His mom, Grace Barrett, had moved on after his father's death, first traveling the country with friends and then a good part of the world with a man she met. Matt was neutral on his mother's decision to date and in her choice of men. The guy she liked the most was the same age as his mom and had ten times the energy his dad ever had. Matt knew she was happy and that's all that mattered.

The trip to the east coast took him six days by car. He stopped in Vegas and in Nashville to hear some good old-fashioned country music. When he finally arrived at the Little Creek Naval Amphibious base, he was ready to get busy again. Matt pulled into the team compound on base and parked his car near the SDVT Two sign.

He was getting used to this drill. Matt ran his hand through his thick blond hair and frowned. The new guy thing. Every six months or so since joining the Navy, Matt was the new guy—checking in and learning the new rules. At least this time his orders were for two years. SDVT Two was home.

Matt completed his check-in and was told to see the operations officer before he left the building. He was shown to a large locker room which held a hundred mesh cages, one per man, for their personal operating gear and anything else they wanted to store in the room. He didn't have anything to stow so he thanked his guide and said he was heading to the operations office.

Matt walked in and looked around. The place was empty.

"Anybody here?" he said raising his voice in hopes he'd reach anybody in the rooms near the back of the main room.

"Be right up!" A voice shot back from the area of the open walk-in safe. All the command's classified material was stored in the room-sized safe. It would be a beast to break into *if* you survived the journey through the command building to reach it.

"You just checking in?" The smiling face was welcoming, not an instructor sneer or a haughty attitude. The man introduced himself. "My name is Master Chief Dellen, I'm the ops chief so I keep things straight for the ops officer." Master Chief Dellen stretched out his hand and Matt shook it, the first time he'd ever shaken the hand of a senior enlisted SEAL.

"Yes, Master Chief. My name is Matt, Matt Barrett, LTJG."

The Master Chief's face twisted a bit. "LTJG? You sure?"

Matt was confused but he knew his rank. "That's right, Master Chief. I hope you were all expecting me."

The Master Chief smiled mischievously. "Oh, we were expecting you, Lieutenant. Congratulations, if nobody told you. Your promotion came through a few days ago, while you were on travel status, I guess. Of course, I can call D.C. and tell the officer detailer you'd rather stay a JG."

Matt was surprised. He shouldn't be eligible for promotion for another eight months. "How did…?"

"It's called frocking. The Navy is advancing all SDV officers if they are within nine months of their normal promotion date. No pay, but you get to wear the rank and do all the work expected of an LT. Now, if you don't mind,

I don't have time talk about your meteoric rise in the teams anymore. I've got important shit to do!" The Master Chief smiled at Matt again as he returned to the secure area.

Matt was happy and a little worried. What did they expect of a lieutenant? He left the ops office and headed for the parking lot. It was Friday afternoon. Time to get his bearings so he could experience the Virginia Beach night life. He had the option of living in the officer's quarters or living off base and that was something to look forward to, feeling more normal again. First stop was the base housing office.

2200 Hours–Cairo, Egypt

The explosion lit up the night sky in a kaleidoscope of brilliant color. An ear-shattering roar reverberated against the nearby cluster of white stucco, upper-class homes, violently waking their well-to-do occupants. The Islamic terrorists had once again struck at the heart of wealth and influence in Cairo. Their message was clear, no one was safe anywhere. The inept Egyptian government could not protect them.

The attack was the work of a new group of young religious idealists. Smaller than the Muslim Brotherhood and unlike al Qaeda, not international in scope, the group had limited aims. Their goal was an infidel-free Egypt. With one quick stroke, the nameless killers had snuffed out the useless lives of those who would let the west dictate Egypt's fate. They believed the attack would help ignite the flame of hope and freedom for the faceless millions of true believers in Egypt.

The five terrorists raced through the courtyard and toward the main entrance. A security team reacting to the carnage sprinted through the gate and ran right into the attackers. The lead security man instinctively brought his automatic rifle up to his shoulder and pulled the trigger. His weapon didn't fire. Too late he remembered that for the sake of safety, the guards were not allowed to load their weapons. The loud report of a rifle echoed throughout the courtyard. Two AK-47 rounds cleared the confused thoughts from lead security guard's mind as he was struck twice in the upper chest.

The lead guard's body flew back violently—right into the other guards responding to the alarm coming up close behind him. Two of the guards dropped to a knee in a futile attempt to chamber a round. The terrorists put several rounds into them and they died with unloaded rifles in their hands. The remaining guards were dispatched in a fury of automatic fire. To an observer, the terrorists would have appeared to simply slaughter the security team, running right through them without slowing down a step.

The terrorist hit team exited the complex and stopped on the street. Two blocks away a green utility vehicle flashed its headlights. The team's leader barked a command and they began to run down the street without encountering further interference. Sirens began wailing all over the city. The five men dove into the small windowless panel van and slammed the double doors shut. They pulled away from the curb slowly and after a few streets turned away from the target, disappearing into the city.

The group's objective was the personal residence of Egypt's newly elected president, fell into itself as the weight of the structure overcame the ability of the melting support beams to function as designed. Ten minutes after the attack, the stately home was reduced to a pile of smoking rubble, the polished white stucco stained by the billowing smoke. Somewhere in the ruins lay the bodies of the president and his family.

By morning, the entire world would hear of this bold strike. The region would hear their message of faith expressed as vengeance as the soldiers of the jihad spread the word of Allah throughout first Egypt and then the Middle East.

The new President, Mustafa Hammet, was Egypt's last chance at reconciliation and peace. Elected by more than two-thirds of the popular vote, he'd been viewed by knowledgeable observers inside and outside Egypt, as a welcome centrist who would comfortably adopt moral rules of national conduct, while focusing on the less fortunate. He'd also sent a message of inclusion to the conservative religious extremists, or holy warriors of Allah—attempting to bring them into an honest and constructive dialogue with the new government.

Hammet's mandate from the voters had been clear. Accept the social demands of the faithful, but not at the cost of dragging the country back to the Dark Ages like was done in Iran. But the new president never had a chance to try. His violent death was unmistakable testimony to the focused and uncompromising agenda of the radical terrorists. There was no room for political bargaining. Who now would take up the banner of peace and moderation?

0200 NATO Headquarters–Brussels Belgium

The staff duty officer rubbed his aching red eyes with his palms in a slow, circular motion. He would be up all night responding to field reports from NATO forces deployed on peacekeeping missions around the world. As usual, the continuous cat-and-mouse activity expected in disputed areas and active war zones demanded that the NATO forces supporting the various United Nations resolutions and core alliance objectives, react to probable worst-case scenarios everywhere and investigate everything. To say the alliance was over committed was an understatement.

Ever since the attack on America in 2001, NATO had been slowly pulled into events and conflicts defined more by U.S. leadership of the alliance than the original charter obligations. NATO forces were deployed in Afghanistan and Iraq and coordinating counter-terrorism efforts in other areas such as the horn of Africa. In recent years, a resurgent Russia challenged the organization to pull back its forces and reassess the security of Europe, the original mandate come full circle.

Egypt of all places! Since when did Egypt fall into the NATO threat horizon? Heavy footsteps echoing down the access tunnel signaled the end of his watch. *Let someone else get a headache trying to figure it out.* He, for one, was ready to let the rest of the world take a flying leap. The initial reports were sketchy—as usual—but if true, the duty officer would have to send out several messages tonight. The assassination of Egypt's new President wasn't a trivial event.

Chapter Six

SEAL Delivery Vehicle Team Two–Little Creek, Virginia

Wham! The sound of the impact startled Matt. He frantically barked out course corrections to his diving partner who, as pilot of the vehicle, was responsible for operating the systems that propelled and steered the SDV. He spoke into the full-face mask's microphone. "Come left, come hard left!"

Ignoring Matt's harsh command, the enlisted pilot of the SDV responded by deftly adjusting the course of the twelve-foot long mini-submarine only a few degrees. Matt knew that small changes yielded significant effects. His command was over the top but he saw his pilot smoothly maneuver in a controlled manner to achieve Matt's intention without jerking the craft around in the water column. Matt was embarrassed.

They both knew the advanced SDV Advanced Operators course, known as AOT, was complete, all except this final performance exercise. After a grueling sixteen-week process of learning the SDV all over again and putting miles and hours of experience under their belts, they were engaged in a complex training mission scenario patterned after actual target plans. Every decision they made during the final exercise was being observed, recorded, and judged.

Matt shouted into the microphone again as the SDV slammed into another underwater obstacle. A row of wooden posts making up the support structure of a harbor pier. As the navigator on this dive, Matt was responsible for detecting objects in the minisub's path using the underwater vehicle's sophisticated sonar system.

The Navy submersible was shaped like a cigar. The vehicle was fully flooded during underwater operations, requiring the men flying it to wear protective wetsuits. The pilot and navigator sat side by side in a cockpit, their low light displays arrayed in front of them. The pair "flew" the SDV above the bottom of the ocean and beneath the surface waves.

This distance above the sea floor was referred to as "altitude." The distance below the ocean's surface was referred to as "depth". If Matt did his job well, the SDV would be cleanly navigated around hazards and through unobstructed water to its destination, usually a shallow water target in a harbor.

"Hey boss. The comms are working fine, no need to keep yelling at me!

Matt realized he'd been overexcited. "Sorry, Pete. I'll get my shit together."

"Sounds good, sir. Maybe you ought to slide back the canopy and check out the damage," Pete recommended.

Pete was Matt's pilot for today's dive. He was a second class petty officer. Few people knew that SEALs used to maintain their original Navy ratings. With the exception of corpsmen, SEALs would only move up in rank if they beat their fleet peers in written tests, a feat difficult to accomplish when you spent all your time learning how to kill bad guys.

After nearly forty years, the SEAL community finally petitioned for their own SEAL rating in the late nineties. They were successful. Enlisted men in the teams were referred to as "Special Operations". For example, a Chief Petty Officer's rate in the teams would be SOC, or Special Operations, Chief.

Pete slowed the mini-sub down to a snail's crawl. Matt didn't miss the edge in his pilot's voice. His enlisted pilot was only twenty years old, a new guy to the teams and still wet behind the ears. But then again, so was Matt. He'd realized during the tough sixteen-week AOT course that flying the SDV was an art requiring precious little commando experience to master. It was all a head game, knowing where you were in the water and knowing what you could expect from the boat's complex systems.

The really great pilots and navigators just sort of evolved with time and training. Matt was one of those who had not evolved as an SDV artist. The way things were going, he'd be lucky to graduate after the final dive of the course. Thus far, except for Matt's stellar contribution—guiding the SDV directly into a pier at high speed—Pete had controlled the entire dive from the pilot's seat.

Matt slid the canopy door back on its track. The SDV had slowed enough for him to stretch his body out of the cockpit so he could inspect the damage. Matt slid down into the cockpit, shut the canopy, and snapped his face mask's communications lead back into the SDV's control console. "Sorry, Pete. The starboard bow plane is gone!" Matt said.

"That's okay, sir," the kid answered back cheerfully. "I won't tell anybody if you don't! Just reach around behind me and grab the extra bow plane I brought along just in case."

Matt smiled and shook his head in disbelief. "Why did you do that?" he said.

"Well, sir. I've had to dive with you for sixteen weeks now. I just estimated how bad things could get with you in here and planned accordingly."

Matt stared hard at his dive partner. The kid was right. After all, Matt truly sucked as an SDV navigator.

Matt reached around the pilot and pulled out the extra bow plane. He slid the canopy back, leaned out, and quickly replaced the critical part of the minisub's steering system.

"Hey, Pete? Can we keep this little fuck-up between us?" Matt asked, sliding back into position next to his pilot.

"You know the deal, LT. Whatever happens underwater, stays underwater."

Matt smiled. "Thanks, Pete."

"No problem, sir. Now, close the damn canopy so we can get on with this dive!"

Matt didn't answer. He was too busy following Pete's order. Twenty minutes later, the rest of the AOT class scampered about the pier area as Matt's SDV broke the surface. Matt and Pete had successfully finished their final dive. Matt and Pete disconnected their comms and exited the SDV. They both pushed the bulky full-face masks off their heads and sucked in the first fresh air in many hours.

It was a short distance to the ramp, so they swam on their backs until they arrived at the edge. They spun around and with the help from a few classmates, were lifted up and onto the dry ramp. With all the diving equipment, survival kit, weight belt, and other essential pieces and parts, an SDV diver was carrying about one hundred pounds on their bodies.

Matt glanced up as somebody shouted down from the quay wall to the right of the ramp. "The crane's hooked up, guys. Any time you are ready is all right with us." As always in the SEAL teams, everybody pitched in to get the job done.

Once Matt and Pete had cleared the immediate area of the SDV the entire AOT class went into motion. The students scrambled to successfully lift the minisub out of the water and onto the waiting SDV trailer where it was strapped down for movement to the SDV Team Two compound.

Matt and Pete were helped to their feet. Behind them a truck was pulling away, the SDV nestled securely on the trailer behind the vehicle.

A fellow student shouted a question from their left side. “So, how’d it go, you guys?”

Matt bet down and picked up his fins. He looked at Pete. The target had been hit successfully and nobody detected the SDV. In the SEAL teams, the standard statute of limitations regarding what really happened on a training mission was six months, another great SEAL rule of thumb.

Pete grinned at Matt in silent understanding. Looking up, the SDV pilot shouted, “No sweat! It was a piece of cake!”

Matt walked up to the place where the ramp and the quay wall came together. He spotted the commanding officer of SDV Team Two, Captain Richards, chatting with the training instructors, getting their opinions of the exercise, no doubt.

The skipper looked pleased and that made Matt feel better. His eyes reflected the pride he had in his men, even these men, so new to the SDV business. Matt approached the captain staggering under the weight of his mission gear. Next to the captain stood a stocky lieutenant commander Matt didn’t recognize. The man was upset about something.

Captain Richards saw Matt and stepped forward, smiling and extending his hand. “Well done, lieutenant!” The captain’s grip was firm and somewhat painful. Matt’s hands were swollen, made soft by the long SDV dive.

"Thank you, skipper," he returned. "My pilot, Petty Officer Pete Simms, completed the operation despite my interference."

The captain chuckled and nodded in the direction of the young pilot who decided he needed to get the hell away—too many officers.

"Well, I'm sure it went well. Maybe in a few months or so you'll share the real story with me!" Captain Richards winked.

Matt was taken aback but then relaxed. All SEALS were operators first and operators always knew the deal. Captain Richards had "been there and done that". He was a SEAL who men could rely on and trust.

The skipper turned toward the stocky lieutenant commander. "Hey, Barrett. I'd like you to meet your new boss."

Matt nodded one more time to his pilot before turning his attention to the officer in front of him.

"Say hello to Lieutenant Commander Sandoval, commander of Task Unit X-RAY."

Matt reached out to shake the LCDR's hand. Sandoval still wore a curious "somebody just took a shit in my cornflakes" look on his face. He wasn't having a good day.

"Pleased to meet you, sir," Matt said. The dry, polite greeting implied neutrality between two unknown professionals.

Sandoval returned the handshake.

"I hear you can't fly an SDV for shit, lieutenant," his dark eyes mocked Matt. His hand stopped pumping abruptly and pulled away.

Matt searched the senior officer's face for some indication he was just messing around. But what he saw instead began to piss him off. "Well, sir," Matt began, trying to change the mood of the moment. "I don't think I'll ever win any points for style, that's for sure." Matt's attempt at charm didn't work.

Sandoval snorted.

Captain Richards chuckled, more to change the atmosphere than as a reaction to Matt's comment. "Well, I don't think you'll have to worry about that anymore, lieutenant, because you are being assigned to Task Unit X-RAY as the reconnaissance troop commander. I imagine my SDV's will be safe from damage with you away playing sneak and peek." The captain continued. "Task Unit X-RAY's almost finished with her pre-deployment training work-up. They lost their recon troop LT to a broken leg. You're his replacement. I'm sure that with your positive attitude you can catch up."

Matt stared at Captain Richards in disbelief. The navy personnel bureau had explained to him it would take over a year for an officer to qualify in all the unique SDV related skills. Only then would a new LT be allowed to start the SDV Task Unit training program. The captain's comment indicated Matt would be operational right away.

Matt looked at LCDR Sandoval. "Thank you, sir. I won't let you down!"

Sandoval scowled. "Don't thank me, Barrett! It wasn't my idea! I'm still not convinced you can make the grade so soon out of BUD/S. Nor am I convinced you can make up for missing so much of the Task Unit's pre-deployment training."

Matt's initial euphoria over being assigned to the Task Unit was fading rapidly. This guy was beginning to look like a grade-*A* asshole. SEAL or not, even a great job like leading the reconnaissance troop could go sideways if the boss was out to prove a point at Matt's expense.

0400 Hagada, Egypt

The Egyptian sergeant froze as a subtle indication of movement off to his left caught his attention. His post outside the American military support facility faced the street affording him a broad field of view. The movement came from just beyond the soft yellow halo cast on the ground fifty meters down the wall by an overhead security light. The sergeant hadn't experienced combat, but he was a well-trained professional and his instincts told him something was not quite right.

It had been six months since the first major terrorist bombing attack in Cairo killed the new president. Since that time, several foreign offices had been bombed and in one case an Egyptian army security patrol had been ambushed. The sergeant shook his head. What did he have to worry about? The Sons of Allah were mad at the Egyptian government, not the Americans. The building he guarded wasn't a likely target.

The sergeant sighed and then forced himself to relax. He learned a long time ago to let loose of the anxiety that something was always about to happen. His experience told him the movement was likely a trick of the light.

He hated pulling double duty, watching the American compound after working all day at his regular assignments. His miserable wife didn't understand the soldier's life. She expected him to make the right kind of friends in high places and then bribe or beg his way out of the shitty assignment.

Sometimes, he thought she might have a point. Quite frankly, he didn't understand why the Egyptian Army was spread all over the country protecting foreigners when the troops could be put to much better use hunting down the religious fanatics. Or better yet, taking time off to spend with their neglected families. First the Muslim Brotherhood and now the Sons of Allah. Too many priorities and not enough manpower.

From his point of view, this latest call for jihad made no sense at all. These disturbed young men who, through their mad acts of violence, threatened to pull all of Egypt down in flames, were better off than his generation had been and—come to think of it—his father's generation, too. The young are never happy and the old are never able to convince the young they have it made.

His thoughts were interrupted when a white Volvo four-door sedan turned onto the main street. He watched intently as the vehicle approached his post, a plush hotel leased by the United States Navy and used as a fleet communications support facility. The sergeant's attention was fixed on the driver's face as the car rolled to a stop directly in front of him.

The driver was a striking young Egyptian woman. Her white blouse was flimsy and nearly sheer, open down low enough to expose a lacy black bra. Very risqué attire considering the crazy religious zealots roaming about these days, the sergeant thought to himself. The sergeant's eyes focused on the woman's ample chest with barely disguised admiration. Ah, if only the sergeant had been a few years younger!

The woman ignored him, focusing on her smartphone. The sergeant could see the stress etched in the pretty woman's face. Was she lost? The sergeant scratched his head. Tourists were rare here in Hagada and it was very late. Maybe she was coming home from a party. He decided to see if he could help the lost little lamb.

Chuckling to himself, the sergeant shrugged and stepped closer to the driver's side of the Volvo. The woman looked up, her face spreading into a brilliant smile. The sergeant bent over to look inside, leaning on the Volvo's hood. He once again took in the view, even more impressive from the new vantage point, so he was surprised when he saw the pistol appear like magic in the young woman's hand. He realized too late that it was a trap. The veteran's last thoughts were of his children as three downloaded nine-millimeter bullets passed through his forehead, exploding through the back of his skull with a dull popping sound.

The assassin had concealed the short automatic pistol and six-inch silencer in the fold of her skirt. Her blouse was unfortunately discolored by the blood that sprayed back on her as the rounds struck home. Only the mechanical sound of the pistol's slide moving back and forth could be heard, but there was no one around. The sergeant didn't see the Volvo's headlights flashing their silent signal. He'd been dead before he hit the street.

The lights flashed twice, paused and flashed once more. Twenty meters away ten darkly-clad men appeared from around the corner of a nearby storefront. The team sprinted across the street and toward the hotel's entrance.

For a split second the group was illuminated by the dull streetlight, revealing that each was loaded down with automatic weapons and haversacks filled with explosives. One figure paused to place a round into the bright streetlight in front of the American facility. His suppressed German H&K MP-5 SD submachine gun coughed once, plunging the area near the entrance into darkness.

The Volvo pulled away from the curb and rolled slowly toward the bright lights of the other major hotels nearby. The staff was arriving in the early morning to get the hotels ready for the long day ahead. The woman reached back and pulled a dark scarf from the rear seat, wrapping it across her upper body to cover up the blood and her overexposed breasts. Her job was done.

The leader of the ten-man team responded to the flashing lights by heading to the hotel and entering the complex, sprinting across the professionally-landscaped front lawn and through the main door of the building.

Muffled gun shots and the sounds of furniture crashing signaled that their pre-rehearsed ballet of terror had begun. The well-trained men set about their bloody night's work with machine-like precision. The few Americans on duty were taken completely by surprise. There would be no survivors.

Chapter Seven

Matt wasn't much of a party animal. What little time he had to himself he spent relaxing, reading, and sleeping. He did go out from time to time with two of the other officers in the AOT course. Todd was from Texas and couldn't even swim the first time he realized being a frogman was the life he wanted. He started college at Texas Christian University and at the same time enrolled in swimming lessons. He graduated in the BUD/S class ahead of Matt as did Wes, Todd's ever-present companion.

Wes was an African American, one of the few in the teams. He was a stellar athlete and a Rhodes Scholar, graduating with honors from Stanford University. His parents, family, and friends were therefore shocked when Wes decided upon graduation to become a SEAL. He was a naturally funny guy, a man's man, but at the same time he came off as shy and vulnerable to the ladies. The combination of brains, brawn, and charisma made him a force of nature.

The third time Matt was goaded into joining the dynamic duo he wasn't in the mood to meet strangers, but that's the night he'd met Sherry. Sherry Thompson was tall and graceful. Matt first spotted her across the dance floor at Peabody's, a favorite haunt of his two buddies. She was sipping a drink and occasionally laughing at whatever her date was saying to her. Matt couldn't take his eyes off of her.

It took three beers and thirty minutes for Matt to work up the courage to talk to her. He waited until her male friend went to the bathroom and pounced. She didn't spot him approaching until he was only ten feet away but when she did, she made eye contact and smiled. Matt almost stopped dead in his tracks. He must have had a weird look on his face because Sherry laughed. Matt had to have this girl!

"I'm glad to see you have a sense of humor," Matt began.

Sherry casually twisted her neck, allowing her long auburn hair to swoosh out of her face. She tilted her head slightly and smiled that damn smile again. "Better be quick, my date will be coming back soon."

Matt glanced in the direction of the men's room, no sight of the guy. It was now or never. "I can't stop looking at you, you are gorgeous! My name is Matt and I hope you're not marrying that guy." The words came out in a jumbled mess, but he spit them all out. There was a dreadful pause.

Sherry's eyes lost their twinkle and she seemed to study Matt closely for a few moments. "Okay, you are very handsome and probably hit on someone new every night in a place like this." Matt began to protest but she raised her hand to stop him. "But."

Matt's heart skipped a beat. She wasn't shooting him down. "But?"

"But I don't get that hunter vibe from you. You're too clumsy."

Matt glanced back at the men's room again. Sherry's date was out but had stopped to order a drink. He was running out of time. "I need to see you again. Are you…"?

"Getting married? I don't think so, and definitely not to him." She looked across the dance floor at her date. "He's a friend from work. I'm sure he has nefarious intentions, but I couldn't turn him down again. He's very persistent."

"Persistent but not the one, right?" Matt hated every word coming out of his mouth. She must think he was a dumbass.

"I don't even know your name and yet you seem very concerned about my future, Mr…?"

"Barrett, Matt. I'm more concerned right now about my future."

"You have thirty seconds before it becomes messy." Sherry indicated her date was closing in with a nod of her head."

Matt stared into her hazel colored eyes and inhaled. "I think you're beautiful and I can't think of why you'd see me again and if you didn't want to, I'd understand but I really need to see you again and how do I do that?"

"I work at the aquarium, day manager. Saturdays and Sundays. If you come to see me there, I can give you my number, there I mean." Sherry's eyes darted to the left. It was time for an extraction.

Matt turned slightly to the left and moved away without looking at the dazzling young lady. His shoulder intentionally brushed hers, ever so slightly. "I'll find you there."

Saturday morning didn't arrive soon enough. The Thursday night encounter had filled Matt with a frenzied energy. He didn't sleep Thursday night and had a terrible time maintaining the pace of training the next day. Friday night was easier, he was exhausted and fell asleep early, but not before he looked up the aquarium's operating hours and set his alarm.

Matt woke up at seven and showered. He changed clothes at least three times trying to achieve the perfect look, casual but not frumpy, tight to show off his physique but not so tight he looked like a dancer from New York. In the end he settled on tan cargo shorts, a mildly clinging tee-shirt, and flip flops.

He was hungry so on the way to the aquarium he stopped to eat at Belvedere's, a tiny out-of-the-way breakfast diner on the Virginia Beach boardwalk. As he ate his breakfast, he watched the small east coast waves take forever to roll in and then weakly crash before hitting the wide beach. Matt used to love the water, the ocean in particular. It felt like the office.

The ocean was always cold for a SEAL. Matt knew hypothermia could set in and cause teeth to chatter even in south California or the Caribbean. It was only a matter of time in the water. It pulled a man's body heat away from him relentlessly until it became a struggle to make the mind work or the body to obey commands. This was a frogman truth not easily conveyed in action movies.

Matt finished his breakfast—the standard ham and egg omelet—paid the waitress, and left the diner. The encounter at Peabody's was becoming more a fantasy than a real memory. Was he reading too much into her request? Work was a safe place to meet a stranger so that made sense, but Wes had pointed out she may have given Matt a false story just to get rid of him. He wasn't ready for that. He decided it was true and she was sincere. In a few minutes he would know.

The aquarium was a large building. Matt parked out front and gathered his courage. Why was this so hard? He wasn't afraid of much and even when he was his internal force of will dealt with the stress of a threat by buckling down and pushing through the anxiety. It worked for him, but meeting Sherry was terrifying. Matt realized it was the fear of failure—failure to impress her in the short time they would have this morning, impress her enough to get a real date. Wes' comments were also popping into his head.

Matt opened the car door and stepped out onto the parking lot. The place was filling up and the aquarium would soon be busy. He took a deep breath and let it out slowly, calming his heart and mind. He did it once more. The second time worked. "Fuck it," he said to himself as he took the first step.

Sherry had worn a loose top that draped down to her upper legs the night at Peabody's. That, the dark yoga pants, and the dim lighting had made it difficult for Matt to figure out what kind of body she might have. He realized he'd stared at her face exclusively. She was tall with auburn hair. As he opened the door and entered the aquarium, he was confident she'd be easy to spot.

The place was huge and comprised of odd-angled walls. A sea otter tank made up the far wall, a gift shop stood just to his right. over here. Matt began his search as a bus load of middle school aged children barged into the space behind him.

After ten minutes Matt stopped searching. She wasn't anywhere. In desperation he went up to the activities desk and asked.

"Excuse me, I'm looking for my friend Sherry. Do you know where I might find her?"

The young lady behind the counter smiled at Matt and her eyes conveyed she liked what she saw standing before her. She didn't answer. Matt began to repeat the question, but the girl snapped out of her stupor.

"Sherry Thompson, right?"

Matt nodded. He didn't know her last name, but it felt right the way the girl said it.

"Yeah, Sherry Thompson. Do you know where I can find her?"

The girl must have sensed Matt's interest lay elsewhere and she sighed. Meanwhile, a line had formed behind Matt and the parents were getting pushy.

"Sherry works out back in the ropes course complex. You'll probably find her there."

Matt followed her finger and saw the double glass doors. He thanked her and moved away from the counter headed for the back of the building. The doors led to a huge park, of sorts. Tall Norfolk pines and other large trees created a green canopy overhead. Scattered throughout the park were obstacles, rope bridges, wood platforms, and wires with metal contraptions designed to allow people to slide from one platform to another.

There was a small building to the right and—further on—an equipment rack covered in climbing harnesses. A crowd of people clustered around a tall auburn-haired instructor. Her eyes focused and her voice projected authority, calm. and light humor all at once. Matt leaned against the railing that lined the path to the park and watched. Wes didn't know shit. He'd found her.

He waited patiently.

Ten minutes went by before the group was finished with the safety lecture and had donned their harnesses.

Sherry and an assistant instructor checked the fit of each participant then waved them on to the beginning of the course. When the last person left the instruction area Sherry looked up, right at Matt, and smiled. She waved him over and waited while he walked the few yards to where she waited for him.

"You came! I didn't think you would." Sherry's eyes sparkled.

"Are you kidding me? My buddy said you probably gave me a fake story to get rid of me the other night. I didn't believe him, though. You seemed too nice to do that to someone."

Sherry's face changed a bit and she glanced over at the crowd of climbing students. "I just have to walk them through the practice area. Then, they are on their own and I'll have a few minutes. Don't go anywhere!"

Matt watched her jog to the group milling about a miniature replica of the larger course. She was incredibly hot. Sherry wore a tight-fitting tank top and her breasts were impressive. Her arms and shoulders were lean and muscular but still feminine. Her long athletic legs went all the way up to a great ass. Matt was stunned. How had he missed all that before?

A few minutes later Sherry returned. "So, you accepted my invitation. Why?"

Matt thought the question made little sense. Was she unaware of how attractive she was? He thought before answering. It wasn't about physical attraction. Women always asked questions. It was a test. "From the moment I saw you across that dance floor I couldn't stop thinking about you."

"You don't know anything about me." Sherry turned, placing both hands on the railing; she looked off into the distance.

Matt knew the truth as soon as she said it. He *didn't* know anything about her. It was time to find out. "Call it faith—instinct, maybe. I have good instincts."

Sherry tilted her head to the side to look at Matt, her waving hair cascading down the right side of her face. She squinted her eyes as she looked him up and down, settling on his face. "I'm twenty-six, I work here on the weekends and Monday to Friday I'm a paralegal. I was a conflicted youth—lawyer or outback trail guide? I split the difference, sort of."

Matt smiled. "That's nice, a good combination. Brains and adventure."

"How about you? Time to share—I only have five more minutes before the next group shows up." Sherry glanced up at a large clock hanging on the exterior wall of the gift shop.

"I'm an officer, Navy. I'm twenty-five. I grew up on the road. My old man was in the military, so we followed him around until he retired. It's always been hard to make friends; I was always leaving."

Sherry frowned for a moment. "Let me guess, your dad was Navy too."

Matt shook his head. "Marine Corps, through and through."

"Yet, you are not a Marine. Interesting. He must not have rubbed off on you." Sherry looked toward the building at the sound of the double glass doors opening as six chattering little adventurers spilled out onto the walkway. "Time's almost up, Matt. Tell me why I should see you again—and make it quick."

Matt saw the humorous twinkle in her eyes, and it gave him confidence. "I'm a solid guy. I don't lie or cheat and I don't play the field. If you and I were to start dating it would be cool. I'm not an asshole, honest."

"Dating? That implies *many* dates." Sherry feigned seriousness and pretended she was weighing his words. Then she smiled. "Wait here a minute."

Matt watched her jog back to the equipment area and rummage through a small back pack. She found what she was looking for and jogged back to Matt. "Here's my business card. I wrote my personal number on the back. Give me a call. Don't make me wait too long, either!"

Matt took the card and turned it over. She must've written the number down before she came to work today. She'd already decided to see him again. He'd need to be on his toes with this one.

Just then another group, older this time, burst through the doors.

"I have to go." Sherry suddenly came close and kissed Matt on the cheek.

"Hey! What was that for?" he said as he touched the spot with his hand.

"First date, first kiss. Second date…"

Matt's mouth opened in shock, but she was already gone. Her hair bounced back and forth as she hurried to the lecture area. Matt turned to go; the smile stayed on his face all the way home.

Chapter Eight

Sherry and Matt saw each other nearly every night for a few weeks then settled into a comfortable rhythm. She confessed she too was a Marine brat and that at some point she'd have to bring Matt by the house to meet her parents.

Matt didn't show the alarm he felt inside. If her dad was a hard ass, he might not like Matt. It might be enough to break the two of them up. Sherry wasn't impressed with the SEAL thing, but she was sure her father would bond with Matt based solely on his affiliation with the elite unit.

With AOT behind him, Matt had looked forward to a break but that wasn't in the cards. He was now a member of SDV Task Unit X-Ray. Even more importantly, Matt was one of four officers leading the Task Unit and he wasn't sure he was up to the job, despite Captain Richard's endorsement. His first taste of command was to remain calm as the operations officer denied his leave request. Matt wasn't going anywhere.

The Task Unit was comprised of three troops. One of them, the reconnaissance and surveillance—or R and S—troop, was manned with SEAL snipers. Traditionally, the officer in charge was rarely a sniper himself.

The precision long range shooting and advanced surveillance training was normally reserved for enlisted SEALs. There were ex-enlisted officers with the coveted skill set but they were rare. When the R and S SEALs operated, they had the use of the submarine-launched SDV, combat raiding craft like the CRRCs, and any other surface vessel or aircraft a normal SEAL Team relied on for mission support.

Matt was now freefall and SDV qualified and trained in advanced over the beach maritime operations using small craft. He wasn't a sniper, but he was indoctrinated in the tactical use of SEALs in this mission category. His major shortfall was not knowledge but experience. He didn't have the multiple years of practice, endless repetitions that made average operators masters of their craft. He knew all too well that the men of his new troop would be painfully aware of this fact.

On the sixth day after the AOT graduation, Matt worked out with the rest of the command and then showered. His first meeting was with Sandoval. Matt wasn't looking forward to the event. The other two troop leaders were away on readiness evaluation exercises. Each troop trained both apart and together. The readiness tests were conducted to ensure the deploying Task Units were combat-ready in all mission areas before being declared C1 war ready.

Matt walked out of the Task Unit office and sighed. The meeting with his new boss had gone as badly as he'd envisioned. Sandoval resented the skipper's choice of a new, untested officer to lead the R and S troop.

He made sure to repeat his concerns again to Matt's face. He'd been directed to follow the lead of his troop Chief and to try and not fuck things up too much. The one-way conversation lasted all of three minutes. Matt was dismissed and standing in the hallway, he wondered what he'd gotten himself into.

Matt walked down the hallway and wondered if Sherry was available that night. He needed a friendly face and her smile would drive Sandoval right out of his brain.

"I guess you're Matt Barrett?" The voice came from behind Matt and it wasn't a voice he recognized.

"Yeah, that's right. I'm Matt Barrett," Matt responded as he turned around.

“I’m Chief Auger, your troop chief. Glad to meet you, finally.” Chief Auger reached out to shake Matt’s hand.

“Chief! Glad to meet you, too. I’ve been advised to keep my mouth shut and my ears open, especially when you speak.” Matt voice was tinged with sarcasm.

“Ah, I see you’ve had some alone time with our fearless leader! Don’t let him get to you. He’s bucking for commander, so he’ll stay out of our way. Operators get wet and nasty. That’s not the path to higher command in this man’s Navy.

Matt smiled. “Thanks, I needed that. He’s…”

Chief Auger interrupted Matt. “No worries, LT. Forget all about Sandoval. Let’s go meet the guys, your fame precedes you.”

“You mean in the AOT course?” Matt asked.

Chief Auger chuckled. “Hell no, they’re curious what the son of a real Medal of Honor winner looks like.” The Chief smiled. Matt groaned. Great, he was going to be compared to the old man again. His curse continued to haunt him.

Chief Auger was an old hand at the special warfare business. Throughout his thirteen years in the teams, he’d participated in various minor and major combat actions ranging from advisory work in Central America to Operation Enduring Freedom in Afghanistan. The chief was undoubtedly the strongest man in the troop. Short and powerful, his speed and quickness made him a deadly opponent during close quarters combat training, a subject he often taught.

His soft-spoken demeanor belied the intensity of his passion and his deep sense of responsibility for the young SEALs he led. The chief had a great bedside manner with the men. He never belittled or chastised the troops in a public forum. He believed you were much more effective as a leader if you praised in public and punished in private. Matt felt especially lucky to have him as his second in command.

Chief Auger took the time to fill Matt in on the backgrounds of the troop members pointing out that each man in Matt's SEAL troop had arrived at that point in his life by traveling a different path. Boone Kilpatrick joined the United States Navy after two frustrating years of local community college where he'd attempted to study commercial art. Boone's six-foot frame was well muscled. While appearing thin in clothes, Boone was deceptively strong. He was one of the only men in the troop without an organized sports background.

Matt found out that Boone had impressed his boot camp company commander with his natural athletic ability during a weekend sports competition in boot camp. After sweeping many of the events, Boone was sent to see the resident SEAL recruiter assigned to the Great Lakes, Illinois, recruit training facility or RTC.

A grizzled old chief talked to him for hours, eventually convincing Boone to try out for the teams. A few weeks later Boone breezed through the SEAL physical screening test and afterward watched a SEAL recruiting film. Before the film was finished, he was hooked. With his sandy hair and boyish charm, he always seemed upbeat and ready for anything. Chief Auger had great confidence in Boone's instincts. He was the recon troop's point man.

Sam Oberman, or Oby, Matt learned, was the troop's overeducated enlisted frogman. He'd lettered in four different sports through high school and eventually earned a full wrestling scholarship to attend Boston College, but he could've got into the prestigious institution on his grades alone. While on Spring Break during his senior year, Oby bumped into a group of enlisted SEALs engaged in a loud alcoholic celebration. He started asking questions.

Matt listened to the chief as he continued to explain the curious details of how Oby finally decided to become a SEAL. The rowdy SEALs explained to Oby who they were and Oby wanted to know more. They explained that it took close to a year after boot camp before a student candidate became a SEAL.

Before that even began there were other pre-requisites such as no criminal record, high IQ, and strict medical screening. One of the SEALs took out his smartphone and showed Oby the SEAL trident. Oby stared at the image of a large gold medallion. The picture depicted a fierce eagle, head looking to the left, with wings outstretched. The eagle held Neptune's trident and a flintlock pistol in its sharp talons. The SEALs called the distinctive device a Budweiser.

After shooting the breeze with the enlisted SEALs late into the night, Oby knew he was hooked. He graduated later that year with a degree in political science and promptly departed for boot camp in Orlando. Oby graduated from the BUD/S course as class honor man.

A distinction bestowed upon the top student as seen through the eyes of his peers. He picked up a loose sniper school slot after SQT by being in the right place at the right time. He completed the course with flying colors and reported aboard SDV Team Two a year before Matt. Oby was the troop's best shooter.

Then there was Doc McDermott, the babe magnet. The other guys loved to hang around him when on liberty waiting to pick up the girls Doc rejected. His smooth charm and movie star good-looks always worked. Doc made it through BUD/S despite his borderline physical condition.

No matter how hard he tried, Doc always found himself at the back of the pack on training runs and ocean swims. The guys loved him anyway because despite being the troop's worst athlete, he never quit anything he started.

As the corpsman for the eight-man troop, he was a graduate of over two years of advanced special operations medical training. SEAL medical personnel were required to attend the army's advanced Special Forces medic school at Fort Sam Houston, Texas.

Doc did extremely well, scoring high enough to be considered for a special Navy program that would allow him to earn a commission and go through medical school, all paid for by the Navy. He'd declined, deciding instead to report aboard SDV Team Two on schedule. Doc wanted to be a shooter, not a cake eater. He was also a fully qualified R and S spotter and surveillance expert.

Matt was introduced to Oby, Boone and Doc a few hours later. Knowing their personal stories helped close the new guy gap a bit. When Chief Auger began to introduce Miguel Cruise, Matt noticed right away that Cruise was one of the few Hispanic-Americans he'd seen in the short time he'd been in the special warfare community.

Cruise was from El Paso, Texas, and was a die-hard Cowboys fan. He was on his second SEAL team having spent his first five years with SEAL Team Four. Team Four was oriented toward Central and South America so it made sense he'd made a big impact there. While at Team Four, his Latino heritage had been invaluable in conducting counter-drug operations.

Cruise noted that he was originally discovered by SEAL recruiters during a language recruiting campaign. The teams were scouring the Navy's boot camp populations as part of their strategic effort to increase their foreign language capabilities. Once found, he accepted the offer to try out for BUD/S and he immediately embraced the lifestyle and attitude of the U.S. Navy SEAL. He graduated as honor man of his SQT training class and was a pit bull on the ass of anyone who slacked off in the R and S troop. Cruise was a weapons specialist in addition to being a sniper.

Mitchell Jorgenson and Tim Wells were the last two men introduced to Matt by the chief. Each was a new guy, but not as new as Matt. They'd finished the AOT course conducted right before Matt's. They were both in the Task Unit's R and S troop for the last seven months experiencing the intensive pre-deployment phases of SEAL readiness training.

Jorgy was a former high school football stud who wasn't quick enough to play college ball. His large frame and remarkable stamina earned him the right to carry the heavy M-240B machine gun and all its ammunition. He was also a qualified R and S spotter and even though not an official graduate of the SEAL sniper course, he was the second-best shot in the troop.

Chief Auger noted that Jorgy never stopped complaining. He hated skinny point men and their elf-like habit of dancing through the woods while he humped the machinegun, getting caught on every bush and tree in the forest. He wasn't fond of runners or officers, either. Matt could see by the look in Jorgy's eyes that the jury was still out regarding the new officer. He saw it as a challenge. If he could impress Jorgy the rest of the team would be easy to inspire.

At the opposite end of the personality spectrum was Tim Wells. He stood five feet five inches tall. Wells was easily the smallest man in the troop, maybe in the entire SDV team. He grew up in Hawaii and professed to be a surfer of some ability though he'd never been able to convince the guys in the troop. His life took a dramatic turn one day when he spotted an SDV in Pearl Harbor. Wells went over to the ramp where the SDV Team One support crew was waiting and introduced himself.

He made it a point to return as often as possible over the next year, trying to learn as much as the SEALs would divulge about the unique underwater vehicle. He didn't learn much. So, he joined the Navy and volunteered for BUD/S. He was a classmate of Jorgy's and the two went through SQT, SDV Basic, and AOT together. Unfortunately, once in SDV training Wells found he was a terrible pilot and a worse navigator.

He was lucky enough to score a slot in sniper school right after AOT so while he graduated near the top of his sniper class, he'd missed the initial pre-deployment training with the rest of the troop. Wells was additionally responsible for radio communications and the technical maintenance of the various devices issued to the SEALs. He was the only guy who could calm Jorgy down once the big man was spun up.

Matt made it a point to shake the hand of every one of his men. These guys were handpicked professionals and smart. He was sure they had all the specs on one Lieutenant Matthew Barrett. He wouldn't be surprised if they had all his training files going back to day one at BUD/S hidden somewhere in the troop office or perhaps one of the cages. Everyone checked everyone out in the teams. Your reputation was your status. A shitty operator, a crybaby, a know-it-all—whatever the label, if you'd earned it you could bet everyone was briefed up. There were no secrets.

Government House–Cairo, Egypt

The chatter of machine gun fire echoed down the long marble corridor leading into the presidential audience chamber. The new acting president and his immediate family were tucked away in a small side room, terrified and expecting the worst. Twelve hand-picked Egyptian army commandos guarded the entrance to their hiding spot, each willing to lay down his life for the new president.

Fifty feet away, another team of commandos stood near the end of the corridor waiting for the attackers to complete their assault of the lower level. The soldiers knew the political decision had already been made. Their officers had explained the basics of the uprising and told the men that the Egyptian army commander had refused to throw in his lot with the rebellious government factions led by the religious fanatic, Bandar. The soldiers were more loyal to their General than to their country but if his orders were to protect the president and his family, they would die obeying those orders if necessary.

Bandar the Faithful, as his followers called him, had grossly miscalculated his ability to influence the Egyptian armed forces. While most of the Air Force and Navy leaders supported him, in a land of thankless desert and sprawling urban jungle, it was the Army that held all the cards. Without them, he was in a desperate predicament. He must push through and win or be exiled to the role of terrorist again. It was the time to take jihad to the next level.

An hour later, Bandar heard the news he'd been waiting for. Only hours ago, Bandar had ordered his followers to find and assassinate the stubborn Army chief-of-staff. The last holdout had been found and eliminated by a crowd of angry citizens.

He'd ordered his troops to open up on the crowd, but they'd refused. He had control of all the Army units in and around the city. He gave several sharp orders and the deputies scurried to comply. Twenty minutes later, a ring of armored personnel carriers and tanks closed in around the government house and presidential offices. Inside the presidential palace, lightly armed fanatics charged up the spiral staircase leading to where the stone-faced commandos calmly awaited their inevitable fate.

Chapter Nine

Headquarters NATO Southern Command, Naples, Italy

Admiral Carden pressed the mute button on the TV remote, silencing the CNN announcer for the time being. The coup attempt had been defeated in Egypt. U.S. air power deployed from the aircraft carrier, USS Theodore Roosevelt, had kept the Egyptian Air Force grounded and ineffective. Egyptian Army forces still loyal to the interim president had defied orders to stay in barracks confinement. Reaching the palace, they successfully drove off the forces corrupted by the Sons of Allah who were staged in lightly armed vehicles around the government building.

The interim president wasn't supposed to sacrifice his life. He'd only agreed to stand in for the assassinated head of state until a new election could be held but that process was taking too long. *His life is threatened daily and now this, an attack on the very structure and legitimacy of their government!*

His personal bodyguard had survived a heroic stand within the palace complex, defeating the terrorists and their limited military support even before outside help arrived. Since the event, all United States citizens in Egypt were on standby to evacuate the country if the situation deteriorated any further. The fledgling Egyptian government calmly announced, via the state radio channel, that the situation had been stabilized.

Admiral Carden stood up and stiffly paced about the room. Stabilized! What a stupid thing to tell the people. Egypt was anything but stabilized. The admiral spent hours each day reading reams of intelligence analysis and what he read indicated chaos in the making, not stability. Egypt was going to fall, one way or another.

"You know that bastard Bandar nearly pulled it off," he mumbled half out loud. A communication officer nearby turned away from his console and looked at the admiral quizzically. The admiral waved him off. He wasn't trying to have a conversation. He just needed to vent. Admirals were supposed to be calm, serene, all the time especially in the face of stress and danger. That was bullshit, of course. Admirals were people, too— only they handled negative input differently. Being in command demanded a focused and objective mindset.

He regained his train of thought and began to push his mind down likely paths forward, running each scenario to its logical end and then starting anew.

Bandar had been agitating for over two years. It started with sponsored student protests, worker rallies, and factory shutdowns. Then the jihadist leader began to flex his muscles in earnest, expanding his rebel network inside Egypt. Small attacks to gain prestige and converts at first.

And then, strategic strikes to eliminate rivals—strong leaders in the military and government at every level—including an overt attempt to overthrow the Egyptian government by boldly targeting the head of state himself. Bandar wouldn't quit. It was only a minor setback. Next time, he wouldn't screw up, the admiral thought. The next time Bandar will bring everything he has to win.

Admiral Carden looked around the Sixth Fleet command and control center to see if anyone other than the communications officer was near enough to overhear his profane rambling. As the man in charge of the U.S. Sixth Fleet, and as NATO's southern commander, he was responsible for providing the national command authority; the president, national security agency, and Joint Chiefs of Staff, as well as NATO high command, with a quick assessment of any crisis situation and his recommended plan of action.

The challenge in Egypt was quite simple. Protect the current regime and continue the status quo, or sit on the sidelines, a neutral observer waiting to make friends with the new government. Another fly in the buttermilk was NATO's insistence this was not their affair. But what kind of government would Bandar install? Something similar to the fanatical religious regime in Iran is what his intelligence folks were predicting. NATO leaders saw the same tea leaves he saw. Why weren't they getting more involved?

If a radicalized Egypt was the high-probability outcome, he could take the new situation and project it forward to a future when Israel had strong, belligerent nations on two borders instead of just one. Syria and a new jihadist Egypt could make things much worse for the Israelis and the United States was pledged to protect the tiny nation. Maybe that was NATO's play. They knew America couldn't standby and do nothing. So, rather than pitch in to make the military intervention a global effort, they would stand by and watch America commit, even without allied assistance.

The admiral knew his history. An overthrow in Egypt would set diplomacy back to the era of cyclical wars of destruction, before the Camp David Peace Accords between Israel and Egypt in the late 1970s and President Clinton's efforts with the PLO in the 90s. There was no way the United States would sit back and allow a resurgence of fundamentalist threats against her only true ally in the Middle East. It didn't matter if NATO agreed, he was a Navy man and he would be drawn into the issue by the orders of his superiors in Washington, even if NATO turned a blind eye to Israel's plight.

After stretching their mandate to protect Western Europe by conducting operations in Afghanistan and Iraq, NATO was wary of blindly supporting U.S. foreign policy everywhere in the world. It was also no secret that many NATO countries were sympathetic to the Palestinian independence movement and hostile toward Israel. If NATO dragged their feet or outright refused to assist, the United States may be forced to act alone to save Egypt's democracy. The admiral knew the feelings back home weren't a given, either. Internal American politics were forever shifting from pro-Israel to a more neutral posture.

The voters back home wanted the police actions to stop. Morale in the military was sinking due to the constant deployment demands and material readiness was being stretched to the breaking point. Admiral Carden couldn't do anything about that. He had a more pressing issue to deal with: the safety of U.S. citizens living in Egypt. As usual, U.S. State Department warnings to leave Egypt were only mildly effective. If a NEO, or non-combatant evacuation operation, was needed to safeguard American lives he would be responsible for the successful execution of that operation.

His other deep concern was for the men and women in uniform who would bear the cost in blood if things got messy. If U.S. forces conducted a NEO before a successful coup occurred, he could hope the Egyptian military would assist or at best stay out of the way. If, however, the NEO operation happened after a successful overthrow of the government he could expect Bandar's newly converted generals to follow his orders. He would direct them to attack any U.S. or NATO forces deployed on, near, or flying above, sovereign Egyptian soil.

The admiral walked back to the low table where the secure phone lines were set up. Placing the receiver against his ear, he dialed with determination. It was time to wake up the idea department and get some things down on paper. He finished punching out the number to his operations and plans office four floors below and waited for someone to pick up.

Isolation Complex–Fort Eustis Virginia

A door slammed somewhere in the dark aircraft hangar. Matt's eyes shot wide open. Damn it! Only minutes had gone by since he'd hit the sack. After planning and rehearsing all day, Matt was dog-ass tired. The mission was complex, requiring several different transportation platforms and a multi-tiered command structure. The rehearsal oversight was becoming a major pain in the ass. Try as he might, Matt couldn't keep the prying senior officers off the backs of his SEALs.

Day after day, the men of Matt's recon troop poured over the intelligence material related to the target and the environment surrounding the target. Physical training, or PT, was conducted every morning to keep his men strong and hard. The early morning sweat drills also served to increase morale and mission focus. The good-natured banter between Matt's men was, at times, sharp and biting. They all knew the deal if they couldn't stand the abuse: just fucking quit!

As a new member of the troop and as a newly-minted LT, Matt wasn't invited into the lively exchanges between his men. At first, it was hard to watch the comradery and know he wasn't an accepted participant. Chief Auger explained it would take time and it was up to Matt to balance being in charge, gaining professional respect as a leader, and creating a personal relationship with each of his seven direct reports. This advice was useful, but Matt missed the tight brotherhood of his training classes. In the long SEAL training pipeline, everybody had one thing in common—they were all new guys.

Matt realized with a sigh that his attempt to catch a few winks was futile since reveille was only thirty minutes away. Instead of trying to get back to sleep he rolled onto his side and surveyed the somber interior of the large hangar. He peered into the dark, looking across the open space at the distorted, sleeping shapes of his men. They lay scattered about, twisted in random sleeping positions on the cold cement floor.

Somewhere near the door a buzz saw was spinning up. Matt couldn't see who was snoring, but it didn't seem to affect anybody. These guys were all different yet the same. Each a specialist, each had his own unique personality, yet they were all able to work together like a group of old friends playing pickup basketball for the hundredth time. Matt never stopped marveling at the professionalism and drive of these fine sailors.

Matt turned onto his back and stared at the ceiling. In the last two months, he'd feverishly worked to keep up with the operational tempo set by LCDR Sandoval. It felt like the entire reconnaissance troop was essentially being punished for Matt's late arrival.

Having missed the early pre-deployment command and control assessments, Matt was being forced to participate in the final operational readiness exercise, or ORE, without the benefit of the six-month-long training program his men had experienced. He was a liability and Sandoval knew it.

He'd studied and burned the candle at both ends to meet the demands of pre-deployment training. Training in advanced demolitions, special weapons, and advanced small unit tactics, demanded sixty-hour work weeks. Traveling to new training locations by air on the weekends. Saturday flight in, a week of hard operating, Friday flight home and repeat. As always, hard work tende d to burn the calendar up, and already Matt wondered what had happened to time since he'd joined the task unit. Although his guys were looking sharp in every category of performance, using the DDS, or Dry Deck Shelter in the final ORE was sucking up precious time remaining before heading to the Mediterranean Sea for six months.

Their method of insertion in the ORE was time consuming but it was what made SDV teams elite. A nuclear submarine with a pressurized storage hangar mounted behind the tall structure that rose up from the deck referred to as the sail, was to launch Matt's troop into the exercise scenario, an enemy shoreline.

The complex DDS was designed to store and then launch either rubber boats or the SDV minisub. Matt had learned a considerable amount about the DDS in the basic SDV and AOT courses but now he was required to understand the complex systems and be able to brief and answer questions related to the special operations delivery platform during the ORE.

His head still throbbed from the effort of memorizing the multitude of valves and gauges associated with the DDS. Each SEAL was required to understand enough about the shelter's operation to help in an emergency and to stay out of the way while the Task Unit's DDS troop set things up for underway operations at depth. The SEALs referred to the submarine-DDS-SDV combination of capabilities as the death star and the label fit perfectly.

As the reconnaissance troop commander, Matt rarely navigated an SDV these days. His primary insertion focus was the combat rubber raiding craft. The SEALs deployed their black CRRCs from the submarine mounted DDS to support clandestine infiltration and exfiltration of mission teams.

All the Task Unit X-Ray SEALs had been required to attend a comprehensive two-week advanced DDS course during the pre-deployment workup. They learned the hangar system's basic operations and refreshed their advanced deep diving skills. They were also selectively chosen to qualify on several DDS operating stations as a backup in case one of the DDS task element's Navy divers was sick or otherwise incapacitated. Since Matt missed the course, he was on the hook to teach himself. Several of the DDS divers were helping him through the rough spots.

A loud snort punctuated the sounds coming from near the door. A boot sailed through the air and landed with a thump against the wall. The snoring stopped for a minute or two and then began again. Hell Week was making more and more sense as his time in the teams added up.

Keeping focused and alert while staying awake for five straight days and nights taught you two important things about yourself; first, if you could survive five days of punishment and zero sleep you could probably handle anything. And second, this survival ability was a rare skill among average American males. The SEAL community's commitment to this Darwinian process was the key to selecting a rare breed of warrior.

Matt realized that BUD/S subtly trained the students in the art of situational reality awareness. Most people went through life learning rules. Rules of conduct, rules for communications, nature's rules and so on. One thing true about combat in all the written histories going back as far as the ancient Greeks, war, and especially combat, turn the rules upside down. Weather, terrain, bad information—any of these aspects could conspire to tear the plan to shreds. Of course, the enemy gets a vote too. He can break any and all rules and create new ones—whatever's required to win.

The BUD/S instructor's method was deviously simple. They methodically challenged the student's comfort in relying on rules. Runs scheduled for four miles were extended to twelve miles. Events were briefed one way and then contorted by the instructors to confuse and dismay the students. Eventually, the students realized there were no rules except the ones defined by the reality they were experiencing. One step at a time, one training evolution at a time, one day, one week, one phase at a time. The SEAL phrase that captured this was enlightening. It's not over until it's over.

Those young men who couldn't handle this orchestrated chaos often decided to drop out, declaring, "The SEAL way of life wasn't for them". Matt wasn't a BUD/S student anymore, but he still didn't expect any slack from Sandoval.

His adversary wasn't going to be fair. Fairness was just another concept tied to one's reliance on rules. He knew Sandoval wasn't going to help Matt succeed. The young SEAL officer could deal with that reality and use that information to defeat the Task Unit commander. He was focused on his performance and that included his growing rapport with the men of his R and S team. Only deeds would prove Sandoval wrong.

Chapter Ten

NATO Command Headquarters–Naples, Italy

Navy Commander Frank Mason sighed in relief. The briefing had been a rousing success. The NATO commander, Admiral Carden, was more than pleased and he openly congratulated his tired operations staff, taking a moment to praise Commander Mason's professional presentation.

"As you know only too well, gentlemen, the detailed mission planning and logistics management required for proper execution of a military operation this complex, often spells the difference between success and failure on the battlefield. I want you all to know that I'm flying to Stuttgart, Germany, this evening to brief the European Command on Operation Sparrow Hawk, the NEO in Egypt. I believe my recommendations will be received favorably, due in no small part to your efforts these last few days."

Admiral Carden nodded and then stood up. He and his entourage exited the small secure briefing room through a side door. Commander Mason followed the group out of the room, trying to keep up with the admiral. He appeared both elated and nervous to those watching.

Despite the clear win scored by his planning team today, no one was as tuned into the obvious difficulties associated with Operation Sparrow Hawk as he was. For that reason, a small part of him hoped the idea would quietly go away once the big boys took a look at it.

Admiral Carden's stride was vigorous as he left the secure briefing center. Although he was still obliged to personally brief the CINC tomorrow, the timeline set by the State Department demanded his quick passing of codeword authorization for Operation Sparrow Hawk to indicate his approval to the President. In this manner, the United States national command authority in Washington, could if required, commit to the initial stages of troop deployment and pre-positioning of combat support assets within the next ninety-six hours.

The admiral pondered the enormous level of effort involved to pull off an operation of this size. In only four days his people had put together an outstanding answer to the Egyptian problem.

Operation Sparrow Hawk would be a lightning raid on a massive scale, seizing key transportation facilities such as airports and harbors to facilitate a massive multinational evacuation of Egypt. Of course, it was looking more and more like NATO was going to delay committing their forces until after the United States was committed to full unilateral execution. He knew that was par for the course.

The plan represented a risk but all military ventures had risks. He was especially concerned about the early special operations phase prior to sending the whole task force into Egypt. The SEALs and Green Beret operators would be inserted in the early hours of the operation to conduct strategic reconnaissance and act as eyes on the ground for the first wave.

They would be exposed for a short period of time without air cover or supporting arms. Their missions were critical to the overall success of Operation Sparrow Hawk so sending them in was a necessary risk. At the door to his private quarters, his chief of staff saluted and left the admiral for the operations center.

The admiral entered his stateroom and walked casually toward the oak credenza behind his ornate desk. His eyes were irresistibly drawn toward the black and white photo of his former squadron mates. The F-14 Tomcat pilots looked invincible in their faded flight suits, their grinning faces hiding the fear and tension of near continuous flying combat missions, day in and day out, over Bosnia.

Only half of the twenty-two men in the picture were still in uniform. The stress of combat and constant deployments since the 2001 attacks in New York drove many to seek a more sedate life with their growing families. He didn't begrudge them that decision. Navy life was hard, and it wasn't the only life of value a man could live.

He missed those days—so simple compared to his role now. Great friends and great pilots. They'd all hear if he failed. The Tomcat brotherhood was strong and only a click away from spreading good news and bad.

Admiral Carden kept the picture close as a reminder of just how shaky it could get at the pointy end of the spear. He'd been too senior to participate in the air campaigns that opened up Operation Enduring Freedom in Afghanistan or Operation Iraqi Freedom, but he would never forget the individual sacrifices asked of each soldier, sailor, and airman going into harm's way.

The picture kept him humble and respectful. Men and women like these were counting on the senior leadership to make the right call. He hoped Sparrow Hawk met the standard.

The flag officer turned away from the photo and slumped heavily into his leather office chair. Rubbing his eyes with the palms of his hands, he began once more to run over the weak spots in the Operation Sparrow Hawk plan. Would NATO go through with their support role as promised? That freed up U.S. forces to be the assault force. If not, he'd have to split fighters between target packages and combat air patrol, protecting the air refueling planes and the stream of inbound forces as the first day unfolded. But what if the European politicians balked?

Would the United States execute Operation Sparrow Hawk unilaterally? And what if the critical first phase didn't go as planned? Too many questions, too many unknowns. Admiral Carden looked over once again at those smiling friends of days gone by. Was it ever any different? The men in the picture didn't answer him.

Autec Naval Training Area–The Bahamas

The dark seawater rushed into the empty dry deck shelter, furiously pumping into the empty space through several small but efficient pipes located in the bottom of the hangar. Matt and the other SEALs couldn't help reacting to the cool rush of seawater, although the water was warm by Virginia standards, it still took a minute to adjust.

When the level of water came close to the line, known as the bubble line, marking the fill line, the hangar operator began to slow the flow of water. Once the level was chest high it became easier for the men to move around. They welcomed the water's assistance. The weapons and other personal mission gear draped and attached all over their bodies were designed to be neutrally buoyant in salt water.

The two CRRCs were stacked flat and banded down to a sled-like device in the hangar. All other nooks and crannies were stuffed with mission equipment bags, outboard engines, and Matt's troop, trying to stay out of the diver's way. There were three operational DDS chambers—an emergency treatment chamber, a submarine access chamber, and a cargo hangar. For tonight's mission, the SDV had been removed to allow Matt's troop to execute a submerged rubber boat launch.

The reconnaissance troop was still behind the energy curve after their whirlwind movement to the forward operating base in Puerto Rico. The operational readiness exercise was designed not only to test the troop's tactical ability but also to comprehensively evaluate the SDV Team's capability to move its operational SEAL troops and support units where needed with little or no notice.

Human biology was a key factor in being successful. Stress affected what little sleep the SEALs experienced and the need to hydrate and consume calories was important enough for the chief to measure and monitor. Even with everyone doing the right things, Matt's group was operating at eighty percent when they arrived in Puerto Rico.

The dry deck shelter-capable submarine met the troop in Puerto Rico three days after Matt and his men arrived to begin live full-dress rehearsals. They used the SEAL training facility on Pineros Island as the target. Pineros was a small, live fire range covered in jungle overgrowth and only a few miles southeast from the main island of Puerto Rico. SEALs were cleared to shoot at the island from the air, from boats, and on land. The flexibility to do all these things made Pineros an excellent stand-in for the real target.

They meticulously practiced the various phases of their mission, the fruits of their collective planning effort in the isolation area back in Virginia. The troop had four CRRCs and the chief's idea was to use two for submarine deployment practice and the other two for maritime navigation and over-the-beach practice.

Chief Auger found a shallow area not too far from the SEAL compound and had two CRRCs weighted down so they would sink to the sandy bottom. The boats were flat and strapped to each other, like they would be on the DDS sled. The mission equipment and bags were simulated by using empty canvas bags that were weighted down.

Water visibility was fifty feet during the day. So, unlike deploying at night from the deck of a moving submarine, the daytime practice was easy. That night they practiced the drill all over again, going by feel. When the chief was satisfied, they checked that box and moved on to the next rehearsal block, open water navigation and clandestine beach insertion.

The second pair of CRRC's were on trailers and rigged with all the real mission gear, fuel bladders, weapons, radios, and an outboard engine. Matt and the chief each took a boat, splitting the troop into two four-man teams. The chief and Boone worked up a multi-leg navigation course that would provide enough practice to make them all feel comfortable with the gear and their ability to move from point A to point B without getting lost.

On the third day, they spent most of their time sending in and then recovering the swimmer scouts. Their job was to get in, move across the beach, and set up without getting caught. They called the boats in and the troop practiced their actions at the objective phase until it started getting dark. They patrolled to the beach and swam out to the two CRRCs waiting off the beach.

Dinner consisted of cold MREs, sitting in the boats, and telling stories. It took another ninety minutes for the sun to go down. Then, Matt and his troop ran through the entire process all over again in the dark. The training evaluators were in their own boat, a safety platform that allowed them to watch and grade the rehearsals. They also sent in one instructor who swam in near the swimmer scouts then shadowed the SEALs as they conducted their operation inland.

The Pineros rehearsal was over and Matt knew they'd nailed it. Matt and his men were beat, and they hadn't even started the real ORE mission. He figured they'd averaged five hours' sleep a night since being recalled to start the ORE.

He realized everything he'd experienced was important and normal for SEAL operations. No one was messing with his guys; SEAL work was exhausting and the meticulous attention to detail drilled into their collective heads throughout their training was a standard that had a high cost. The BUD/S instructors had been sincere when they told the students that basic SEAL training was just the beginning, a warmup for the real thing.

On the fifth day they cleaned and packed up all their mission gear and weapons. Around noon the submarine pulled into Naval Station Roosevelt Roads, the U.S. Navy's protected harbor on the southeast coast of Puerto Rico. Chief Auger directed the onloading and after several hours reported to Matt.

"Sir, we're all good to go here. I told the guys to stick close, no going into the base. Has the skipper told you when he plans to set sail?"

Matt nodded. "Yeah, the executive officer sent me a note saying they wanted us inside and all tucked in by fifteen hundred hours." Matt checked his watch. "That's only twenty minutes from now, so may as well round everybody up and get them inside."

Chief Auger nodded. He knew it took a full hour for a Navy ship to detach from shore power, disconnect land line communications, get a full head count of the crew, fully man the control room and the fair-weather deck on top of the sail. Once all that was complete, they would throw off the thick ropes secured around large steel cleats on the pier and begin to slowly edge backward until free of the pier. Then the submarine would pivot, pointing its nose to sea and slowly pass through the harbor traffic until arriving well beyond the harbor mouth.

Chief Auger whistled and caught Wells' attention on shore. He pointed his index finger in the air and began to move it around in a circle. Wells waved showing he understood the muster or rally-up hand signal. A few minutes later the men of Task Unit X-RAY's R and S troop were safely nestled in the crew's mess, eating snacks.

Matt and Chief Auger were last to enter the vessel. They counted heads then climbed down the ladder into the area just off the control room. Matt was curious and had received permission to watch the team as it maneuvered the submarine out of the harbor and into the channel between Vieques Island and Puerto Rico.

The chief nodded then headed back to the chief's mess to watch a movie. From here on out, the SEALs would struggle with boredom and the ship's crew would struggle with SEALs in their way as they tried to do their job.

The submarine submerged two hours after pulling away from the pier in Roosevelt Roads. It made good time, covering the just over eight-hundred-mile trek in a little less than two days. Once off the Autec Training area in the Bahamas, the submarine began to navigate in a large circle. They were ready to commence special operations.

The Troop was notified they were to man the DDS shelter in two hours. Most of the men went back to the crew's mess to get a cup of coffee and snatch a couple of chocolate chip cookies. Matt could sense his men were at ease, ready to get the ORE over and done with. They'd all caught up on their sleep and were keen to begin the mission. At the appointed time, the submarine's 1MC public address system blared the message "ALL SEALS TO THE DDS SHELTER. I SAY AGAIN, ALL SEALS TO DDS SHELTER."

A shiver ran down Matt's back. This wasn't a real mission, but he had a lot riding on his performance. He instinctively knew if they failed in any way, he would own the failure. Probably because he second guessed his team's judgment. If Matt relaxed and let the team flow through the problem set, they would succeed, and he with them. Matt met his chief at the ladder leading up into the DDS.

"Full head count?"

"Yes, sir. You were the last one." The chief smiled.

Matt didn't mind the barb. He'd purposefully lagged behind to give everyone in his team a chance to squeeze down the narrow passageway that led to the ladder. "Sorry, chief! Let's head on up."

The two men climbed the ladder and entered the hangar. The troop was staged all the way back near the huge DDS outer door. The divers from the DDS troop were moving around, checking that gear was secured properly and the multiple air bibs running down both sides of the hangar's roof were turned on. The bibs were SCUBA regulators attached to long hoses and fed air directly from the submarine. This meant the SEALS didn't have to wear SCUBA tanks inside the DDS.

Inside the DDS, Matt reviewed their efforts so far and was pleased. He believed the rehearsal training had hardened his troop and kept his guys focused. He knew the proper execution of the pre-mission planning and briefing phase was a critical and graded part of the entire mission cycle, but it was time for his team to face the meat of the exercise.

No matter how well they'd planned and rehearsed, his troop must succeed this mission or they would fail the operational readiness evaluation—and failure meant no combat readiness certification for the troop or their parent, Task Unit X-RAY.

While the confinement and close living arrangements at the Virginia isolation complex tended to agitate the young SEAL warriors, the open-air live-fire environment of Pineros Island facilitated a return of their professional passion and an intense desire to succeed. It stirred in all of them a primal hunting instinct. The pre-game show was over, it was time to put up or shut up!

Chapter Eleven

The navy diver assigned as the hangar operator stood in the DDS control bubble spinning a fourteen-inch diameter, horizontal disk known as a wheel valve, shutting off the water flow into the hangar.

The small space was called the control bubble because air pressurization in the small space prevented seawater flooding the Hangar from rising up, placing the hangar operator underwater. The bubble of air allowed the operator to be dry from the waist up—free to manipulate the shelter's controls and use the communications link to the control room in the submarine as needed.

Matt heard rather than saw the seawater stop entering the large space. The hangar supervisor stood in the control bubble next to the hangar operator keeping dry enough to watch everything. The supervisor controlled everything in the DDS from behind a clear plastic window using hand and arm signals the SEALs and Navy divers understood and passing information to the submarine's control room through the control bubble's two-way communications system.

The hangar supervisor directed the hangar operator to equalize the shelter by pumping air into the hangar then rapped the side of the steel hangar three times using a wrench. He paused a few seconds, then added one final tap. The divers and SEALs were patiently waiting, breathing on bib regulators. When they heard the signal, they used their fingers to pinch their noses and began blowing hard against their nose to open their ears, this technique allowed the inside chambers of their sinuses to relieve the steady buildup of air pressure.

The first and second-class divers assigned to Task Unit X-Ray's DDS troop were handpicked from throughout the U.S. Navy and were graduates of rigorous advanced special operations training. The divers and the SEALs from the R and S or SDV troops worked as a cohesive unit with the divers to load, unload and operate the DDS system. The divers were physically fit and could pair up comfortably with any SEAL if he needed assistance underwater.

There was a senior diver in charge of the hangar cargo area who maintained a position halfway between the control bubble and the huge DDS door. He coordinated launch/recovery activity both inside and outside the DDS using hand and arm signals to the hangar supervisor. He received direction from the supervisor standing behind the window the same way, passing the instructions to the hangar dive team and SEALs getting ready to leave the submarine.

The remaining hangar divers received okay signals. Fingers indicating a closed loop using the thumb and index finger, from each of the SEALs before flashing the same signal to the senior diver who in turn flashed the signal to the hangar supervisor in the control bubble. The hangar operator indicated the hangar was equalized with the sea pressure outside the submarine. Once pressure equalization between the hangar and sea pressure was confirmed, the hangar supervisor directed the hangar operator to hydraulically pump open the huge dry deck shelter outer door.

The entire series of activities from initial loading of warm, dry and very overloaded SEALs into the hangar, to flooding, to pressurization and finally opening the DDS door, took practice and skill. In thirty minutes or less, the mission team was moving onto the deck of the submarine.

As the door opened fully and locked into position, soft starlight began to filter down from the ocean's surface to the deck of the submarine below. The divers and Matt's eight-man team moved smoothly about the submarine's deck coordinating their various functions like a well-rehearsed underwater ballet. The Navy divers moved out carrying canvas bags filled with rigging lines. They swam to the hard points; stainless steel pad eyes attached to the submarine deck and snapped the rigging lines in place.

Once the lines were ready, a diver took a large deflated salvage buoy out of the hangar and swam out to the middle of the deck. The loose ends of the rigging lines were snapped into the bottom of the large buoy. Then a toggle was pulled, activating the carbon dioxide cylinder attached to the buoy. The buoy rapidly inflated and shot to the surface of the dark ocean, taking all the attached rigging lines up with it.

The track was slid out of the hangar and locked into place allowing the boat-laden cradle to roll out of the hangar and into the starlight. The cradle was controlled and then locked into place by two divers. Boone, Wells, and one of the divers quickly unsnapped the retaining bands holding the flat boats to the cradle.

Cruise and Jorgy went back into the nearly-empty DDS and brought out the thirty-five horsepower outboard engines, protected in special rubber waterproof bags. The engines were placed into the top CRRC and secured to the boat with metal snap link connectors.

Matt and the remaining SEALs ferried out the additional mission equipment, snapping the bags into the top CRRC. Soft rubber fuel bladders were then removed from the submarine's aft line-locker and secured in place next to the outboard engines. The entire process took no more than five minutes during which the submarine maintained perfect trim and depth control. An ascender line was connected to the vertical rigging line that led up to the salvage buoy on the surface. When the silent dance on deck was finally complete, Matt signaled his mission team to assemble on one side of the flattened rubber boats using a red chemical light stick.

Using a hand signal, Matt directed Chief Auger to pull the handle of the carbon dioxide bottle attached to the first CRRC. Four members of the troop held on as the CRRC gently inflated and began to lift off the deck toward the turbulent surface above. The second boat was deployed to the surface in the same manner with the last four SEALs ascending. The SEALs insertion phase was complete. Infiltration into "enemy waters" was next on the mission schedule.

White House Situation Room–Washington, D.C.

The President sat quietly listening to the commentary provided by his National Security Advisor. The chief executive was weary of these sessions. His campaign for president had been based on an America First theme. He'd promised the American people a drawdown of the military and substantial reinvestment of the peace dividend into his rather aggressive domestic agenda. But as with countless presidents before him, he was now being forced against his will and better judgment to dance to a different tune.

It never ceased to amaze him. No matter how bad things were in America, they always seemed to pale in comparison to the crisis of the decaying new world order. The President rubbed his tired eyes with the palms of his hands then took a deep breath. He needed to force himself to focus on his close friend and National Security Advisor.

"So, in conclusion, Mr. President, it's the Security Council's collective opinion that the problem in Egypt will get worse before it gets better. It's our consensus recommendation that you grant authority to conduct preliminary operations in support of Admiral Carden's contingency plan for the rapid evacuation of American personnel from Egypt. We further request your sanction of Operation Sparrow Hawk with a one-hundred-hour contingency response window effective one week from today."

The President looked intently at the Chairman of the Joint Chiefs and Air Force General "Bull" Swanson. He addressed the chairman. "General, I know you and the Chiefs have reviewed and approved the Sixth Fleet contingency plan. But what's the downside in doing this before these people in Egypt demonstrate hostile intent? I mean, there's no indication, that I'm aware of, that we should expect a new fundamentalist government to actively seek out and target United States citizens. Aren't we being a little paranoid?"

The president watched as the ruggedly built general officer choked back his first response. Although by law the president was the commander in chief of the armed forces of the United States, and therefore the chairman's superior, it was well known through leaks in the beltway press, that the general believed that the president's policies had directly led to the decline of American power, prestige, and influence overseas.

He was quoted in one interview read by the president several weeks earlier, that the commander in chief appeared weak to the tyrants and jackals of the world. This weakness had opened the door for a crisis to occur, maybe even in Egypt. The last comment in the article hit the president hard. The general made the point that he'd never spent a single day in uniform before being elected president.

"Mr. President," the chairman began. "Operation Sparrow Hawk is a smart, economical plan using only minimal force to achieve the primary evacuation objectives.

The force package required utilizes our special operations forces early on and relies on Army Rangers and Marines to establish the evacuation sites and safe corridors in and around Cairo and Alexandria. If we do not start the evacuation operation's timetable now, Mr. President, I fear many Americans could become involved in a negative way. Kidnapping and murder come to mind, and we won't be in position to do anything but watch."

The President was distracted; his eyes drifted toward the window. The chairman was carefully insinuating that he was ignoring the military's input intentionally. As if following the orders of military men was the president's job and not the other way around.

The frustrated senior officer proceeded anyway. "Mr. President, in my professional opinion, there is no downside to the contingency plan submitted by Admiral Carden. Of course, the flow of sufficient pre-mission intelligence will determine how surgical and bloodless the operation can be and will be. This, of course, must be collected well before the one-hundred-hour period begins. With all due respect, Mr. President, without your authorization to collect such information now, the potential casualties will be higher among our lead units."

The President clenched his teeth. He shifted his gaze from the window to a painting on the wall to the left of the window. He so disliked these military types. So willing to throw bombs at every challenge. His eyes strayed to the left some more, to the impressive piece on the wall depicting a scene from the Battle of Gettysburg. What a terrible couple of days that must have been for President Lincoln. A horrific and costly battle in a terrible war. All because politicians couldn't find a way to solve their problems.

"I wonder what old Abe would think about the chairman's plan?" he thought. "What advice would he give me now? I bet Lincoln would say suck it up! This is what a president gets paid to do."

The President sighed. Every president all the way back to George Washington had their domestic agenda derailed by war or impending conflict. And now, he realized, it was his turn in the barrel.

The President refocused his attention on the military men and advisors sitting across from him in the Oval Office. "Very well, General Swanson. The Sixth Fleet contingency plan for Egypt is approved. Let Admiral Carden know he can proceed with logistical and intelligence preparations immediately. I still fervently hope this whole thing blows over before we have to commit our boys to combat."

The President scooted his chair back and stood up. The meeting was over. He hurriedly moved toward the door and his next appointment as the assembled advisors and military officers scrambled to jump to their feet. Egypt was an important issue but the fires currently wreaking havoc in California were becoming a major media event. As president, he had an obligation to show the proper level of concern, personally. He spoke over his shoulder as he departed the room. "Have the Secretary of the Interior notified that I'll pick him up in Air Force One en route to California."

The White House chief of staff responded. "Yes, Mr. President."

The President of the United States put Operation Sparrow Hawk out of his mind and left the room.

General Swanson smiled. He stood at attention while the president cleared the oval office. The president and his pack of butt-kissers scampered down the hallway. What the general didn't know, mused the president, was that the CIA had already informed him of the joint chief's preemptive moves to set the operation in Egypt in motion, this before seeking approval and sanction from him.

There was no way as commander in chief he would have stood by like some weak functionary letting Admiral Carden and his team sit on their hands until given permission to prepare. He felt it best not to tell the military they were being watched. He needed an advantage in this high-stake political game.

The forces of change in Egypt would have taken advantage of the delay caused by this any hesitation. Now that the Pentagon had their official green light, the chairman and his service branch leaders could get down to business and really start to move some tonnage around. As the president entered the executive limo he made a mental note to visit the tank in the Pentagon. He wanted a detailed briefing on the status of the special operations forces in the area of the Mediterranean.

Autec Training Area, The Bahamas

Chief Auger directed Jorgy to detach the snap link holding the second CRRC to the bottom of the salvage buoy and reconnect it to the steel ring at the top. Matt's boat had already disconnected from the tether point and was casually maintaining a position ten yards away. The submarine was moving slowly so it wasn't difficult to stay close while his second group crawled into their CCRC.

Jorgy gave the chief a thumbs up, acknowledging the Chief's order, then waved to the diver hugging the buoy at the surface of the ocean. The diver didn't respond, but he reached up and grabbed the snap link connecting the CCRC's bow line to the buoy and unhooked the device. The bowline went slack and Oby pulled it into the small rubber boat. They were on their own.

Matt watched the second boat disconnect then pointed to Wells to get moving. Wells gunned the outboard and they took off. Chief Auger's CRRC roared across the waves behind them and in seconds he'd caught up. Once alongside the first CRRC he maintained a five-yard separation between the boats.

Matt could see in his mind's eye what the support divers were doing behind him. The dangerous dance in the ocean took skill and courage to execute. The team of divers on deck would begin to winch the buoy and rigging back down from the surface allowing it to collapse to the deck.

It would take them ten minutes to stow the rigging lines and salvage buoy back into their bags, secure them down to the DDS cradle, and then slide the whole rig back into the DDS. Once the divers ensured all gear and personnel were accounted for, they would signal the hangar supervisor to pump shut the big door. Matt turned his focus to the mission.

Chapter Twelve

The two black rubber boats streaked across the surface of the calm sea. Matt's mission team was ready to get ashore and get down to business. The submarine was comfortable, but the SEALs were always in the way. The crew enjoyed the novelty for the first day or so and then the grumbling began. It was a good thing for everyone that there were eight fewer bodies in the submarine for a while.

Officially it was day eight of the ORE. But the real game had already started. The SEALs were tired of endless planning and briefing—studying DDS launch procedures, target parameters, timetables, and all the other issues related to the ORE mission.

At some point, it was time to just get it done. As the veterans in the troop knew all too well, Murphy's Law was in effect the minute they inserted. Whatever could go wrong, would go wrong. SEALs were trained to expect that and to manage the chaos—even coping with target conditions that often were considerably different than what had been briefed earlier.

They were also sick of being watched daily by staff pukes grading the pre-mission phases. LCDR. Sandoval, in particular, had been a royal pain in the butt for everyone involved. He should feel lucky to have grabbed an operational leadership position. Most combat units in the teams were led by Lieutenants and below.

Task Unit X-Ray was one of only a few exceptions. The micromanaging leader of the Task Unit had contested every detail of the operational plan contrived by Matt and his men. Whatever they thought up, the old man countered with an emotional reaction and veto. It was a miracle, Matt thought, that he hadn't demanded a seat in the CRRC!

LCDR Sandoval was so unlike any SEAL officer Matt had ever met or worked with, that sometimes he wondered if the man had somehow faked his way into the teams. He had a terrible reputation and a personality like a wet fish. Matt looked over at the second CRRC now trailing slightly behind and to the left of his lead boat. Boone was using a night observation device, or NOD, to pick out coastal navigation lights and tossing the information back to Cruise who was validating each fix against the GPS' electronic navigation board.

Even though Chief Auger was in the trailing boat, Matt directed him to make sure he paid attention and backed up Matt's primary navigation team, just in case they made a mistake. The chief was to confirm their progress by using old-school techniques that didn't rely on a satellite or batteries.

The submarine the SEALs with their launch point coordinates, so Matt knew that all the Chief had to do was draw a line along their planned bearing and mark off distance in one thousand-yard increments. Then he would use a tool referred to as a whiz wheel to convert their known speed and time of movement to a distance to be plotted. Lastly, the chief would shoot bearings to the navigation lights near the Autec facility's coastline to cross check his location on the plotted track.

The technique in its entirety was called "dead reckoning." It had been good enough for the Vikings which is one reason Matt felt better with the chief getting a running second opinion.

An hour had passed since the successful dry deck shelter launch. Matt looked down at a nautical chart segment made of special waterproof paper. The chart showed the launch point, the intended course by magnetic bearing, and the coastline. His calculations indicated they were about a mile offshore. Matt turned to Wells.

"What's up, Wells? Any chance we'll get out of this damn boat before the sun comes up?"

The troop's primary navigator was a professional. Although only a third class petty officer, he excelled at nearly every aspect of SEAL operations.

"Keep your pants on, sir!" Wells whispered. "All we have left to do is continue on this track and speed for another five minutes then zig ten degrees to the right of track. That offset will place us near the reef five minutes later and then we turn hard left to follow the coastline for five hundred yards or so, then presto! The gap in the reef, our entry point." Smiling, he added, "What's the matter sir, don't you trust me?"

Matt regretted raising the question in the first place. One of the strangest things about the teams was the quality of individual you found working alongside you. Men who excelled at anything they set their minds to. All of them, content to be on-loan to Uncle Sam's Navy. Each man doing it for their brothers-in-arms and for the right to be called a SEAL. They certainly weren't there for the pay.

"Thanks for the update, I'm good to go." Matt pulled out his encrypted UHF radio and turned it on. The waypoint message was going to the orbiting command and control aircraft who would then relay the status of the mission to the submerged submarine and to higher headquarters, back at Little Creek, Virginia.

As predicted, Matt soon spotted the reef, marked by the foamy turbulence created by the ocean rushing over the three- to four-foot depth of shallow water covering the reef. The natural barrier could have been breached by driving the CCRCs over the reef—there was enough depth according to the chart, but all it would take was one tall coral head to take out an outboard engine and screw up the mission.

Wells directed Oby to come left onto a course that ran parallel to the reef and the beach.

Matt couldn't see the shoreline, but he knew Wells' partner in crime, Jorgy, was using a night observation device to track their progress.

As the boat maneuvered around to its new base course, Jorgy whispered, "Mark!"

This call indicated to Matt that the boat's nose was now on the correct course, parallel to the shore. Wells nodded to Matt once he confirmed the magnetic heading and told then Oby to hold that course. The second boat slid around to the left after executing the turn and continued to maintain its offset position.

Matt knew the chief was continuing to work on the backup navigation to make sure his LT didn't screw up. Matt pressed his push-to-talk button on the UHF radio.

"X-RAY SIX, this is FLIPPER. UTAH, I say again, UTAH, over." Matt waited, hoping he didn't have to repeat the call. Time on the radio was a negative behavior that in real combat could spell disaster, especially against an enemy capable of triangulating the source of the emissions.

"FLIPPER, this is X-RAY SIX, roger, out!"

Matt put the radio away. He glanced over at the other boat and saw his Chief showing a thumbs up.

It was a question.

Matt gave Chief Auger a thumbs up in return. Matt didn't take his Chief's request for confirmation personally. If Chief Auger hadn't been checking on the key events in their plan, he'd be derelict in his responsibilities as second-in-command. Chief Auger's value as a sounding board continued to help Matt anticipate potential problems and prepare for them. As mentors go, Matt knew that Chief Auger was one of the best.

The overhead photography didn't show the exact edge of the coral reef at low tide, so there was no way the SEALs could know for sure whether or not they were hitting the gap in the reef just right. The darkness was an issue since the night vision gear couldn't make out the reef formations under water. Wells raised his hand. He made the navigation call since they were at the gap. It was now time to turn right and head to the beach landing site or BLS.

Matt signaled to Oby to slow down by gently pressing his open palm toward the surface of the water. It was a land patrol signal, but it still worked out here. As both CRRCs backed down, Matt raised his night scope up to his face to check things out for himself. The view afforded him by the sophisticated night vision device elicited a low groan from Matt. The tide was at just the right height to allow the offshore waves to mark the reef line, but the tide was rising causing the turbulence to dissipate. It was near impossible to determine where the reef ended.

The bitch of it was, Matt knew their timeline demanded forward movement to the BLS. They didn't have the margin to mess around out here. Wells raised a clenched fist indicating he wanted the boats to stop. Matt lowered the scope and patiently awaited the navigator's verdict. Wells glanced back to respond to the lieutenant's unspoken question.

"I just took a global positioning fix, boss. Best I can figure we're close enough to the edge of the reef for government work!"

Matt checked his watch. One thirty in the morning. That left three and a half hours until nautical twilight began. At sea, dawn came early, offering increasing visibility an hour or so before the sun actually broke the horizon. The SEALs needed to be off the beach and underway en route to the submarine rendezvous before this early illumination began.

Matt watched Chief Auger maneuver his CRRC along the port side of the lead boat. It was apparent from his backup team's analysis that they were at the right point. "Why aren't we going in, LT?" His chief gave Matt a thumbs up indicating that his crew's back up navigation concurred with the technology in Matt's CRRC.

Matt reached out to grab the carrying handle of the chief's boat, stabilizing the two boats immediately. Wells hissed a warning to Chief Auger. "Hey, chief! Put your engine in neutral, you're shoving us toward the coral!"

The chief glanced shoreward and quickly gestured to Cruise to kill the outboard on the second boat. The chief then turned his attention back to the reason he'd pulled alongside in the first place.

"So, what gives, boss? Are we going in or what?"

"Stay hitched to us, we're going in through the gap. Tilt your outboard out of the water a little just in case."

Chief Auger nodded. "Roger that, sir!"

Matt signaled to Boone that he could begin the approach to the BLS. Boone looked at Wells for confirmation, Wells nodded. Matt didn't miss the exchange. He was still the wild card on the team. Unproven, unknown. That was something only time and success would change.

The two CCRCs moved toward the beach slowly, making very little sound and creating no visible wake. The SEALs in both boats knelt or laid down to reduce their silhouettes. There was no doubt in their minds that they were already under the watchful eye of the training cell folks hanging out on the beach. Everything they did was scored, including how they landed on an enemy beach.

After ten minutes of slow movement, Matt felt Wells ease over closer to him. “Bingo, big cheese, we are definitely right off at beach-center. Chalk up one more for the kid!”

Matt smiled at hearing the good news from Wells. No matter how much the troop planned and worked to get this stuff right, there were a million ways to screw it up. Every SEAL had a seabag full of horror stories from previous training missions. The tradition was to convert the bad experiences into hilarious self-deprecating humor. SEALs didn’t talk about the perfect missions, what was the point?

Invariably, all SEAL stories included dramatic elements which increased the scale of the experience being recalled such as fierce storms, freezing temperatures, unbelievably long forced marches, and nighttime ocean swims in presumably shark-infested waters. As one might expect, these sea stories became more tragic and fantastic with each telling. Matt learned to both enjoy and to learn from these tales. SEALs were always ready to share their lessons learned with other frogmen.

Matt nodded and patted Wells on his arm. “That’s good news, Wells. You did a fine job getting us here.” Matt’s comment stated the obvious. Nobody in the teams took this shit for granted. The lieutenant was speaking for the entire troop.

“All right, Chief,” Matt whispered as he turned once again to look directly at the senior enlisted man. “The way I see it, I don’t want to bury these boats the way we briefed back in isolation. We have a better chance of crossing the beach undetected if we anchor the boats out here, leave two men behind to protect them, and swim the rest of the mission team in from here. It’d save us a lot of time.”

“How far a swim ya figure that’s going to be, LT?” Chief Auger asked.

"It doesn't really matter how far, chief," Matt replied a little too sharply. "It's our final exam and we don't have a choice in the matter. My gut tells me the training cell is just waiting for us to land and start digging. They'll hit us when we're covered in sand and vulnerable. Then we'll have no choice but to abandon the boats to break contact. That's an abort criterion, mission's over, Sandoval wins. Besides, the swim out to the sub will be a ball buster."

The chief thought for a moment. The new kid was making sense. "I spent a year in the training cell and what you're describing was par for the course. The instructors loved to screw over the new officers and with Sandoval out there somewhere trying to make his R and S troop commander look bad, a BLS ambush is certainly s a high probability tonight." He held up both hands and shook his head. "You're the boss, LT. Whatever you say. But let's get going, we're burning moonlight just sitting here."

He watched as the chief worked to secure the boats to each other. The boat pool would stay anchored just thirty yards seaward of the first breaker line. The waves were relatively small, but things could change when the tide shifted. Best to be safe. The two guys in the boats could move anywhere on the coast to pick up the troop after the actions on the target were completed. The idea added flexibility, even if it meant swimming to the beach.

On Matt's order, he and five of the troop's fearsome gun-slingers slid quietly out of their respective combat rubber raiding craft and into the dark ocean. The chief and Cruise stayed with the anchored boats. Matt gave his chief the UHF radio. He would act as the communications link to the airborne command post while the rest of the troop moved inland. He was also the emergency extraction leader should Matt be required to haul ass to a different area of the beach for an expedited pickup.

"Good luck LT!"

Matt nodded and disappeared in the inky darkness. The mild chill of the water reminded the SEALs, now swimming steadily toward shore, of how depleted their energy reserves were already. The time spent immersed in the DDS had taken a toll on the fluid levels in their bodies.

In the warm waters off the Bahama islands, a swimmer's body would continuously sweat. Within an hour or so a man could lose enough water through perspiring to flirt with mild hypothermia. Add an open-air boat trip, followed by a pleasant night swim to the beach and you were looking at a condition that could negatively impact mission success.

Chapter Thirteen

Boone and Doc led the swimmers into the reef, all of them straining to see if the training cell was indeed camped out on beach center. However, it was impossible at this stage to see any details of the shore. What had seemed simple navigation from the raised platform of their boats was now made difficult by their low position in the water.

Matt watched as his point man tried to use the angle of the wave sets to determine a good heading to the BLS. Boone backed this technique up from time to time with a quick check of his wrist compass. Just finding the shore was easy, any piece of crap tossed overboard ended up there eventually. Matt's team needed to be near the designated landing spot on the far-right flank of the BLS.

The problem the SEALs had, in this case, was to prevent being swept far left or right of the intended BLS. Large rocks protected this section of the coastline everywhere but in the area of their BLS.

Matt felt a twinge of anxiety as the group pushed through the first line of breakers by diving down and under the surface turbulence. His concern was erased, however, when the team all managed to pop up on the other side together. The men had instinctively bunched up prior to negotiating this first challenge. They spread themselves out again, all eyes scanning the dark shoreline.

Each SEAL operator wore the old reliable UDT inflatable life jacket developed by early frogmen in the 1950s. Less complicated than the diving gear used for combat ship attacks, the UDT lifejacket was designed to be slim, light, and easy to wear. It was a backup safety device only. Old Vietnam-era SEALs swore the piece of gear had saved lives during that war by keeping them from sinking to the bottom of the muddy delta rivers they frequented.

This critical piece of equipment had remained in the team's inventory for longer than anyone could remember. While it was a great way to compensate for the weight of bullets and guns if you fell overboard, it was a pain in the butt if used as flotation support during a swim.

The jacket could be inflated manually through a breathing tube or by pulling a lever that shot carbon dioxide gas into the empty bladder. If used in this manner it created a tight and restrictive doughnut around the wearer's head and chest turning a SEAL into a hard-to-control one-man raft, subject to the movement of every wave and current that came along.

SEALs were trained from day one in BUD/S to respect the sea. Full combat equipment swims—carrying ammunition, food, water, demolition packs, and radio gear—were routine events in the last phase of basic SEAL training and SQT. Throughout this educational process, the men learned how to sew high-density foam into their assault vests and line associated pouches with thin material.

This compensated for the dead weight of combat equipment. For additional mission equipment the SEALs might repurpose the inflatable bladders found in demolition haversacks. With all this preparation making the men neutrally buoyant in the salty ocean the UDT life jacket was only viewed as an emergency piece of equipment.

Boone signaled for Matt to swim closer. Matt reduced the distance with a few powerful, short strokes of his fins.

"What's up?" Matt whispered.

"No dice, boss," Boone sputtered. "There's just no way through but straight over the top of these rocks."

"Where's the BLS?" Matt asked.

A small wave smacked Boone in the face before he could respond. He twisted his head just in time to avoid getting a mouth full of seawater a second time. "Well, boss. It looks like we missed threading the needle. I know we're to the right, so we won't bump into any assholes waiting for us at beach center. I say we head in, climb up and over these rocks. Get on dry ground, send the feet dry code word, and get on with it!"

Matt's face reflected his concern. All the frogmen were again clustering in a dog pile around him, kicking and kneeing each other in the process. They were only in four-foot-deep water. The shallow beach gave the wave action more authority, swooshing and swirling the operators around each other. It was time to make a decision. Matt's consideration of Boone's assessment and recommendation was accelerated by a sharp knee in the lower back.

"Sorry LT," Jorgy whispered.

Matt made his decision. "Okay, Boone. Take us in before we kill each other out here!"

Matt quietly passed the word to Wells who then whispered it to each man and so on until they were all informed of Matt's decision to go in over the rocks.

As he turned and gave Boone the signal to move out, Matt shivered. It was the third time in less than a minute. He also noted that Boone's voice was quivering. They were all starting to get cold. The rocks or hypothermia—it wasn't much of a choice. At least they could warm up once ashore. Matt glanced back to sea looking for the CCRCs. They were invisible in the inky darkness.

Satisfied, he kicked harder to catch up with Boone who was only five yards from the rocks defining that part of the coast. His knee slammed into a rock a few seconds later. Matt winced at the pain, caused not by the impact with the immovable object but because of the small cut created by mollusk shells cemented in place all over the submerged obstacle slicing across. *This is going to suck!*

The first cut was small. Matt's knee vaguely registered pain. That was until the saltwater seeped into the tiny wound. Within seconds he banged into another rock and then another, feeling the sharp edges of the mollusk shells cutting into first his shin and then his thigh as he ran out of water depth and started crawling across the rocks.

Matt heard muffled profanity off to his left, a sure sign he wasn't the only guy getting beat up. The thin, standard issue aviator gloves he wore were not designed to protect his hands against something like this. As he moved farther up the rocks and out of the water, he experienced cuts on both hands.

Soon, Matt crested the rocks and spotted Boone's silhouette just inside the edge of the tree line. The rest of his team was assembling around him, laying prone on the sand along the edge of the shoreline. Their bodies blended in with the shapes of the rocks.

The trees there, on the windward side of the island, grew at sharp angles to the ground. Matt calculated the time and distance travelled by the troop since leaving the rubber boats. He guessed they were approximately fifty yards to the right of the pre-selected BLS. Matt signaled Boone and the other SEALs to advance on line across the beach. Boone and Jorgy moved ahead of the rest as planned. Everybody drained the water from their weapons and then silently moved forward.

To call the foliage trees was being generous. They were more like gnarly six-foot-tall bushes all interwoven and as dense as steel wool. Pointing the waterproof night vision scope inland, Matt swept first right, and then left. He could clearly make out the continuous line of low brush and bent trees, but he couldn't identify the BLS from his vantage point.

Matt watched as Boone moved farther into the trees with Jorgy and his M-240B machine gun close behind. They pushed into the dense trees, half-crawling, half-crouching, until ten yards later they broke through the trees and into a cleared area.

The swimmer scout pair patrolled slowly and carefully in a diamond-shaped pattern. At each point of the pattern, Boone and Jorgy would pause to look and listen to the night sounds. After a moment or two, they moved to the next point and repeated the process, walking about fifteen yards per leg of the geometry until they arrived once again at their starting point. Matt checked his watch again.

Boone applied pressure to the push-to-talk button on his small tactical VHF radio. Each man carried the encrypted Motorola communications link, safely inserted into a clear waterproof bag.

Matt was waiting for the signal that all was clear, three presses on the button created a sound referred to as breaking squelch—the odd sound made when the radio was ready to transmit. He didn't have long to wait. Boone signaled the all clear by repeating the squelch pattern and Matt moved deeper into the tree line with his team trailing behind him.

When the SEALs exited the trees and into the clearing Boone twirled his index finger over his head, the signal to create a rallying point. As each man arrived, Boone pointed to the exact spot for each man to go to ground. The end result was a defense perimeter and an opportunity to confirm a full headcount. The team finished forming a circle around Boone and Jorgy.

Each SEAL was responsible for the field of fire in his slice of the pie. Matt moved into the center and the SEALs began the standard ten-minute drill. Look, listen and wait. Matt slid his sleeve up to sneak a quick look at his luminescent dive watch to see how they were doing with time. His brow knitted in consternation as he calculated the rest of their transit quietly in his mind. In every special operations mission, the planning team tossed in a little extra time to allow for screw-ups.

This "fudge factor" allowed the team leader to expand or contract the mission timeline once he was on the ground. Unfortunately for Matt and the troop, the unexpected night swim to the beach had used up any slack they may have expected originally. The ten minutes passed without incident. "Boone, how does it look up ahead?"

Boone leaned in a bit closer. "Opens up quite a bit fifteen yards or so from here. We need to get a solid GPS fix and determine where we are in relation to the target. After that, we can move out and make up for lost time."

Matt nodded and took a moment to consult his GPS navigation system. He could see they weren't too far off the original BLS-to-target bearing. Matt squeezed Boone's arm and used his fingers to pass on the course bearing.

Boone nodded and looked around one more time before standing up. He walked out of the circle followed by Matt.

The rest of the team eased out of the defensive perimeter, uncoiling like a dark green serpent. Each man, in turn, stood up and assumed his position in the patrol. The SEALs moved in a single file, carefully placing every step. Their quiet passage barely registered a complaint from the jungle life all around them.

City of the Dead–Cairo, Egypt

Bandar relaxed under an ancient olive tree. Its twisted branches offered welcome shelter against the intense Egyptian sun. In that magical place, the sunlight played subtle tricks, casting curiously-shaped shadows on the ground in front of him. The effect was as soothing as it was mesmerizing. He sat cross-legged, quietly contemplating his most recent action, calculating what effect his collective acts of violence were having on his intended audience.

Since the beginning of the struggle, his interest was to raise awareness in the Egyptian people of their true power and their destiny. They needed to see and understand what the infidels were doing to their country. The western world had made a whore out of Egypt, and Egypt's leaders were no better than high-paid pimps selling the people's legacy to the highest bidder. Even the brief attempts of the Muslim Brotherhood to raise consciousness and a call-to-action had fallen short. They'd neglected to enlist all the people. A secret society, while well-intentioned, wasn't large enough or strong enough to affect real sweeping change.

There was also a personal reason to destroy the infidels. Bandar's uncle had died while after the first bold, but ill-fated strike, of the jihad a few years earlier. The government, with the help of American and European spy agencies, had uncovered the insurrection's network. One at a time Bandar's people broke under interrogation; the trail eventually led to his uncle. The old man's weak heart couldn't handle the stress of interrogation and he died without betraying the name and location of his nephew.

Bandar needed space and time to think. He required enough time to carefully consider the next phase of his plan. He wanted violence, yes, but he couldn't afford wasteful losses. There would be time enough for martyrs.

Violence was only one tool and it soon lost its psychological impact as people grew to expect it. What he needed was patience. The patience to wait for an appropriate opportunity to deal a serious strategic blow.

Bandar's silent army was frustrated and skittish. The attack against the American communications facility was a great boost to morale. It also had the added impact of focusing Washington's diplomatic pressure and attention on the weak Egyptian government.

The authorities were cracking down, going door to door and rounding up criminals, journalists—anyone on their long list of complainers and irritants. What he'd failed to do on his own, the foolish government now accomplished for him. They needed to show the Americans and Europeans that they were in charge, that everything was under control and this would be their undoing.

The Egyptian state radio and television networks broadcast the government's decision to declare martial law throughout the country. This step was taken only hours after a stern call from the U.S. State Department telling the Egyptian President that things had evolved to a crisis of governance.

Americans in Egypt were being threatened and placed in harm's way by a meek response to the internal threat of the jihad. What could the President do? America was a major economic partner and a source of military resources such as aircraft and battlefield management technology.

From Bandar's point of view, the response was just what he needed, far surpassing results from any of his provocative attacks. The government was turning his little jihad into a national crisis right before his eyes. The media blitz alone was providing him and his cause a sort-of celebrity status, stimulating a flow of new recruits—men and women who wanted freedom from the west's tyranny but hadn't been aware of Bandar's movement. The numbers joining his cause had been but a trickle was a torrent. It was unmanageable but exhilarating at the same time.

What the government and business leaders had failed to realize was the depth of resentment and loathing residing in the hearts and minds of the Egyptian people. Most were uneducated and unaware of the specific cause of their plight, so they complained and sulked and suffered. But they were being made aware of an option, a way out of their misery, courtesy of his enemies.

The press was doing one more thing that assisted Bandar. They were crafting a ridiculous, near-mythical image of him as a great spiritual leader—a leader whose single-minded purpose was to rule the nation by the code of Mohammed. They were calling him the new Bin Laden.

They painted him as a ruthless killer, a warrior for God who would stop at nothing until Egypt was the center of the Muslim world, a new caliphate for the twenty-first century. A mad man who would stop at nothing to tear down the existing fabric of Egyptian society in order to build a new society based on the teachings of the Koran and governed by sharia law.

This assumption was spot-on. In their minds—and the minds of their target audience—Bandar was an enigma. He liked that contrived public profile very much. An enigma to his enemies and a holy warrior to his people. *Well, then. S*o be it! He couldn't have written a better marketing plan. He stood up, yawning and stretching his wiry frame. Time to focus his thoughts on the day's scheduled activities.

Chapter Fourteen

Bandar picked up a dozen bodyguards and two assistants as he left the olive grove. The entourage trailed behind him at a respectful distance. Soon he'd travel to a dusty gathering place just south of Cairo, a secluded location far from the prying eyes of the police and the government's intelligence operators.

Several influential leaders in the Egyptian Air Force and Navy indicated they were ready to negotiate with him. Again, a boon from the media hype. The generals were survivors and the paranoia fueled by the government's crackdown and the press had indicated the winds of fate were blowing in the direction of the jihad.

The military leaders wanted a place in his new fundamentalist regime. More simply, they didn't want to lose the social status and comfortable lifestyle they'd grown accustomed to living.

Bandar was willing to give them—well, to promise them—anything they wanted to gain their support for the final phase of the jihad. However, once the deed was done, he could remove the dogs and place his own loyal lieutenants in command. At the time, it was prudent to let them think they were controlling the deals being made.

A rustling noise caught his attention and he looked to his left to find a man in his security detail pointing. "Beloved one, the truck is ready behind that wall." The husky former soldier gestured to the east where a wood access door provided a way out through the six-foot-high rock wall that surrounding the olive trees.

"Is everything else in order?" Bandar's voice was, as always, just barely audible. An effect which he knew forced others to listen more and talk less in his presence. The trusted bodyguard stared back, his eyes dark brown and expressionless. He swallowed hard before answering.

Bandar noted his behavior and realized even those closest to him were afraid of him. Good! Fear was a powerful incentive.

"Yes, my Lord. All is in order. The generals will be there ahead of us. I suggest we arrive and keep you safe in the vehicle until my team has swept the area for surprises. This meeting could be a way to lure you out into the open. The military leaders fear you."

Bandar nodded. "Have you contacted our advance people at the meeting place?"

"Yes, of course. Nobody has arrived yet. If you'd like, I can call them again now to get an update. They are not trained security people so they cannot verify the site is safe, but we use them to provide notice when the other parties arrive."

Bandar looked up at the big man. The bodyguard's hard exterior was offset by the twitching in his left eye. The man was not comfortable. Should he worry about this man? It was the little things that people conveyed that spoke volumes in Bandar's experience. Besides, he must remain suspicious of everything and everyone if he wished to survive.

"Fine, I would like that. Call them now and tell them to move the generals from the meeting place to the Askari quarry once they arrive. Tell them to take the Trans-African highway and wait at the entrance to the quarry for further instructions. Make the generals follow instructions if they refuse to change locations." With that said, Bandar moved purposefully toward the waiting truck.

Autec–The Bahamas

Matt could see that Boone was in his element. His point man slid to the left and then glided to the right deftly negotiating the trees, bushes, and open spaces. The file formation behind him maintained an interval of six to seven feet between each operator, just far enough not to lose sight of the man in front.

Each SEAL operator mimicked the motions of the man in front of him. One of the most difficult positions in the formation was rear security. This responsibility required close attention in two directions while moving, the forward-looking field of fire and the area directly behind the combat patrol. The maneuver of rotating back and forth while simultaneously placing each foot down without stumbling was an art.

The fact that SEALs were experts at maritime infiltration and exfiltration was well-established. What wasn't as well-known by many was the SEALs natural ability to blend into almost any terrain or environment. SEALs loved to play sneak and peek. They were good at it. Despite the opinion of their Marine and army brothers-in-arms, SEALs believed they were the best elite light infantry in the world.

The center of this part of the island sloped up from the east to form a spine-like ridge running north and south. Matt grunted as his toe struck an unseen rock. The terrain had changed from sand and scrub brush to a landscape of sparse trees. The ground was covered in a mix of small rocks and broken coral. A few steps later he kicked another rock. He tried lifting his feet and placing them down in a more vertical manner to avoid the abuse. This wasn't much better. The technique caused him to turn and twist his ankle every few steps. He decided to kick rocks instead.

The SEALs stumbled up the dark incline, the broken rocks covering the ground challenging all of them. Matt followed close behind Boone, maintaining the proper interval in the inky darkness. The men were warmed up now, the heat of their bodies and the external heat of the Caribbean night had dried their wet cammies; the risk was over heating during the climb.

Twice during the two-thousand-yard climb, they were forced to detour around campfires lying directly in their path. Even though the island's inhabitants were out of play, they didn't want to be spotted by anyone. The SEALs' pride was at stake. Besides, the training cell graders would still mark it down as a failure to remain undetected on the way to the target and mission compromise would likely mean a failing grade for the ORE.

Boone stopped and held his fist up in the air. The patrol was just short of the top of the ridge. After listening for a moment, Boone turned left, heading north.

He began moving parallel to the ridgeline with the patrol following in his footsteps. It took another half hour to reach the highest point on the island.

Once there, Matt moved up to Boone and squeezed his arm. Then he put his fist up in the air, halting the patrol. He took out his night vision scope. Scanning intently, Matt looked back and down toward the BLS. He noticed a flickering light. Taking the scope from his eye he turned and offered it to Boone to see if his point man could also pick it out. "See if you can spot anything strange down there."

Matt gestured, pointing toward the beach. Boone nodded and took a knee. With this added stabilization. Boone looked and gave Matt a thumbs up, he too could see the same phenomenon.

"Well, what do you think?" Matt whispered."
Anything to worry about here?"

"Only if you consider a bunch of opposing force assholes hiding at our original beach landing site something to worry about," Boone said dryly.

Matt snatched the scope away from Boone and knelt down to take a better look.

"Sure, as shit! Now, how in the hell did those bozos figure out exactly which part of which beach to set up on?" Snickering from behind caused Matt to turn.

Wells grinned at Matt in the darkness. "Well, boss. I wouldn't put it past those staff pukes who were observing your final mission brief to hand color copies of the PowerPoint presentation and annotated maps to LCDR Sandoval just to screw us over! All he had to do was get the information to the training cell guys playing the opposing force role out here for the exercise. We might as well act like those turds know the whole plan."

It was the same old game. The older staff guys resented the young operators because they were the shooters and the staff personnel's days of operating were ancient history. So, they pulled bullshit stunts like this one. Sandoval wanted Matt to fail. Fail so badly he'd lose the troop and be replaced before the deployment. Matt didn't want to believe that, but Wells was right—their plan as briefed was compromised.

Wells wasn't finished handing out pearls of wisdom. "I remember one time the Echo troop guys got in a pissing contest with some of the training cell guys. They were in Blackstone, Virginia, in a bar and the shit really hit the fan. Echo won the fight, of course. When their ORE came up six months later, the training guys set the troop up to fail. Echo had to do the ORE all over again."

"Yeah!" chimed in Doc. "I remember hearing about that too. The skipper heard a rumor of what went down and reamed the training department. Echo troop still had to repeat the damn ORE, though. You know LT, the training guys don't like us much, either. And Sandoval has a serious case of the ass for you, and that's a fact. No, sir. I wouldn't put it past these guys to jerk us around tonight!"

Matt nodded in silent agreement. LCDR Sandoval had been gunning for him ever since his dismal performance in the advanced SDV operator course. That wasn't the whole story, though. The Chief had brought Matt up to speed on the Task Unit commander's flat out refusal to see the potential of the new reconnaissance troop concept.

The Chief pointed out that Sandoval had another reason to want Matt to fail. By allowing Matt to carry the ball, LCDR Sandoval was sure the concept would fail. Then, SDV Team Two could get back to the bread and butter SDV ship attack mission he so dearly loved.

As far as Sandoval was concerned, if you were not a top-notch minisub operator you needed to just go somewhere else. The fact that during the long pre-deployment workup, the R and S troop was responsible for actually proving the new idea could work—which pissed Sandoval off even more. *If tonight the odds had been stacked against us, we will just have to level the playing field somehow.* Matt motioned for the men to circle up. It was time to improvise!

"Listen up, guys. This is where we give the goons on the training staff a royal headache. As you know, back in isolation we told the big wigs we were going to conduct a demolition raid. But you also know I made Oby lug along a fifty-caliber sniper rifle. An old SEAL instructor back in BUD/S training told my class that back in Nam they always had to worry about their mission plans leaking out in the base area. So, they had a saying. A plan for show, and a plan for go! Sandoval and the headquarters pukes listened to our original plan. They memorized that plan and they're prepared to defeat that plan. Listen close, here's my plan for go."

After Matt's quick patrol brief, the SEALs shifted back into a file formation. Every man knew his role in the new plan. It was simple and that always made enlisted SEALs happy. Complex plans always hit a snag in the real world.

Matt called for Oby to come up and join Boone in the lead. Oby needed to select his final firing point, or FFP. The two men moved forward a bit and began studying the target area. They were specifically looking for lights that would mark their target's exact location.

A few minutes later Oby signaled to Boone that he had acquired the target. Boone pulled out a night vision scope and confirmed Oby's identification. Boone nodded to Oby and the sniper moved about ten yards farther to the right; he'd found a good shooting position.

He kneeled down and pulled his long gun off his back. In minutes Oby had his fifty-caliber rifle out of its drag bag, spotting scope set up, and five high explosive rounds laid out on a small piece of deer hide he carried for good luck. Boone moved up quietly to join Oby and act as spotter and loader for the sniper rifle.

The fifty had a heavy removable bolt, which was loaded by hand after each shot. Oby and Boone had trained back in the States to keep the time lag between shots as short as possible. Matt took the rest of the SEALs and set up a wide semi-circle behind Boone and Oby. For the remainder of the actions on target, Matt and the others would provide security and leave mission execution to Oby.

Matt used a high-power night vison scope designed for sniper rifles but this time it was a detached tool allowing him to see the target site. The four "enemy" soldiers were clustered together near the missile site. They were a mixed bunch, and they appeared to be a mix of three new SEALs and the command's navy career counselor trying to get out of the office for a change.

He observed they'd been placed at a safe distance from the target by the training cell so they could technically be a part of the environment but not close enough to be in any danger. Even though they were sitting on a demolitions range, safety was still paramount.

"Boy, these missiles sure look real!" Matt whispered to Boone and Oby lying nearby.

"Yeah, they even fill those nose cones with gasoline so they'll look cooler when the demolition charges blow!" Boone whispered back.

The four guards looked bored out of their minds. The training cell probably dropped them off an hour before sundown, Matt mused, and there was absolutely nothing for them to do but wait. That was to his troop's advantage. Tired and bored, the opposing force down below would be less likely to spot his position above the target area.

The chief had warned Matt about getting screwed by the training cell. In this case he had LCDR Sandoval to worry about also. The troop's consensus was Sandoval would direct the training guys to saturate the perimeter of the target with booby traps. This would create a three-hundred-and-sixty-degree barrier to the troop's assault on the missiles. An assault they all expected. Mission planned, mission briefed, mission executed. But Matt had a surprise for all of them.

The guards returned to an earlier debate on the classic question of which training class went through a tougher hell week. They were completely unaware each had—for a brief moment—occupied the center of the optics sitting on top of Oby's Macmillan fifty-caliber rifle.

With a final nod from Boone and a quick glance at his dive watch, the SEAL sniper moved his point of aim to the first nose cone. He tapped the side of the rifle and Boone inserted the bolt with bullet attached into the weapon's breech. Boone pulled to lock the bolt down, putting the night vision scope up to his face.

"The OPFOR guys are a safe distance. Clear to shoot." Matt heard Boone communicate to Boone. Matt and Boone closed their eyes waiting for the report of the gun. The rifle's muzzle blast was impressive and would white out the night vision scopes for a second.

Oby began to squeeze.

Chapter Fifteen

Matt looked up in time to see the shockwave of the explosion knock the guards forcefully to the ground. They scrambled away from the missiles, but they were in no danger. Matt knew they must be confused. How did they get close enough to destroy the missiles without tripping the booby traps?

Before the guards could stand back up, a second explosion rocked the night. The five-inch-long, fifty-caliber explosive-tipped RDX round was originally designed to destroy aircraft parked on enemy airfields. Military aircraft were normally staged ready to fly, fully topped off with fuel to avoid condensation build up in the fuel systems. However, the explosive round was useful and highly effective against other hard targets, too.

Though the mock target wasn't as difficult to attack as a real enemy airfield, the effect on the gas-filled missiles was just as spectacular as nailing the real thing. The six-man ambush team, hiding near the originally-briefed beach landing site, abruptly stopped talking and together looked back toward the center of the island as the bright ball of fire rose up in the air.

From the originally briefed beach landing point the second blast was even brighter than the first, this time they were staring in the direction of the blast. The training cell instructor acting as the opposing force leader checked his watch. The timing of the attack was precisely what the team's leader had briefed. He came to the sudden realization that somehow the troop had evaded their beach ambush and moved into the target area.

"Hey, those fucks landed somewhere else! Pick up your shit, we're going down the beach path to catch them at their extract point!" the frustrated training cell leader yelled. He grabbed his rifle and gestured for the others to follow him inland. The ambush team picked up their weapons and radios, following the team leader.

"What about the boat, chief?" his partner asked. "Shouldn't we leave someone back to guard the boat?"

The chief looked at the long black boat they had inserted administratively by the F-470 rubber boat earlier that day. It now sat nearby, high enough to safely avoid the tide. "No, I'm taking all of you with me. The locals won't fuck with it. We'll be back as soon as we hit these guys. Leave it and move out now!"

With the discussion over, the training cell operators trotted along the island path as fast as the limited light and jungle growth would allow them. The path curled towards the ridge inland for about fifteen minutes then swung back to the beach near the troop's originally briefed extraction point. The training department instructors were going to pay a little surprise visit on the upstart SEAL troop. Huffing and puffing in the lead, the leader checked his watch. Twenty minutes since the attack. He didn't see the trip wire until it was too late.

The jungle night erupted in a flash of light and sound as Matt's well-hidden SEALs opened fire with blanks. Grenade simulators exploded all around the training cell—who had wisely hit the deck. The troop, led by Matt, swept through the kill zone spread out in a line covering ten yards, simulating putting rounds into each body they found. Although they were only using blank ammo, Jorgy's M-240B machine-gun was on full rock-and-roll and it still inspired respect.

Completing their sweep through the kill zone, the SEALs consolidated and moved down below the path before heading north. The training cell instructors were scattered all over the path playing dead. Matt hoped they would stay that way. Chief Auger had stories about instructors rising from the dead only to pop up somewhere else to attack again.

Quietly the troop turned right and intersected the beach path again about fifty yards away from their hasty ambush site. Matt hoped that if the instructors still wanted to mess with his troop, they would go to the briefed extraction site expecting to catch Matt and his men loading CRRCs. Matt had other plans.

Matt pointed north and pumped his fist up and down. Boone nodded and took off at a fast jog on the beach trail, heading back in the direction of the original BLS. After making good time, Matt judged they were getting close to the BLS.

He sped up and tapped Boone on the shoulder. It was time to go back into combat patrol mode. It wouldn't be cool to avoid one ambush only to run right into another one. The rest of the SEALs matched the new patrol speed, feeding off the body language of those in front of them. The sweat was flowed and Matt had a fleeting thought of Sherry. What would she think if she saw what he did for a living?

After traveling carefully for ten more minutes, Boone stopped and signaled for Matt to move up. The point man gestured toward the clearing straight ahead. Matt signaled the patrol to move to the side of the dark trail. Boone stepped into the thick undergrowth. Each of the team members did likewise. Once inside the foliage, the SEALs turned to face the path. The SEALs would rest a minute and be able to hit anyone following them from the target site.

Matt pulled out the VHF tactical radio. He'd already passed the target destroyed code word via UHF before the troop left the top of the ridge. His next call was feet wet signaling his troop was heading out to rendezvous with the submarine—he needed the chief to pick up the team in a different location that he anticipated.

"TANGO UNIFORM BRAVO this is TANGO UNIFORM ALPHA. Extract changed to the BLS. I say again the original BLS. How copy, over?"

"Good copy, TANGO UNIFORM ALPHA. BRAVO is inbound, ETA two mikes, over."

Matt was pleased. Two minutes was just about right. "See you soon. ALPHA, out."

Matt expected Chief Auger and Chase to arrive at the original insertion BLS and he saw confirmation of this when the boat pulled up on the beach. He watched the chief pull out a pair of night vision goggles and scan the area. He seemed comfortable that there were no training cell aggressors visible. Matt heard the radio break squelch three times, the signal from the chief that the beach was clear. Matt returned the signal by squelching his radio three times. It was time to get the hell off the island.

Matt followed Boone down to the beach and had the rest of the patrol wait at the end of the beach trail, just out of sight. He signaled the chief by flashing a green light, dit – dah, Morse code for the letter Alpha. Chief Auger moved in slow and quiet stopping his boat in five feet of water while Chase stayed back thirty yards or so. Matt pushed Boone forward then waved at the rest of the team to consolidate on the two CRRCs. The six SEALs got into the one CRRC and when everyone was accounted for, Chief Auger headed slowly out to rendezvous with Chase in the second boat.

Matt directed Chief Auger to steer a bit to the left. He could see the other CRRC at the rendezvous point using his night vision scope. Oby helped by leaning out over the bow watching for sections of the reef. No use screwing up a great operation by being careless. Matt knew the rising tide gave them more and more room to pass over the tricky barrier with every passing minute. The other rubber boat was close enough to see without the use of night vision. Chase turned his boat toward them and closed the distance before he throttled down.

The boats bumped into each other and the troop was reunited. Chief Auger growled and Matt and several of the SEALs climbed over and into the second boat. Matt did a quick head count then gave Chief Auger a thumbs up before directing Chase to turn his fully-loaded raiding craft to sea. Matt observed as the chief took the lead this time, turning over the steering arm to Jorgy before sliding into the center of the boat.

The chief pulled his rucksack toward him and pulled out his GPS navigation system. Matt saw that the chief was ready to commence movement to the extraction site so it was time for his boat crew in the trail position to back him up using dead reckoning plotting and compass work.

He gave Jorgy a bearing and the big machine gunner grunted acknowledgment as he looked down at the large domed compass bubble mounted on the portside tube near his thigh. Once oriented he twisted his wrist and shot more gas into the outboard, heading for the submarine rendezvous point. Within five minutes only Matt, Wells, Jorgy and Chief Auger were awake. Most of the guys were sacked out. It'd had been a long night's work.

On the transit to the submarine, Matt went over the entire mission in his mind, phase by phase. He knew his troop had executed well. He also knew Sandoval and the other staff-types were going to be pissed to no end about his troop's success. Matt didn't care. In the end, only Captain Richards' opinion counted in an ORE. The training department and Sandoval, in particular, were going to say the troop cheated by not following the mission plan. Matt knew in his heart that the CO would see things differently.

They couldn't take this victory from him or his men. Not only were they ready to deploy, in his mind, they were ready for anything. Matt thought about Sandoval's many attempts to make Matt look bad.

In the end, the LCDR had failed to prove Matt was an incompetent SEAL officer. His efforts to challenge him were childish and weak compared to what Matt had endured as a boy. *Sandoval, you're a rank amateur compared to my old man!* He smiled and then snuggled lower in the boat. The adrenalin rush of the ambush and extraction was diminishing rapidly, and Matt began to shiver. Being a SEAL meant freezing your ass off, all the time.

Ninety minutes later, Matt was kicked awake.by Wells. "Submarine's dead ahead, sir."

Matt couldn't believe he'd allowed himself to sleep. He rose up and tried to see the dimly lit periscope. He waved at Wells. "Move up alongside the chief."

Chief Auger was on the encrypted radio and giving instructions to Jorgy. "Welcome back to the living, sir." The sarcasm wasn't harsh. Matt was still feeling the high of executing a difficult training mission.

"Situation?" Matt asked.

"I spotted the periscope lights with the night scope then I used that to steer by. We're close enough now to see the salvage buoy when it pops to the surface," the chief said.

"How long, you think?" Matt wasn't as experienced at DDS operations as his troop.

"I passed the code word that we were in position twenty minutes ago so they know we can see them, and I bet they can see us. We've been maintaining fifty yards aft of the periscope for a few minutes now so when the buoy deploys, we should see and hear it about halfway between us and the periscope."

Matt peered through the darkness and still couldn't make out the periscope or its lights. The starry sky extended down to the horizon and that far offshore the lights were bright. "How much longer do you…" Matt stopped in mid-sentence.

"Bingo!" Chief Auger said.

Matt watched the large salvage buoy burst to the surface with a bundle of bright green chemical light sticks tied to the top. The chief was right, Matt both heard and saw the event without the night vision assist. A few minutes passed before the shape of a man's head emerged, and then an upraised hand waving a green chemical light next to the buoy.

"That's the signal, guys! Sir, take your boat up first. They'll take you all down and into the sub before deflating the boat and bringing it down. Then, we'll follow you."

Matt wasn't happy with the chief's change of plans. He'd briefed that he'd be the second boat down. What happened if, in a real operation, things went to shit on the surface? An enemy patrol boat or coastal patrol aircraft? No, He was going last. "Sorry, Chief, but that wasn't the plan. You take your boat up there and get your crew into the sub."

"Sir, I know you briefed it one way, but don't you think you need to get down there and begin debriefing the op?"

Matt shook his head, doubting his chief could see the gesture in the dark. "Nothing to debrief until the job is done—and the job isn't done until all my men are safe inside that submarine."

“Okay boss, it's your call of course. Jorgy! Get our asses up there to that buoy!”

Matt continued to assume position aft of the rigging for another twenty minutes before the diver surfaced and waved the green chemlight again. He was the last man in the troop to descend to the deck. Once there, he was handed a SCUBA regulator by a diver. Then he was escorted into the hangar where he was met by another diver who handed him a new SCUBA regulator. All of the SEALs were shuttled in this way, one at a time, until they were safe and dry inside the submarine.

The diver spent another thirty minutes recovering the second boat and pulling the track and cradle back into the DDS before closing the big door. It had been a long night for these professionals as well as the SEALs. Twenty minutes later, the hangar was equalized with the submarine’s internal air pressure and the DDS was drained of seawater. The mission was officially over.

Chapter Sixteen

The Pentagon–Washington, D.C.

The on-duty Pentagon logistics officer absentmindedly sipped the slightly warm cup of bad coffee. The major placed the weathered cup, bearing the Joint Chief of Staff 's symbol, back in its normal resting place on the stained desk. The collection of old coffee stains served as mute testimony to the monastic life led by thousands of military functionaries.

These duty-bound gatherers and distributors of information performed their thankless routine far from the view of an unaware and disinterested public. The major was doing his time deep in the heart of the nation's five-sided military headquarters, only eight months left on his two-year assignment. But he couldn't complain, it was a better posting than many of his peers around the world.

The Joint Chiefs of Staff deployment order 102.1B was a marvel of simplicity and directness. The inch-thick stack of commands would communicate the orders of America's highest military leaders to every corner of the globe. If the plan required assistance from any service, any unit, any supply depot, the order would make sure they understood their role in helping make the operation a success.

This particular order was special to the major. He and a hand-picked team of mid-level officers from several branches of service, worked on it day and night for two weeks. While the timeline was tight, the major felt proud of their work. Now it was up to the designated units to execute.

In keeping with tradition, JCS Order 102.1B had a proper code name, Operation Sparrow Hawk. The name was the major's idea and he was stunned when the brass agreed to use the name. His teenage son was interested in birds. Especially predators. The sparrow hawk was a small, yet ruthless, and effective, hunting bird. His son had been working on a school paper when the major began developing the JCS mission order. The lightning strike envisioned in the mission order reminded him of the aggressive little predator.

Operation Sparrow Hawk called for maintaining a low profile in the expected theater of operations during the preparatory phase. The element of surprise was an advantage they needed to make the plan work as envisioned.

The U.S. would work vigorously behind the veil of normalcy in the Mediterranean Sea to stage all the military forces required to conduct a quick action in Egypt close enough to move fast. Smaller combat and combat support elements were in place in the theater of operations that would form the backbone of the Americans' first-strike capability.

Other U.S. follow-on forces—from England, Spain, and Italy—would be used along with selected airflow support out of Germany. While talks were still ongoing, it did not appear that the NATO nations were going to offer anything by way of help except permission to deploy U.S. military forces from existing NATO bases. The joint staff planners were directed to create their plan assuming unilateral U.S. operations.

The designated Army Special Forces—or SF as they were called—and Navy Special Warfare units assigned to Sparrow Hawk were going to rotate into the Eastern Mediterranean under the cover of regularly scheduled NATO interoperability exercises. The commando units would maintain their normal schedules of forward deployment activity with no actual knowledge of the CONPLAN, or contingency plan, they were designated to support. This would help to maintain OPSEC, or operational security for as long as possible.

Other more unique units such as Army's psychological operations teams and civil affairs units would have to be ordered up from the reserves and National Guard units. These groups would be sent to staging bases in Italy, also under the guise of NATO peacetime exercise play. They were already scrambling to follow their recently-received orders to deploy. The orders had been issued only three hours earlier.

While declining to participate in the initial police action in Egypt, NATO was putting together a second, much larger version of Sparrow Hawk. Their plan would relieve the American forces in place and establish a prolonged presence on the ground. The Europeans would stay in-country after the Americans left in order to stabilize the region and peacefully return the legally elected government to power. If all went well, NATO would eventually turn over stability operations to the United Nations if needed.

The major closed out his secure computer and kicked the main power switch off with the tip of his shoe as he pushed himself out of the clumsy swivel chair. It was the kickoff date for the operation. Whatever happened, good or bad, he was sure he would come out smelling like a rose due to the exactness of his work on Sparrow Hawk. A fine ballet of moving parts that most of the medal-hunting grunts actually participating on the ground could not possibly appreciate or understand. There was a medal coming his way, for sure.

Little Creek Amphibious Base – SDV Team Two

Matt stood at attention. He'd been in the position for ten minutes while LCDR Sandoval ripped him apart. It started professionally, a rundown of Matt's basic flaws as an officer, his AOT performance, then it dialed in, his failure to successfully complete the ORE.

"I never wanted this task unit bullshit! It's undermined the very reason this command exists! And to have you, a failed SDV Pilot/Navigator in a position of leadership…" Sandoval was so worked up he began to stutter.

Matt was mad and scared at the same time. Sandoval was shouting shit and Matt was smart enough to know his task unit commander wasn't drinking the R and S Kool Aid. Captain Richards had a different take on things, and he'd have to sign off on anything Sandoval recommended. Matt was willing to place his trust in the skipper.

"Do you have anything to say for yourself before I kick your ass out of my office?" Sandoval was apparently finished with his scathing personal attack.

Matt thought a moment then decided anything he said would be a waste of breath. "No, sir. I disagree with your professional assessment of my leadership. This is the Navy, whatever happens to me, happens."

Sandoval snorted. "You're damn right it's the Navy!"

Matt was dismissed. He walked down the hallway and then through a side door near the locker rooms and into the bright sunlight outside. He heard the door open behind him. Chief Auger stepped outside and stretched. "Pull-ups lieutenant?"

Matt looked at his chief like he'd gone crazy. "Pull-ups? Do you know what just happened to me? Sandoval's kicking me out of the troop, probably out of the team—hell, the teams, period!"

Chief Auger casually brushed past Matt and walked over to the training area that consisted of multiple dip bars, pull-up bars, rope climbs, and ladder climbs. He placed his hands on the horizontal bar. "You think you can kick my ass? Come on, max reps to failure. No kipping and dancing, only full pull-ups count."

Matt shook his head. His chief was clueless for once. He shrugged and walked over to the bar. He had no idea how many pull-ups the older man could do, but it was something to do while he sulked. "Okay, fuck it! You go first."

The chief smiled. "All right. You count them out loud." The chief jumped up on the bar and immediately began pounding out perfect pull-ups. Each time he went up his chin froze just over the metal bar and each time he went down he extended his body to a full dead hang.

At a count of eighteen the he started slowing down, the pull-ups were still regulation in form but slower, more deliberate. At a count of twenty-six, he stopped and executed one pull up at a time. His entire body was shaking and quivering with the strain. At thirty-one he dropped off the bar.

"It's all yours, sir!"

Matt was impressed. At BUD/S he was able to do twenty-four or so pull-ups on a regular basis. That was quite a while ago, but shit! The chief was thirty years old. He stood under the bar motionless, trying to clear his mind of the scene in Sandoval's office. As he tried to calm down the opposite happened. The rage welled up and he decided to take it out on the pull-up bar.

A few minutes later Matt dropped off the bar and winced. His biceps were screaming, and he was still shaking.

"Impressive performance LT." Chief Auger began a soft clapping. "Thirty-six but I have to take three reps back that were piss-poor attempts. So, thirty-three for the record and the championship!"

Matt regained his composure and grinned. He'd beat the old bastard. Thirty wasn't really old, but in the teams Chief Auger was a senior citizen.

The chief took a few steps away from the pull-up bars and sat down on the concrete curb. "Come over here, lieutenant," he said in a friendly voice.

Matt walked over and sat down.

"What you did in Autec was brilliant leadership. Sandoval was rigging the game and you beat him—not by cheating but by executing the mission with the team and the capabilities you had at hand. You're the kind of thinking officer the teams need, especially this team.

Sandoval and his ideas are relics of the past. R and S is the way of the future. Captain Richards knows it. When he gets back from his trip in a few days he'll decide if our troop passed or failed. My bet is on the skipper. So, chin up and don't let Sandoval see he got to you. Okay?"

Matt heard the logic—the same logic that had rattled around in his head during the chew-out session. If the chief thought he was a good officer it was a positive sign. He agreed; Sandoval shouldn't get the satisfaction of seeing Matt demoralized.

"Okay, chief. Sounds like a plan!"

Chief Auger pounded Matt on the back with his hand. "A great plan! Now, let's get back up on that bar, best out of two!"

Matt groaned in mock protest.

U.S. Naval Air Station–Sigonella, Sicily

The hot blast of the Navy jet's exhaust seemed to linger a few feet above the blacktop as the troop, cramped and sluggish from the long flight, struggled to climb out of the aircraft. Looking out of the tiny cargo window, Matt could see the rugged terrain of Sicily shimmering in the afternoon sun. Shit, he thought to himself. It looks just like fucking San Clemente Island—the lifeless rock off the California coast where the last phase of BUD/S was conducted.

It had been only a week since the troop's successful ORE in the Bahamas. Matt's men should have been enjoying a well-deserved pre-deployment leave but instead, they'd been told their deployment start date was moved up so they could participate in an unscheduled training exercise in the Mediterranean. Teams and shit.

Captain Richards had been apologetic when he'd plucked Matt's R and S troop from Task Unit X-RAY and sent them to respond to the surprise tasking. He explained it would be a short duration exercise and that the rest of X-RAY would join them before they knew it. Matt and his men accepted the Captain's words without complaint. This was a part of the deal and they knew it. The best part of the trip was no Sandoval.

Soon after Captain Richards' return to SDV Team Two a week earlier, he'd reviewed the ORE results and listened to Sandoval's recommendations. No one knew what was said between the two men. The meeting was held behind closed doors. All anybody knew was the outcome—Sandoval had been relieved of his task unit command. There was no explanation or follow up. As far as the team was concerned, Matt's troop had passed their ORE.

Sandoval's replacement was likely going to be the executive officer of SDV Team Two. There wasn't enough time to get anybody else.

It was normal practice for an officer to get off the plane last to thank the aircrew and smooth out any problems caused by his team during the flight. SEALs travel one of two ways; either they sleep like the dead or they pace about like caged tigers. This last option usually pissed off the Air Force-types.

They were used to passengers staying put, belted and docile. However, this time on the long flight over from the states Matt was happy to see there hadn't been any incidents. As he finally stepped down and off the wide C-141 tail ramp, he paused for a moment to look around at the scenery. His men were already putting it into words.

"This place sucks!" Boone's pointed critique caused a smattering of voices rising up in agreement.

Chief Auger's voice cut through the whining. "All right, lads, let's get that flatbed truck over here and start unloading this bird!"

The SEALs knew the drill. Do what the chief wanted, and liberty would come that much sooner. Screw around, and you pay the price. Chief Auger took care of you if you put out and pitched in. One of his favorite mottos was, "There are always good deals for good SEALs." So, without a gripe, the men of the R and S troop dropped their kit bags, daypacks, radios, and computer cases to begin offloading the huge cargo plane.

Jorgy ran over to the local man sitting in the cab of the flatbed truck and started directing him toward the cargo plane. Meanwhile, the Chief and Wells went back into the plane to work with the crew chief and his loadmaster. A forklift appeared out of nowhere and Boone's intervention prevented the flatbed truck and forklift from colliding at the back of the plane.

Chapter Seventeen

A dark-haired man in casual khaki slacks and a short sleeve green golf shirt stood on the edge of the runway on the other side of the red security line. He waited patiently, tapping his toe absentmindedly as he watched the SEALs work together. Matt saw the official-looking individual standing alone and figured he must be the welcoming committee. He and the chief took the time to say goodbye to the aircrew and provide guidance to the troop. The dark-haired man repeatedly checked his watch.

"It looks like the welcome wagon has arrived!" Boone noted, tilting his head in the direction of the stranger.

Matt and Chief Auger finally turned toward the visitor and sized him up. Even at a short distance the mirage caused by heat danced about the man's legs. Chief Auger crossed his arms across his chest as he stared at the stranger.

"Well, boss. He doesn't look like a grunt. My guess is he's an agency guy."

Matt wasn't as worldly as his chief, so he hesitated to ask a question, concerned he'd look stupid. The chief helped him out of his dilemma.

"There are a few agencies we'd expect to work with, the standard three-letter groups. Intelligence collection and analysis is their primary mission but sometimes we help them, and they help us. I worked with a few in Iraq."

"Yeah, okay, chief," Matt replied, now happy to have some idea of who the man might represent. "I think Boone's got a handle on things here. Let's go see what this guy wants. Seems a bit odd if you're correct in your identification."

"Odd?" The chief asked.

Matt nodded. "We were rushed over here for a training exercise, right? If that's the truth, why is he here?"

Matt thought about it for a moment. He didn't have a lot of experience in the teams let alone the navy but his instincts were screaming that this wasn't an exercise and if it wasn't, he might be leading his troop into some real shit.

The two SEALs casually walked over to the gentleman standing impatiently on the tarmac. They walked through the gap in the red security line, waving at the airport security team sitting in a van nearby. Matt approached the government man and extended his hand, smiling. No use pissing this guy off, he thought. The man returned Matt's smile, but it felt plastic, a con man's smile.

"Welcome to Sigonella, LT Barrett. I hope your flight was comfortable."

Matt glanced at the chief before answering. "Well it was okay, I guess. I take it you've never spent any time in a military cargo plane, Mister…?"

"Oh, yes. I'm sorry! My name is Stewart Jackson. I'm a cultural affairs officer with, shall we say, a rather small department of the U.S. government. I specialize in geography. In particular, North Africa."

Stewart reached out to shake Chief Auger's hand. "I'm anxious to get you two somewhere where we can speak—somewhere a bit more private." Stewart wasn't doing a very good job of pretending to be an analyst or data geek. His stance and bearing implied athleticism, even a martial arts background, perhaps. Matt studied the man. He had the bearing of an operator or a former member of an elite military unit.

Chief Auger glanced at Matt and then spoke. "Come on, Stewart. I'm too damn old to play games. I've got a troop of tired, pissed off SEALs over there who want to know what training exercise is so important that it justified recalling us from our homes in the middle of the night back in Virginia and ordered to load out for Sigonella in twenty-four hours. After seeing you, my guess is this isn't an exercise. Am I right?"

Stewart Jackson eased back a step or two. "I assure you my intention is not to play games, chief. I'm sorry if no one felt it necessary to tell you two the truth before coming here, but I have my suspicions why it was a prudent decision not to do so. I need to brief the lieutenant so he can start planning how you will handle the challenge that now lies before you. As soon as you read the mission situation, Mr. Barrett, you'll understand why you've been kept in the dark." Jackson had shifted his attention to Matt as he finished.

Matt wasn't about to cut his chief out of anything this important. "My chief is the brains of this outfit, Mr. Jackson. I don't make decisions without his guidance and feedback and I certainly don't conduct mission planning without his experience. That *is* what you're referring to, correct? A mission plan of some sort?"

Jackson seemed to choose his words carefully before he answered. "As you wish, lieutenant. I don't have a problem briefing both of you if you insist. However, we do need to get to a secure location fairly soon so I can bring you, I mean both of you, up to speed on the mission tasking."

Matt smiled. "Well, I do insist, Mr. Jackson. So sure, let's hit the road!" A glance back showed him the guys were on autopilot unloading the plane.

"Chief, let Cruise know we'll be out-of-pocket for a while. Don't let him in on what we're doing. Just have him carry the ball until the guys are settled."

“What about liberty for the boys?” the chief asked.

Matt paused to consider the request. “Well, Mr. Jackson, do my boys have time to unwind tonight?”

“Yes. Yes, of course, Lieutenant Barrett. You can tell your men it’s okay to let their hair down so to speak. I mean, what could possibly happen in one night?”

The chief winked knowingly at Matt. “Yeah, boss. What could possibly happen in just one evening?”

“Nothing we can’t handle. Right chief?”

Chief Auger nodded back. “That’s affirmative, LT!” With that, he turned and walked to the red line gap and then moved toward the SEALs working next to the cargo plane. Matt’s concern over why they were here was growing by the minute. If senior SEALs weren’t in the command structure for whatever was coming, his troop might be misused or not receive the mission support it needed to be successful. Unconventional units with conventional levels of help usually spelled disaster.

Matt knew that Chief Auger had worked with Marines in Ramadi Iraq and they were great, a real team fight from the grunt in the street all the way up to the general. But he’d heard stories of other scenarios where the SEALs were treated like second class infantry. It was his and the job to make sure that didn’t happen.

Matt watched his chief walk away or a moment then turned back to the agency man impatiently rocking back and forth in front of him. Matt didn’t like the guy. Not one bit. He decided it was better to stay detached and not make assumptions until he knew what this was all about. Within minutes the chief was back, giving Matt the thumbs up.

Many career military types in the Army and Marines ridiculed the SEALs for their apparent lack of discipline and military bearing. However, when they had the opportunity to actually observe the Navy's finest in action, they were puzzled by the way the enlisted frogmen seemed to work together with precision, requiring little or no direct guidance from their leaders.

The simple truth was SEALs rarely gave any outward appearance of operating under classic military order and direction. That was because every man in a SEAL unit knew his job, his scope of responsibilities, and he knew the mission. Each SEAL operator was personally committed to the successful attainment of the troop's assigned task. They didn't need an officer or an NCO to give lofty speeches or deliver veiled threats to get things accomplished.

Matt knew the men of his SEAL troop were going to finish the off-load work and get all the gear and weapons secure—followed by the shortest route to a bar. They were probably going to get drunk, maybe even tear Sigonella apart. Matt wasn't going to restrict their play.

His men had pushed hard for the last ninety days of the pre-deployment schedule and instead of a well-deserved vacation before leaving the States, they'd been pulled in, boxed up, and sent across the Atlantic and halfway across the Mediterranean. If this Jackson was there for some real shit, Matt wanted his men to have a chance to relax before it was time to focus and maybe risk their lives.

Matt's mind began to engage. *What is this all about?* SEALs were in combat in the Horn of Africa, Afghanistan, Iraq, and the Philippines but not in the Mediterranean. He calmed his heartbeat; it was rising as his adrenalin kicked in. He needed to be rational, logical. He was in command of an R and S troop. The job, wherever it was going to be, was in all probability a recon/surveillance mission. That didn't necessarily mean combat.

Their specialty was submarine and SDV mobility—to sneak in under the coastal RADAR and insert over the beach and get shit done. But the submarine, DDS, and SDV were still back in the States along with the other two-thirds of Task Unit X-RAY. He kept that key observation in mind as he and the chief piled into the back of a dark sedan.

Matt tossed his computer case on the bed. He was bushed from the long trip but felt the need to stretch his muscles. The classified brief he and Chief Auger had received from Stewart in the secure center was straight forward, but the variables were left unspoken. Matt and his chief spent a few minutes after the presentation comparing notes. They both decided to allow the troop to get their liberty time. A full mission briefing for everybody would be scheduled for the next day. Until then, they would keep the project to themselves.

Stewart was nice enough to arrange for a ride back to the barracks where the troop was assigned. Once in his small room, Matt realized he was still wound up. He definitely needed to expend some excess energy, so he changed into running shorts and a T-shirt and headed downstairs.

The Navy base at Sigonella was flat and boring. Matt steadily picked up speed and made a game of running intervals from block to block, alternating the pace. When Matt turned a corner and spotted the dominating majesty of a dormant volcano he almost stopped running. It was impressive—and to Matt, it looked evil, ready to go ballistic at any time. The military aircraft departed and arrived like clockwork as Matt continued his run, getting to know the lay of the land. His legs started out stiff from the long plane ride, but they were feeling better now. The exercise also helped to clear his head. Matt saw the sign for the base gym and cut his run short. Time to hit the weights. Later, a long shower and then a good meal and a few beers with the guys in the troop.

The pounding wouldn't stop. Matt wrapped the pillow tighter around his head and curled into a little ball. It seemed to help. He'd been dreaming about the day. Every few months the same dream forced its way into his sleep. The coffin, the rain, the uniforms, the flag. His mother's face. As he began to drift away again, a deep booming voice cut through the fog.

"Get the hell up and answer the damn door, sir!"

Matt uncurled, bolted upright, and then tried to balance on the edge of his bed without falling over. His eyes snapped open and he looked to the right. The clock showed eight o'clock in the morning. He panicked. "Oh shit, I'm late!"

He jumped off the bed and kept on going, his sock-covered feet skating across the hand polished, parquet floor. Matt's feet went out from under him and he unceremoniously lost his balance and landed on his ass with a loud thump!

"Fuck!"

Matt rolled over to his side and then went to one knee, stabilizing his body by grabbing the bed. The pounding on the door started up again, he still couldn't tell if it was coming from the door or between his ears. He checked his wristwatch against the alarm clock and confirmed he'd screwed up big time. The loud voice sliced through his mental recriminations with another demand to open the door. This time Matt could hear other voices in the hallway outside. He stood up and wobbled across the room.

The SDV troop commander unlocked and opened the door to reveal Chief Auger and Boone standing in the hall. The bachelor's quarters used local Sicilian cleaning ladies to keep the temporary quarters livable. One such elderly employee was now blankly staring at the SEALs. Just down the hall a younger American woman, probably a dependent spouse on transit to or from Sicily, was ushering a small red-headed boy into their room as quickly as possible. Everybody stared at Matt.

"Shit!" Matt glanced down, then up, then back down again. He jumped backward, removing his naked body from the hallway, and kicked the door shut.

"Our fearless leader rises!" Chief Auger laughed loudly at his own joke. The cleaning lady apparently understood English fairly well, because she got the point right away and began blushing. He opened the door again and walked into Matt's room.

"Come on, Boone, let's get the boss in the shower! We're going to need him in prime shape today."

Boone nodded and followed the chief into the room. "Hey, chief, how do they pick guys to be officers anyhow?"

The older man turned and chuckled. "I'm not sure, buddy. But when you find out, let me know, okay?"

Chapter Eighteen

The chief and Boone helped Matt into the bathroom and started the shower. Matt was shoved roughly into the booth. The cold water flowed over him, helping to clear his aching head. He couldn't believe he'd missed a troop muster. Chief Auger shoved a thirty-two-ounce container of liquid into the shower. "Drink this, all of it!"

Matt grabbed the container and tilted his head back. The water was salty. "Hey what the hell is this shit?"

Chief Auger didn't have time to lecture his Lieutenant on the merits of mineral-infused water. "It's a proven tonic for hangovers. Your symptoms are caused by dehydration. You're brain basically dries out. So, do everybody a favor, sir, and just drink the damn thing!" Chief Auger's voice betrayed his irritation.

Matt heard the words but more importantly, he heard the tone. "Aye, aye chief!" He tipped his head back and finished drinking it all. He burped loudly and handed the container back out through the shower curtain.

"Thank you, sir! Now shut that water off! We need to get you shaved and dressed. I was able to get a thirty-minute delay, but Jackson's pissed. Better not waste the favor."

What Matt learned in the briefing the day before had justified letting the troop have a night on the town. The chief had swung by Matt's room to invite him out, help him to relax a bit. After a light dinner Matt was ready to back to his room and hit the sack, but he allowed his chief to talk him into meeting the troop at a bar for a drink or two.

Once at the bar, Chief Auger and the rest of the troop kept the rum and cokes coming. Matt tried multiple times to peel himself away but every time someone forced him to share a toast to some odd event or person. As Matt tried hard to remember the night's festivities, he wasn't sure if he'd witnessed the chief swallowing any of the mixed drinks.

A classic tactic used by senior enlisted SEALs to slow down their energetic young officers or to show a leader their acceptance and approval, was to ambush them while on liberty. This normally occurred the night before a distasteful training event, or just to knock an officer's ego down a few notches. Unfortunately for Matt, his troop had decided they liked him. The ambush was a form of tribute—a hazing that marked his official membership in the R and S troop. Last night had been an ambush, but it was a good one. Matt never saw it coming.

The drill was simple; an officer was first surrounded by friendly SEAL enlisted men. Once in position, these fine fellows proceeded to throw compliments and words of praise at their witless but rather pleased leader. Then, one of the men would propose a toast to the troop, or to the Navy, or to their mother. Whatever the toast, a bottle of some dreadful and powerful concoction would miraculously appear along with enough glasses for everyone. The officer would be so disarmed by the warmth and affection of his men that he gladly, and blindly, joined in.

The tactics continued to evolve as the night wore on. One approach was known as the one on one drill. Over the course of an hour or so, an officer would be approached by a SEAL and asked to discuss some personal issue of great importance. The enlisted man always arrived for his audience with a full can of beer or glass of some poison which was gratefully received by the empathetic officer. Once the advice was received the enlisted SEAL would thank the wise officer and disappear, only to be replaced by a new, and even more confused member of the troop, looking for guidance.

This process was punctuated from time to time by a roving pair of SEALs who would crash in on the counseling session to propose a friendly toast. Of course, they just happened to be carrying an extra shot glass. On average it would take the troop about two hours to render the targeted officer incapacitated.

As a result of all the fucking around, Matt, and the rest of the troop, were severely behind the timeline. After speed shaving, Matt scrambled to get dressed in civilian clothes as directed by Chief Auger. The troop was going to the briefing site in civilian attire.

Boone came into the room with a cup of black coffee he'd scored from the base snack bar a block away. Matt guzzled the dark liquid despite burning his tongue. His mind was clearing, the adrenalin generated by his shock and fear of missing the briefing window caused his heart to race. The strange drink forced on him by the chief seemed to be helping, also. Matt finished dressing, pulled on his shoes and nodded to the chief.

"I'm ready."

The eight SEALs of Task Unit X-RAY rode quietly together in the back of a dark green Italian Army van. It left the base and wound its way down and around through the narrow roads in the city of Sigonella. Within thirty minutes of leaving the base, they arrived at the briefing site. The secure facility was actually a NATO operations center located in a hotel leased by the United States Government. The SEALs were allowed to bypass the desk security check-in courtesy of their new swim buddy, Mr. Jackson, who met them at the entrance of the hotel.

"Nice of you to show up, Matt!" Jackson gave the SEALs a quick and quiet protocol brief about how to behave in the building. No rank, first names only. No mention of any military nomenclature or activities outside of the secure classified information facility or SCIF, on the seventh floor. He got everyone to nod in understanding then led them to the elevator. He sent half up first and then went up in the second load to the seventh floor.

Wells looked at Jorgy and shook his head. “This isn’t an exercise.”

Jorgy raised his eyebrows and walked out of the elevator. “No shit, Captain Obvious.”

After checking in and allowing the security team to validate the identities of the SEALs, Jackson walked them through a set of double steel doors. The men found themselves in spacious briefing auditorium. The seats were slanted at a sharp angle, more like a college lecture hall than a military briefing room.

Matt walked down through the row of stairs following Jackson to a podium set up mid-stage, as the chief and the rest of the troop found a place to sit down. Matt sat in a chair on the left side and sat down. He suddenly shivered uncontrollably. He hoped the shakes weren’t easy to pick up on. What he really needed was another cup of coffee to settle his nerves. Matt looked over to where the troop was sitting in the first two rows. They stared right back, all smiles.

Matt couldn’t help smiling himself. He was now officially initiated in the nocturnal drinking tactics and tricks of the Navy’s finest. Luckily, the chief had suggested the day before that the two of them should create the pre-mission warning order brief right after their briefing with Mr. Jackson. Matt wasn’t sure he could think straight enough to create a warning order right that second. The faces turned serious when Jackson hit the projector’s display button.

The machine splashed a topographic map of northeastern Egypt, twenty feet high on the screen behind him. “Gents, this is not an exercise. The political situation in Egypt has been deteriorating steadily now for two years but recently this has accelerated. A rebel leader named Bandar has infiltrated the Egyptian military to the point where it's only a matter of time before the new government rolls over."

Jackson paused for effect. "The United States is going to invade Egypt within seventy-two hours. Our mission tasking is to infiltrate Egyptian territorial waters six to eight hours prior to the main invasion event. We are going to move without detection to the commercial airport in the coastal city of Alexandria. Once there, we are to conduct a cursory reconnaissance of the target, report on its status, and then standby to support the initial Army Ranger strike force as it takes over the airport. Matt."

On cue, Matt stood up and walked to the podium. He took a deep breath and dove right into the details of the warning order. Warning orders were used in the military as a preparatory mechanism to issue lists of mission-essential equipment, identify rehearsal requirements, direct gear testing, and to provide other guidance related to the team's pre-mission preparation. It lay out an hour-by-hour schedule to accomplish all the tasks to ensure the operation had the best possible chance of success.

Matt also assigned duties and tasks related to the logistics of moving to the mission area, as well as subordinate leader tasks associated with the final planning and rehearsal phase. With only a few hours left, every detail had to be perfect the first time. Most of the troop's attention would be spent on the chalk talk—a SEAL solution design process where the members of the troop sat together debating the hundreds of possible outcomes of each and every potential action they might take, phase by phase, until the mission ended.

Every man in the troop had a right and a duty to bring up their concerns, observations, or ideas. Anything that might help the troop to succeed. For the next two days, Matt and his SEALs poured over Mr. Jackson's detailed target folder containing the Egyptian naval, ground, and air order of battle.

They analyzed topographic guidance on preferred routes of infiltration and exfiltration. They also reviewed a mix of signals intelligence data, intelligence estimates on enemy order of battle, and general background information from mostly public sources related to Egyptian society and her people. The gaping hole in the assessments was a lack of any accurate data related to the force strength on and around the target itself.

On the face of it, their portion of Sparrow Hawk was a simple operation. The planning was straight forward enough. Matt's troop would rely on generally accepted SEAL and SDV Team Two specific standard operating procedures or SOPs, to execute virtually all aspects of the mission except dealing with the unknowns on the target itself.

If American forces went in and performed as expected, the Rangers would be on the airfield target within thirty minutes of Matt's team setting up their observation point. The rest was simple—provide terminal guidance to assist the Ranger's insertion aircraft in finding the airport and landing safely. The troop assumed they would be providing an overwatch for the first twenty to thirty minutes after the Rangers hit the deck. They could watch the exterior avenues of approach and provide sniper support if and when needed. After that, the SEALs would pack up, round up, and load up. The extraction method was being left unanswered since the airflow into the seized airport had priority over outbound flights. The R and S troop might be stuck there for a long time.

Matt was confident the larger Sparrow Hawk plan would work as designed. It was a basic evacuation project—known in military jargon as a Non-combatant Evacuation Operation or NEO—it was similar to dozens of others conducted by the U.S. military over the years. What he didn't have a handle on was the enemy's reaction to being pushed off the airport.

Once it was clear the Americans were on the ground, would the jihadists rally up and counterattack the Rangers? Or would they attempt to ambush and kidnap the American civilians, the unarmed evacuees directed by the State Department to get to the airport? Would this Bandar kill them or take them hostage? And what about the Egyptian military? Whose orders would they follow?

When Matt finished his points, Jackson sighed. "Matt, I understand the desire to know all things. It makes the darkness of the unknown shrink smaller and smaller. But you have all the answers we have. Your questions are solid, but we do not have the answers. And of course, there's always Murphy's Law."

Matt wasn't impressed. Murphy's Law was: anything that can go wrong will go wrong. That was no way to plan. These spooks weren't as good as they thought they were. He and his team would have to find the answers the hard way.

Every SEAL mission was unique because every target situation was unique. The airport mission wasn't that difficult a task on the face of it. Matt considered the assigned R and S mission to fall squarely within their competency. He was comforted that there were other U.S. military assets doing what each did best.

Rangers were specialists at airfield seizures. SEALs were not. The teams were trying to recapture their original charter in a time when all special operations forces were deployed in combat zones deep inland, conducting sustained operations. The SEALs were happy to help but they knew that in the long view, they were not a good fit for conventional infantry missions.

Matt's troop would be positioned in a manner that enhanced the success of the Rangers and that was appropriate. He was aware, through his training, that there were times in the history of the teams when SEALs were given combat missions they were not suited for.

SEALs were lightly armed and normally did not carry heavy weapons or a lot of ammunition. They were perfectly aligned with fast, deliberate, small-scale raids, and low- to no-visibility reconnaissance of key strategic objectives. In those few historical anomalies where they were misused, the SEALs performed heroically and were ultimately successful—but not before taking significant losses.

Time flew by as the troop struggled to cover all the logistics and tactical issues at hand. Matt and Chief Auger continued to mentally check off the primary concerns as they were addressed and resolved. First and foremost was the safety of his SEALs. His responsibility for them had been the driving force behind the rigorous training conducted by the troop back in the States. Matt believed that the harder they trained, the more likely each of them would react correctly and therefore survive combat.

Matt took time to inventory his strengths, his weaknesses, and his personal responsibilities as a leader. He was, of course, a product of the same combat training as his men, so he felt personally ready for the rigors and basic challenges associated with surviving and winning a fight.

He knew that enlisted SEALs did not tolerate weak officers. They quietly demanded that their officers at least keep up with them, and even better, excel. Matt was average enough to not represent a liability to his men, but physical fitness, shooting, and carrying a load were not the standards he'd be measured by on this mission. His men only cared that he led well—they'd take care of everything else.

Chapter Nineteen

At the end of the preparation the troop collectively came to the conclusion that they were in a good place. The mission planning to execute their task was solid. Even though it had been no more than two days of study, Matt felt like he knew the objective area like it was his old neighborhood back home. The communications package—containing primary, secondary, and emergency frequencies, and all the event-by-event code words—was simple and functional. Every communications device had been tested twice.

One thing SEALs hated was overbearing supervision via the radio. It was far too easy for higher commanders to micro-manage the mission remotely. Matt would make sure the command and control network supporting the mission was informed as to key steps in their progress, usually by sending execution checklist code words, but it wasn't going to be a play-by-play narrative.

The communications plan as constructed was bare bones by modern special operations standards, but Matt didn't want to have to lug any more radios around than were absolutely necessary. He was mindful it was a reconnaissance job.

Matt's thoughts were interrupted when Chief Auger placed his hand on the lieutenant's shoulder. "Well, boss. The boys look sharp. I wouldn't run them through rehearsals again unless you see something I don't see."

Matt tilted his head in the chief's direction. "Yeah, I think you're right, chief. We'll let the guys take a break. I don't want them to peak too early. Let's get the parachutes packed up and the mission equipment staged at the hangar before we stand them down for some rest."

"You got it, LT," the chief agreed. "Hey, something chewing on you? The lights are on but it doesn't look like anybody's home."

Matt looked right at the older man and smiled. "No, I'm as ready as I'll ever be. Go ahead and get the guys moving. I'll catch up with you later. Oh, yeah. No liberty tonight. That also means no beer in the barracks, understood? I don't know when they'll launch us so better to be rested and thinking straight."

"Roger that, boss!" The chief turned and casually trotted over to the assembled SEALs to put the word out. Matt watched him leave. He felt lucky to have such a great chief. Matt knew it all would have been a lot more difficult without Chief Auger's experience and guidance. Matt tried hard but couldn't think of anything he'd missed. He knew from his training experience and all the harsh critiques of his leadership that second-guessing his decisions was his Achilles heel. He had to learn how to relax and focus at the same time. Was that even possible?

The struggle in his mind was over that very issue. It wasn't training but he was aware of that fact. The plan was good but was the intelligence it was based upon? There were two plans and every SEAL leader needed to remember that. Your plan and the enemy's. So, the enemy always gets a vote on target according to Master Chief Brown back at BUD/S.

He was a multiple tour combat veteran with two purple hearts and the silver star for heroism under fire in Jalalabad, Afghanistan. Despite all the training and all the advice from those who knew the deal, Matt couldn't stop imagining any number of disasters. The flashback of himself as a young LTJG struggling to cross a road on San Clemente Island in BUD/S third phase was a reoccurring thought. Would it happen again? Would he freeze up or make a call that got his men killed?

He also couldn't stop thinking about his dad. Was he sitting up there somewhere watching the show? "I bet he's already predicted I'll fail," Matt mused. The old man would have handled a job like this without a hitch, cool as ice. But then again, Arthur Barrett had never been a SEAL. Special operations aren't straight forward or often predictable.

Matt refocused once again. He felt he should spend a little more time on the geography of the emergency exfiltration route since the terrain was so different from the built-up urban area around the airport. He considered it for a second and then decided to blow it off. Matt needed a break. He was sure he could cross that bridge when he came to it. He cleared his mind and then Sherry's ass popped into view. Matt smiled. That was a much better thought to ponder.

The White House – Washington D.C.

The duty officer, a Marine colonel, sat in the White House Situation Room nodding while he listened to the flash report. The American embassy in Cairo was forwarding their interpretation of the most recent act of terrorism. The crowds of European and American tourists were always large this time of year. The devastation wrought by the large blast near the pyramid of Giza efficiently and viciously struck down one hundred and twelve people within seconds.

A mobile food kiosk, loaded with explosives with nails and other small pieces of scrap metal taped to the inside panels, was the epicenter of the carnage. These events happened all too often around the world, but this one was different. This one could mark the beginning of an overt jihadist uprising in an unstable Egypt.

The colonel continued to take detailed notes until the report ended. He was responsible for logging the information into the database prior to forwarding it to his superior so all interested parties had access at the same time. Just then, he heard the embassy staffer's voice on the other end of the communications link suddenly rise to a high pitch. Something new had happened. He flipped the notebook over to a new page and began to take notes for a new report. The new data, would have to be passed up the chain of command in a more discrete manner.

The colonel scribbled as fast as he could, trying to keep up with the often-rambling narrative. Then, without warning, the link was broken. The White House duty officer directed the communications technician to reconnect with the U.S. Embassy but after several attempts, he shook his head.

The system was working, there was just no one on the other side responding. He stared at the technician for a second then jumped into action. The senior officer stepped forward and took over the console, pressing the button that connected him with the senior communications technician in the basement below.

The duty officer turned to a junior officer sitting nearby. "Captain! Take this note to General Hawkins. He was scheduled to meet with the National Security Advisor ten minutes ago in his office so you should find him there. Interrupt them and give them this note. Tell them I consider the content of the note to be an immediate operational priority. Go!"

The captain jumped up, grabbed the note, and rushed out of the room. The colonel picked up the phone and dialed the White House switchboard, an archaic label for the sophisticated communications center, but a nickname that wouldn't go away. "I can't get anyone in the basement communications center to answer my calls.

Please try through your system. Tell them it's an operational imperative that they connect with me in the situation room, and one more thing. Try to connect with our Embassy in Cairo, Egypt. Start at the top and work your way down until you get someone on the line, then patch it through to me."

The operator acknowledged the two requests by repeating them back, the colonel hung up and then sat down.

Ten minutes later, there was still no communications with the senior technician. The colonel was getting ready to go into the basement and hunt the guy down when a call came in from the White House switchboard. He jumped up and grabbed the handset himself startling the enlisted man manning the console. "What do you have?"

"Sir, we've tried to patch through every way we know how, as you requested, starting at the top and working our way down the chain of authority at the Embassy. We can't get through to anyone in Cairo. Nobody is picking up or responding to secure email requests, land line, or radio transmissions."

The Colonel was confused. "Do you mean to say all the communications links to the embassy are busy?"

The reply came immediately. "No, sir. I'm saying that from what our technicians are saying to us is that all communication with the embassy has been cut off at the source."

The words stunned the Marine duty officer. How could the embassy's communications capability be interrupted? The U.S. Embassy in Cairo was a state-of-the-art communications station. Hell, the facility had more broadcast capability than the host country! His thoughts were abruptly cut short by the noisy arrival of General Hawkins, JCS senior duty officer at the White House.

"Dan! What do you make of this report? Is it possible that both the Egyptian Air Force and the Egyptian Army have rolled over to that madman Bandar?" Apparently, the colonel's messenger had found the general in the office with the National Security Advisor as expected.

The colonel turned to face the general squarely. "Sir, not only is it true, but I have reason to believe our embassy in Cairo may be under direct or indirect attack even as we speak."

General Hawkins looked shaken for a moment. Then his face transformed as resolve took hold. "Dan, go to the National Security Advisor and ask him politely to come down here and join me. Don't go into great detail but tell him enough to realize his presence is urgently required. Then call the JCS operations center at the Pentagon and have them initiate a code blue recall. When you have that rolling, call NATO command and exchange information. I hope our NATO friends contact Admiral Carden through their channels and tell him to standby for execution of that Egypt plan. What was it called?"

"Sparrow Hawk sir. Operation Sparrow Hawk."

"Right, also have the Pentagon boys send a flash message to the Admiral. I have my doubts about our allies. They may choose to delay action while they weigh the politics of the situation. Make sure the message is clear. He's to move forward on Sparrow Hawk, make it a unilateral Sixth Fleet U.S. operation. Let the Europeans catch up if they want to help.

Hangar Thirty-Five, Sigonella, Sicily

The schedule had just been moved up by twelve hours. The SEALs scrambled to collect their personal items and then run them to storage containers at the airfield. Their operational gear had been ready and staged in a hangar for some time, so once they arrived in the hangar Matt received a head count.

Matt looked around him. Each member of the team made his final preparations in his own, private way. After weighing all the choices and the availability of support assets in-theater, the SEALs had determined the best method of insertion without detection was by air. The Egyptian coastline was covered with a smattering of fishing and commercial vessels of every size and shape making the classic Navy boat insertion and infiltration a problem.

Often, the locals slept on their boats at anchor rather than travel all the way back into the port of Alexandria. A couple of CRRCs would be spotted quickly. They'd be abnormal, both in sound and shape, alerting the fishermen—who were required to report strange activity to the harbor tower or coastal law enforcement. Matt couldn't risk running into an inquisitive Egyptian coastal patrol so the troop would avoid the issues and fly over the fishing fleet to the beach instead.

Matt watched with interest as Chief Auger put the finishing touches on the troop's flight plan covering their movement in the air once under canopy. He deftly manipulated the laptop navigation console's controls as he flew practice runs using the system's mission simulation mode. This drill also allowed him to verify that all the various course legs from high altitude down to the surface were input correctly.

The console's computer would allow the primary navigator—during the high altitude, high opening, or HAHO, parachute flight—to make the best use of the prevailing winds at different altitudes during the team's descent. Once the men jumped off the aircraft's tail ramp, the HAHO technique allowed the SEALs to descend under specially designed, rectangular parachutes, riding the winds and following precise course changes at specific altitudes as if traveling down a series of escalators.

The insertion aircraft shared the hangar with the SEALs. The black MH-53 PAVLOW special operations helicopter loomed over everything in the small space. The impressive array of weapons and antennae gave the twenty-five-foot-long helicopter a sinister, business-like appearance. The elite Air Force aircrew members tinkered here and there, trying to make efficient use of the remaining time before mission takeoff.

Matt knew the aircrews could be counted on to do everything right. The Air Force PAVLOW helicopters had been the first aircraft to enter Iraqi airspace and initiate the massive air campaign in Operation Desert Storm and they were the workhorse tactical aircraft operating in Iraq and Afghanistan at the time.

Their unique electronics package included state-of-the-art electronic jamming and electronic countermeasures systems. Their weapons could be slaved to an internal flight and gunfire control system and directed by an onboard weapons officer using a joy stick or fired in the conventional mode by door gunners. These aircrews were the best in the world at what they did.

Matt saw the helicopter crew chief was looking at the troop trying to pick out the officer in charge. The enlisted man in charge of the load planning and logistics held up his hands flashing all ten fingers to the SEALs, two times. Matt understood the message, only twenty minutes until wheels up. It was time to get the guys together. The hangar door began to open as Matt yelled to the chief to round up the troop. He gathered up his personal equipment and moved over to the pre-selected jock-up point just behind the tail ramp.

The term jock-up was taken from the early days of Navy deep sea diving. When Navy working divers put on the heavy canvas and brass suits, it required everybody's assistance and multiple buddy checks to ensure the diver was ready to go.

The SEALs were all combat divers and the phrase aptly communicated the need for teamwork and attention to detail as each SEAL first donned his mission equipment and then his HAHO parachute rig. Each man checked his gear before putting in on then waited for another SEAL to double check by inspecting everything. Once the buddy checks, all that was left were the jumpmaster inspections.

Chapter Twenty

The boys were lined up behind the helicopter and they followed the aircraft as it was towed by a utility truck out of the hangar and placed in a large red circle where the aircrew and pilots would finish their pre-flight checks and start the turbines. The troop stopped fifteen yards away from the helicopter to allow the crew to do its thing.

Matt could see everybody was anxious to get rolling, but the gravity of the situation was also weighing on the entire mission team—both SEALs and aircrew. There wasn't anything left for Matt or his troop to do. The SEALs were going in with whatever capabilities and skill they had. No more training—too late to make up for lost opportunities to improve. It was time to execute. The troop's mood was upbeat and confident despite the seriousness of the moment. They were still warriors, and warriors lived for that shit.

Matt smiled at the faces arrayed around him. "Okay, gentlemen. You know the deal. Let's go over it one last time. Boone, run down the checklist until we're under canopy." Matt had to shout over the sound of the helicopter to be heard.

"Yes, sir!" Boone's voice was all business as he covered the jump inspection check list. As the troop's jumpmaster, he was responsible for final equipment and parachute checks prior to boarding the Helo. Wells was the assistant jumpmaster for the drop. "You guys get first checks from Wells right over there."

Boone pointed to a spot near the back of the Helo. "When Wells is done, come over to me at the ramp for a final look. Everyone will enter the bird in reverse order of the exit plan. Go as far forward on the starboard side as possible. Make sure you have all your shit with you, we ain't making any Seven-Eleven runs if you leave something behind!"

This last comment brought a chuckle from the assembled jumpers. Boone continued. "We'll be executing a tail ramp exit, jumping off the green light. I'll go first followed by each of you in your assigned order. The LT will be the last man out. We have a ninety-minute flight to the drop point. Exit altitude will be at fifteen thousand feet. Expect to be under canopy and in flight formation by thirteen thousand feet." He paused for a moment to check his watch.

"As usual, muster on the low man and tighten the stack up as soon as possible. You guys know how this goes down, so let's start this show off right. The LT and I will discuss any problems en route to the deck over the headsets but everyone else, stay off the net unless it's an emergency. I guess that's it, LT. It's not like this troop hasn't executed this drill a few times before. We're all good!"

Matt nodded. "Good job, Boone. Thorough, as usual, chief. I want you to go over the mission phases one last time."

Chief Auger grunted, acknowledging the request. "Alright, guys I'll make this short and sweet. Boone covered phase one pretty well. Phase two begins when our flight formation hits the water. If Boone's navigation is any good, we will be fifty to one hundred yards off the insertion beach. Get out of your harness and swim away from it. The weights in the harness pockets will take that crap straight to the bottom and out of sight. The team will muster together in the water and get a good head count. Don't forget to put a few puffs of air into your life vest to compensate for all the mission gear."

Matt checked his watch and twirled his finger to give Chief Auger the signal to speed up.

The chief nodded. "We'll swim in, four to a side in a parallel column toward the beach landing site. Boone and Jorgy will detach to recon the beach. The rest of us will buddy up in the shallows. One man covering the recon team while his partner takes his fins off. When the first guy's ready to go, switch roles. Boone will signal us if the beach looks okay using a flashing red alpha code. That's dit-dah for you boneheads!"

Auger waited for the laughter to subside before continuing. "Once the LT gives us the thumbs-up, the rest of us will leapfrog ashore two at a time. We'll set up a perimeter near the high-water line, then wait and listen for a while before moving inland. You have anything to add LT?"

"Yeah chief, remember we need to send the feet dry codeword by UHF burst transmission before we move out. So, Boone, you need to wait for my thumbs up before leaving beach center."

"Roger that, boss," Boone responded.

The chief moved on. "That ends phase two. Phase three is the patrol to the airport. We just need to stick to the timeline and avoid contact. Remember, a firefight is probable cause for a mission abort, so keep your eyes and ears open. We'll adhere to standard patrol procedures and deal with any surprises based on our SOPs. This is not a war zone; it's not Ramadi or Kandahar so don't kill everything you see. There are civilians between us and the airport so dial it down."

"Phase four covers our actions on target. Our mission task is to conduct reconnaissance and surveillance of the airport. We have purposefully kept this part of the phase loose and flexible. Our final actions on target are to assist the Ranger's raid on the airport if possible. Now, we aren't going to get in a fistfight trying to help the Rangers—those assholes can take care of themselves. But we can help spot targets for the air support guys. Let's stick to what we know. Keep it simple. The name of the game is stealth all the way on this one."

The chief pressed on with the briefing. "Phase five is patrol movement to our primary extraction point near the airport if something goes wrong with the Ranger raid. Of course, if the Rangers complete their task at the airport successfully, we'll be riding back in style, courtesy of the U.S. Army! You guys need to keep thinking about what ifs and be flexible at all times. We are good at what we do. That, and teamwork will get us through this operation. That's all I've got, LT."

"Thanks, chief. Remember guys, the first casualty upon contact with the enemy will probably be the plan, so we'll stick to what we rehearsed, as long as it fits. As soon as the shit hits the fan, we'll just have to use our heads and our firepower to gain us a little time and distance to figure things out. Any questions?"

Wells raised his hand. "Yeah, I mean, yes sir, what are the chances these Army guys don't show up at all? You know, get lost or something stupid like that?"

Matt smiled. "Don't worry, Wells. I think we'll be able to count on the cavalry arriving this time." Most SEALs knew the track record established from previous special operations missions in Grenada, Panama, and Afghanistan. During the invasion of Grenada, SEALs waited under fire for twenty plus hours for a relief force that planned to relieve the SEALs one hour after the invasion began. The same thing happened again in Panama and in later in Afghanistan.

Wells' smart-ass response was cut off by a high-pitched whine coming from just outside the hangar door. The troop looked toward the sound. The PAVLOW was winding up to full power and ready to fly. It was time to go. The crew chief motioned energetically for the team to board the bird. Matt waved back to acknowledge the crewman's signal. "Okay, guys. This is it! Let's load up!"

The troop broke up, each man grabbing his helmet and goggles. Matt and the enlisted SEALs walked stiffly to the tail ramp, their rucksacks strapped tight across the front of their thighs and their weapons strapped to their torso on the right side.

At the ramp they quickly organized themselves and, as briefed by Boone, began to enter the aircraft in reverse order. Two of the aircrew pulled the chocks holding the wheels from rolling and ran up the ramp tossing the chocks to the side. The crew chief walked up and down to confirm the SEALs were belted in place before telling the pilots through his headset that all was ready for takeoff.

With the team securely seated inside the bird, a crewmember pressed a button that lifted the tail ramp to its fully raised position for flight. Within seconds the helicopter rose slowly into the night sky. As it passed the tail end of the runway, all of the aircraft's lights blinked out. Operation Sparrow Hawk was underway.

There was nothing quite like it. The powerful blast of cold air at fifteen thousand feet sharpened Matt's senses. It was always a thrill for him to watch the tail ramp slowly open in preparation for a jump. There were few things he enjoyed more in life than the thrill of leaping into open space and flying. The first time Matt jumped out of a perfectly good airplane had been at a small private airfield in southern California. Contractors, all former SEALs, were hired to train the SQT students in static line operations and then advanced freefall.

Static line jumping was a technique that was, for the most part, unchanged from the days of World War II. A jumper wore a harness with a round parachute folded and packed into a rectangular backpack. A nylon cord with a locking metal hook was attached to the back of the pack.

This “static line” was then hooked onto a wire cable in the jump aircraft.

When the jumper stepped out of the aircraft, the static line went taut and the falling jumper’s body weight ripped the back of the pack open, deploying the parachute. Matt was happy the SEALs focused on advanced freefall parachute techniques such as HAHO. He hated the idea of being attached to the plane. Many SEALs referred to static line jumping as “rope-a-dope”.

Matt re-focused his attention on the men in his troop. They were as ready as they could be considering the limited time allowed them. He knew that the parachute jump was the most fragile of the various mission phases. He and the other SEALs had to rely on the skill of the aircrew to get them to the right exit point.

An exit error of only a few thousand yards could translate into mission failure by adding miles to the beach swim—putting them too far away from the proper beach crossing point to stay on schedule. If that happened, the SEALs wouldn’t be able to support the Rangers.

The flight had gone by quickly. Matt was tapped on the shoulder by the crew chief who then held up ten fingers. Ten minutes to jump time. Matt nudged Cruise who in turn passed the signal down the line. Boone unbuckled his safety belt and stood up.

He walked awkwardly to the tail ramp and stood next to the crewman who was already standing in position. A minute later the crewman pressed a button and the helicopter’s tail ramp slowly lowered, revealing the inky blackness beyond. Boone put on the headset offered to him by the crewman and he spoke with the pilots. When he was satisfied, he gave the headset back to the crewman and gave him a thumbs up signal.

Boone placed both palms up and raised them toward the top of the aircraft. This was the signal for the commandos to stand up. He waved the troop over to the other side of the helicopter and signaled the first man to begin equipment checks. Boone checked his gear and then had Wells check his gear for him again.

The rest of the SEALs were going through the same final pre-jump buddy checks. It was difficult to see that the tail ramp was open, as the pilot had turned off all interior lighting. Boone led Jorgy, who was the second man in jump order, to the edge of the ramp leaving a small space for himself to assume the first position. Boone turned to face the tail ramp.

The crewman tapped Boone on the shoulder and showed him an index finger curled downward, the signal for thirty seconds left to go. Boone passed it to Jorgy who passed it back down the line of waiting SEALs.

The red light mounted near the ramp door changed to green and Boone stepped into the lead spot even as he launched himself out of the helicopter. Jorgy moved a step forward rapidly with the over six men coming up tight behind him. He followed Boone off the tail ramp and disappeared into space. Matt, as team leader, jumped last.

Falling from a helicopter was a completely different feeling than jumping from a fixed-wing airplane. The MH-53 PAVLOW created minimal downdraft with its one multi-blade rotor, compared to the powerful jet or turbo prop storm generated by many standard, fixed-wing military jump aircraft. As a result, once out of the helicopter it took a second or two for the SEALs to stabilize their bodies in free fall.

Boone was responsible for wearing and operating the laptop navigation console and as the first man out he fell the farthest before pulling his ripcord. Each SEAL muttered a different delay count before opening his chute.

This allowed the group to create an initial dead space between each jumper. Once under the seven-cell rectangular parachute, a reasonable gap had to be maintained while flying to the designated landing site—so the jumpers didn't collide or drift too far away to see the troop in the darkness.

The trick was to stay close enough to gather together in the air from the very beginning so they could create a vertical flight formation. If things were done correctly, each jumper would stack directly above and slightly behind the man in front of and below him. The troop's training paid off as each chute popped open with a loud crackling sound and the SEALs found themselves in a near-perfect stair step column formed by their high-performance canopies.

Matt was the last man out of the aircraft and as designed he found himself at the top of the stack after his chute opened. He looked down and counted the chutes before reporting into his throat mike. "Solid head count!"

"Roger," Boone responded, using his best golf commentator voice. Staying calm was important but sounding in control was even more important.

With the team was assembled, Boone could stop guiding the stack in tight left and right turns and proceed on the first leg of the course.

"Turning left. Four, three, two, one, execute!"

After giving the command Boone glanced at his laptop navigation console and gently pulled down on his left steering toggle. He watched the digital reading adjust slowly and stopped when the first leg's bearing was displayed. The night air was dry and becoming warmer with every foot of the troop's descent. Each man was close enough to chat, but they didn't speak. The live microphones would pick up the conversations and only

Boone and Matt were authorized to break silence unless there was an emergency.

No further than six feet away from the man in front of them, they maintained formation by using low power light panels. The panels were mounted on each of their parachute harnesses. Red on the right, green on the left. Match them up and you knew the guy in front of you was flying away from you and not at you. It was all the control they needed as long as they stayed close. After five minutes of flying the initial course bearing Boone executed his second turn and steadied up on a new course for the second leg of the aerial journey.

"Right turn in five, four, three, two, one, execute!"

There was no need to respond, the SEALs in the stack were on comms and could hear the preparatory alert, allowing them to tighten up their place in the formation in anticipation of the turn. If Boone turned too radically the troop's reactions would be delayed and the stack would accordion, spreading out and doubling or tripling the distance between the men. During the day this mistake could be rectified quickly but at night someone might whip out far enough to lose visual contact of the light panels of the man in front of him.

Chapter Twenty-One

As the SEALs descended from fifteen thousand feet of altitude to the water entry point, the direction of the wind changed with the change in altitude. Sometimes they changed radically with winds at high altitude moving in the opposite direction of the winds that affected a landing approach near the surface of the ocean.

The wind speeds at each altitude were also different. The higher course legs were shorter because the wind speeds might exceed forty to fifty miles per hour. Stay on a high wind speed course too long and you added miles of error to the landing point on the ground. The navigation computer incorporated weather data for the area, date and time, and a final download by the aircraft flying in the high-altitude air space. That was the science. The art was knowing when the computer's calculations became sketchy—usually at lower altitudes. That's when the navigator earned his pay.

Boone continued to ride each pre-planned wind line to a new pivot point and executed a change in direction. The flight computer calculated these courses so the SEALs could take advantage of the prevailing tailwinds and descend as if walking down a series of stairs pointing in different directions.

The trick to staying in formation was attention, focus, and canopy maneuvering skill. Each SEAL needed to set his canopy angle in a way that mimicked the man in front and below him. It started with Jorgy copying Boone and so on up the stack. Failure to monitor the precise adjustment and a man might sink faster or stay aloft in a way that destroyed the formation's integrity. It was intense and challenging, just the way they liked it to be.

Once the troop was below five thousand feet the navigation became simpler. With slower winds, the margin for error relaxed and Boone had more time to set up the next course leg. He would attempt to maximize the team's altitude so they'd have more height rather than less when they arrived offshore. If he brought them in too low, they might find themselves farther from shore resulting in a long swim. He could always bleed off excess altitude—regaining lost altitude was impossible.

The troop continued its descent without incident. At two thousand feet, Boone began a lazy swing left and right in order to descend faster. At one thousand feet, he turned the formation into the wind for landing. He checked his navigation display and paid close attention to the bearing while also watching the yardage to the landing point counting down. At five hundred feet Boone chose a spot in the water and focused, aiming right for it.

Matt paid close attention as the stack slowed down and began to sink almost vertically downward, toward the water. This was the last maneuver as they all sank down to land more or less on top of Boone. Straight ahead, the city lights of Alexandria shone like a bowl of polished diamonds in the distance. To the left stood the outline of the great port of Alexandria breakwater that once held Cleopatra's fabled palace. Looking out at the beautiful sight, it was hard for Matt to believe this wasn't a training operation. Would he ever be able to tell Sherry about all this?

The stack stayed tight until the last few feet. Then, just prior to contact with the ocean, each man jammed his steering toggles down hard to stall his chute right over Boone's entry point into the water. As air dumped out of the canopy, it stopped any forward movement and dropped each SEAL straight down into the water. The troop was in enemy territorial waters and there was no going back. The arrival of the armed American SEALs in Egyptian territorial waters was an act of war.

Pentagon Situation Room–Washington, D.C.

The high-pitched sound pierced the quiet and startled the Air Force Major. He recovered and oriented his gaze to the operations status board on the wall. The audio alarm indicated receipt of another phase execution codeword for Operation Sparrow Hawk. So far, the status boards concerning phase one of the operation all displayed positive initial reports.

Air refueling assets and communications relay platforms were up, in position, and on schedule. Unmanned assets were also in position at lower altitude, orbiting in circles offshore until released to penetrate Egyptian air space and pursue their tasks.

They should be seeing the actual lead special operations elements moving in-country to their objectives. The Major spent a moment searching for which mission and which event for that mission had generated the alarm. He identified the event on checklist three, the Green Beret HALO team had passed the code to signify they were feet dry in Egypt. He knew their team's mission was to seize an important radio relay site, override the system, and begin broadcasting propaganda to calm the Egyptian people. There were five such Special Forces units doing similar operations that night.

A second alarm went off. The Major was looking at the wall and spotted the mission update immediately—another special operations unit communicated their progress. The SEALs were "feet wet" in the water offshore the city of Alexandria. The codeword SPLASH explained it well enough. "Now things are really going to start hopping around here," he thought. Another alarm kicked off.

Sixth Fleet Headquarters – Italy

Admiral Carden sat in the combat information center and watched the codewords pop up on his command center's mission status boards. His team of twenty officers and enlisted personnel were experts in air, sea, and land logistics, communications, intelligence, and the capabilities and limitations of the units being deployed into Egypt. His job was to provide resources when the assigned mission packages were shown to be insufficient to get the job done. That, and wait for things to go sideways. That's when an admiral earned his pay in an operation this big.

All military operations were complex, high-stakes activities. Everyone planned for the reality of the combat environment, but that environment was often a fantasy, a constructed reality based on guesswork—the guesswork of intelligence professionals. Weather always played a part and of course, the enemy had a vote. Tonight, it was this variable that most worried the admiral. The U.S forces were expected to meet light resistance at all locations. The Egyptian government knew this was a humanitarian evacuation, not an invasion. It should be a calm and orderly process. Unless…

The jihadists could cause mischief, but his forces were more than a match for any lightly-armed belligerents. It was the jihadists potential influence over the Egyptian military that bothered him. Special operations teams weren't designed to fight protracted battles against heavy infantry and armored vehicles. He knew that if the men on the ground found themselves in a major fire fight, the U.S. would have to unleash its airpower on the antagonists. Even if those antagonists ended up being the Egyptian military.

The admiral watched as the codeword "SPLASH" was sent by the SEALs. They were swimming into a relatively easy objective with a simple purpose. Put eyes on the airfield and report back to the incoming Ranger battalion flying in to seize the target. He was more concerned about his Green Berets. They were farther inland, prosecuting targets in the large cities and vulnerable to attack from almost everywhere. He remembered the SEALs briefing—if they got into a pickle, they could always run into the Mediterranean, jump in, and call for extraction. He smiled. He liked SEALs—they didn't seem to sweat the small shit.

Beach Landing Site - Alexandria Egypt

The water was warm and salty, especially if you swallowed some, which is exactly what Matt did while struggling out of his parachute harness. Nearby, he heard the grunting and sputtering of someone else working the straps and buckles. Matt looked around at the bobbing head silhouettes and took a quick headcount. So far, so good. In four minutes, the troop was assembled around Matt thirty yards offshore and ready to swim to the beach through the light surf.

Boone's navigation the fourth and final leg of their flight put them smack dab in the area between the beach and the much larger line of surf fifty yards further out in the sea. The regular crashing of the breaking waves validated Matt's early decision to infiltrate using HAHO instead of using the SDV or CRRCs. Even if there had been no fishermen to compromise their approach by boat, the surf could've done damage to the small boats, underpowered as they were with small thirty-five horsepower outboard engines.

Matt looked around for Wells and saw him nearby, next to Jorgy. Before he could say anything, Wells gave Matt a thumbs-up signal. Matt smiled back at the radioman and returned the hand signal. Wells had already sent the "feet wet" codeword via a secure waterproof UHF radio he carried.

Matt waited for the radioman to put the hand-held communications device away then started to count heads again. He stopped. This wasn't BUD/S or SQT where an officer's highest and best use was marshaling and moving loose formations of bodies through the training day. He needed to stop worrying about the small shit and start leading the mission.

Matt worked his way over to Boone and when he found his point man, he grabbed his arm and squeezed. Boone didn't respond, instead, he grabbed Cruise and repeated the arm squeeze. Matt watched the two SEALs start swimming to the beach. This close to the action required the two men to swim on their bellies, weapons in hand, scanning the backshore for movement.

Matt knew he could count on his troop—it was his performance that was in question. While not everyone was a combat veteran, Matt was new to the teams, the Task Unit, the Troop, and new to leading men. His anxiety ebbed and flowed periodically without warning.

Chief Auger had told him everyone gets butterflies and it was a good thing. Adrenaline created by the fear response made the brain razor sharp. Matt took a deep breath. No more second guessing, no more headcounts to justify his presence on the team. He needed to get into the zone and flow with the rest of his men. Their lives may depend on it.

Egyptian Air Base Outside Cairo

Bandar uncrossed his legs and pushed himself off the floor with one smooth motion. It was obvious that the leaders of Egypt's proud military services weren't used to sitting on a hard floor. Each uniformed officer had to roll around a little before struggling to their feet—in a few cases, gasping for air. Their concern for their appearance was comical. Once on their feet, they each took time to fuss with their clothes until they were satisfied they were presentable. "If any of these swollen pigs survive this revolution," Bandar mused, "I will enjoy making them re-learn the hard ways of their desert ancestors."

Bandar stood to one side, quietly acknowledging each officer as they left the room. But his thoughts were far away. Bandar was now certain everything was ready and in place as he ran through the final steps of his grand maneuver in his mind. He checked his watch. The first exercise of his newly negotiated power would take place within hours. The action would signal the beginning of the end for the tyrants—and like a sudden desert wind, usher in a new beginning for his people.

Bandar walked outside and looked up into the clear night sky. The Egyptian Air Force commander had warned him there was a rising tempo of offshore aircraft activity at several operating altitudes. He believed the patterns were consistent with military operations and stated it was most likely NATO or the Americans preparing for something big.

He'd asked Bandar for permission to send reconnaissance flights out to investigate but Bandar had denied his request. Whoever was maneuvering out there in the night wasn't expecting the response he'd planned. Surprise would be his ally. By morning the infidels would know that he and his followers were a force to be reckoned with and the whole world would know that Egypt was free at long last!

Chapter Twenty-Two

Boone's flashing red "alpha" light signaled to Matt that the immediate area of the BLS was clear of enemy presence. Matt couldn't see Boone and Cruise in the shadows along the high berm, but he knew they were there. It had taken all of twenty-eight minutes for the swimmer scout team to swim to the water's edge and stealthily crawl the perimeter of the large diamond pattern SEALs used to inspect the BLS and a short distance inland.

Boone and Cruise were positioned at the six o'clock position of the diamond pattern with Boone facing the water and Cruise staring into the interior of the Egyptian landscape and holding security. They were the only effective defense if a military patrol caught the rest of the troop crossing the beach to join them on the high berm.

The remaining members of the troop quickly swam the thirty yards to the beach. Without looking backward, Matt pointed with his index finger toward the berm and Wells and the chief immediately began crawling toward Boone's position.

The rest of the SEALs paired up and followed suit, each buddy team scurrying across the open beach as fast and as low as they could. Once at the top of the berm Boone directed each pair to a cardinal position, forming a three-hundred-and-sixty-degree perimeter. Each pair took up defensive positions addressing the flanks and inshore approaches.

Doc and Matt were the last to join the perimeter. Matt watched as Wells transmitted the codeword "SANDFLEA" indicating they were "feet dry." As soon as Wells finished packing up the radio, Matt signaled Boone to kick the team into gear. Matt noticed he felt uncomfortably cold. Although they were in a desert country, the long process of getting to the BLS in Egypt from Sicily had sapped him and his troop of vital energy.

To make things worse, the human body continually perspired when placed under stress. So, even though they had pre-hydrated prior to the flight, he was sure he wasn't the only one who had pissed away a pint or two during the ocean swim. All of the stress and perspiration had combined to create an onset of mild hypothermia.

Matt motioned for Boone to take them inland. Boone tipped his head slightly in response. He was all business as he unwound to his full height. The point man cautiously scanned the unknown terrain in front of him from left to right and back again. His movement was copied in kind by the others in the patrol, as the rest of the team stood up and looked to their individual fields of fire. They all knew the drill. The troop had thousands of hours of patrolling practice behind it. But this time—for most of the men—it was different. This time it was real.

Chief Auger turned and signaled for Doc to get Oby's attention. The chief had shared his experience with Matt and the members of the troop, that on combat mission, where tensions were high, frequently SEAL rear security men would be so intent on looking backward they would be left behind when the patrol moved out. Oby turned when tapped by Doc, nodded, and got to his feet. Matt watched his rear security for a moment then turned his attention forward again. He didn't think anyone was going to fall asleep on *this* operation.

The SEALs fell into their standard single-file order. Boone was at point and therefore responsible for navigation to the target and contact reaction forward. Matt, as patrol leader, was positioned behind Boone and slightly ahead of Jorgy and his big machine gun. Matt's field of fire was to the right because Jorgy's M-240B was belt fed. This meant Jorgy had to point his weapon to the left in order to operate it properly. By doubling the standard distance between men in the patrol, Matt and Boone became a two-man lead element.

Wells followed Jorgy and carried the team's communications equipment. He also carried a short model M-4 carbine with an M-203 grenade launcher attached under the rifle's ten-inch barrel. His field of fire was to the right. In addition to the SATCOM radio, Wells carried a primary and a backup UHF handheld radios to control U.S. aircraft, special marking beacons, and panels for use in marking landing zones and airstrips to support MEDEVAC of casualties or emergency team extraction.

The first four men in the patrol were designated fire team one. Cruise was the first SEAL in fire team two, right behind Wells. His job was to maintain the pace count. By counting every step of his left foot Cruise could calculate when the SEALs had covered a distance of one hundred yards. He then marked the distance by sliding a black bead down a rawhide string tied to his combat vest. Every thousand yards traveled, was passed up to the LT via hand signals.

The old Ranger trick was simple and effective. By passing the information up and down the patrol in this manner, all the SEALs were kept aware of their current position. In addition, at each temporary halt, Matt and the chief would show each fire team where the patrol was on the map and indicate the location of the closest emergency linkup point on the map. If separated due to contact with the enemy, the SEALs would move as pairs, groups, or individually if necessary, back to the last designated rendezvous point.

In addition to his primary M-4 rifle, Cruise also carried specially rigged anti-personnel mines called claymores. SEALs have always had a love affair with the claymore mine and they were especially gifted at modifying the devices to suit their needs. The SEALs usually primed the back of the weapon with very short lengths of detonating chord and time fuse. The time fuse was inserted into a firing assembly.

When a patrol was being pursued, these "stay behind" devices could be set up quickly to cover their retreat. Anybody running up behind them would suddenly eat six hundred steel ball bearings traveling at subsonic speed as the short time fuse burned out and set off the device. The claymore mine was so devastating it could easily take out four to five enemy soldiers in one whack. Cruise carried two mines. His field of fire was to the left.

Doc was right behind Cruise. His job as team medic was to guide the work of others and attend to any extreme injury that existed—such as amputation or life-threatening chest wounds. Doc carried a field surgery bag and every kind of bandage imaginable. The first SEAL on the scene handled the initial response to trauma. Each man was a graduate of advanced trauma care and qualified to start an IV to prepare a wounded comrade for MEDEVAC.

Historically, when a man was hit, his swim buddy reacted before the corpsman even knew there was a problem. The SOP was to use the wounded man's med gear, not your own. The same thing applied when using water to clean the wound. If this procedure wasn't followed, your personal loadout would depart with the wounded SEAL as he was flown out via MEDEVAC helicopter, leaving you on the ground with less water and an empty med kit.

Doc had made trauma "blowout kits" for each man to carry. The kits consisted of an IV, morphine, an ace wrap, a zip tourniquet, a packet of anti-coagulant, and one medium sized battle dressing. The SEALs in Matt's troop all kept their blowout kits in an extra M-4 magazine pouch attached to their equipment belt. The kits were designed to provide the first SEAL on-scene with the minimum equipment required to quickly stop bleeding and stabilize a wounded man until Doc could look them over.

Ironically, it was often the machine gunner or rear security who saved your life while many of the SEAL corpsmen evolved into the most adept killers in the teams. Doc carried the short, ten-inch barrel M-4 carbine with an M-203 grenade launcher. He and Matt were responsible for carrying and, if needed, launching forty-millimeter illumination and signaling flares. Doc's field of fire was to the right.

Chief Auger followed Doc in the line of march. As the assistant patrol leader or APL, he was responsible for taking continuous head counts and conducting backup navigation. He would also take command of the team when Matt and Boone went off to scout around or if Matt was hit.

The chief carried extras of everything: two claymores, compression bandages, radio batteries, and various items a man of his operational combat experience could appreciate. He also carried a silenced MP-5 SD submachine gun. The chief and Cruise were used for quiet elimination of sentries and silent room entry. The teams were beginning to get tricked out M-4 rifles with silencers or "cans" as they were called, but SDV Team Two hadn't received theirs yet. Chief Auger's field of fire was to the left.

Finally, there was Oby. The best sniper in a team of snipers brought up the tail end as rear security and was responsible for checking the SEALs trail to detect evidence of enemy trackers or pursuit. He carried a breakdown fifty-caliber sniper rifle in a soft case strapped diagonally across his back and a short barrel M-4 carbine rigged with a four-power scope. All the SEALs' M-4s were outfitted with picatinny rail systems that allowed the easy attachment of flashlights, handgrips, and the AN/PEQ 2 laser designator.

Oby could be teamed up with Boone for long scouting trips when Matt felt it was necessary to make waypoint calls to higher headquarters or confer with his chief on the progress of the mission. As their best sniper, Oby was the troop's first choice where long-range standoff weapons were required. He could be paired up with any other SEAL in the troop as required. Usually, in this mode, Oby and his partner would find a high observation point and control enemy movement covering a large area. He was the last SEAL in fire team two and the last man in the patrol.

The patrol moved quietly and easily over the rolling Egyptian terrain. Each man's eyes moving in coordination with his weapon, the environment was about what the SEALs had expected from their intelligence briefings—windy, dry, and for the most part uninhabited; an industrial wasteland that covered most of the terrain between the sea and the airport.

The low scrub scattered all around them stood about four to five feet tall on average. This was somewhat of a surprise. They had expected knee-high foliage; the overhead photography had misrepresented their height substantially but this was a bonus for the patrol. It allowed them to stoop slightly, allowing the bushes to mask their movement to the target. The SEAL troop swept their weapons back and forth smoothly, covering their fields of fire in a menacing ballet of death.

The SEALs patrolled slowly and carefully for forty-five minutes, closing the distance to the objective but not risking ambush by a casual Egyptian military patrol. Matt's early chill was rapidly replaced with sweat rolling down his back as the exertion of stealthy walking over the broken ground in the dark took its toll. It felt good to be finally approaching the target, Matt thought. The long rehearsal and briefing process always seemed to take the adventure and thrill out of the job by over thinking and over planning every aspect of the mission. On Egyptian soil, it seemed wild and exciting again.

Matt wondered for the first time in a long time what his father would think of all this. Matt could envision the old man sitting up in heaven somewhere, probably in a lawn chair, with a few marine buddies, drinking scotch and telling tall tales. His dad would bring up his son the SEAL and commence to critique the hell out of Matt's life, his choices, his abilities as a leader—betting that in the end, Matt would screw things up. "Well, Dad," Matt thought, "this is my life and my challenge and it's not over until it's over."

In the back of his mind, he kept thinking about the sunrise. By sunrise, the Rangers would be on the ground and Matt's job would be over. He had until dawn to not make any critical mistakes. The forty-five minutes went by without incident and they were getting close to the airport. Matt saw an odd plane land or take off once in a while which was a good sign. He also clearly saw the lights of downtown Alexandria ahead. At their careful pace, it would take them another thirty minutes to reach their objective.

There were more and more signs of human habitation to the east and west with every step they took. Matt knew that moving so close to the population increased the chances the troop would be detected before reaching the objective. Matt considered ordering a short water break. He didn't want the team to get fatigued or zone out and stumble into trouble. Boone's form just ahead of Matt suddenly disappeared, interrupting his train of thought. Without thinking about it, Matt's body reacted in kind, hitting the deck and rolling to the right.

Instinctively, all the SEALs followed Boone's and Matt's example. The SEALs had practiced these contact drills over and over until they were able to execute them without verbal commands. Matt settled into his firing position next to Boone. Without speaking Boone had communicated a lot of critical information to the entire team. Whatever was ahead of them was a direct threat and whoever they were, they were apparently unaware of the SEALs or they would've opened up by now.

They were very close. Matt's quick glance to the left confirmed that the rest of the team was also in position facing the road. He was about to ask Boone what the hell was going on when he heard the voices. A million thoughts rushed through Matt's mind as he frantically searched the darkness for the source of the sounds. The low bushes obstructed his view. He could barely even make out the outline of Boone's body nearby. Matt's heart pounded louder and louder. It seemed to get so loud he was sure those approaching their location would hear it and compromise his team's hasty ambush.

The SEALs stayed perfectly still. As the voices grew louder, the men remained focused and in control. This was it! The Super Bowl and World Series all rolled into one. They had each waited, what seemed a lifetime, to prove they had what it took to excel in combat with the enemy. The hasty ambush site was set, and they had a good kill zone clearly defined by the roadbed in front of them. Matt and the others knew the mission imperative was not to get caught, to not engage the enemy unless—and only unless—fired upon prior to arriving at the airport. If this turned out to be a regular military patrol, they would hold their fire and let them pass by safely. Regardless of their instincts to attack, the mission must always come first.

Matt's wildly spinning thoughts quickly began to organize themselves. His training took over as he ran down his tactical checklist. Apparently, Boone had not been spotted and the team had responded correctly to Boone's body language by forming the hasty firing line on the edge of the road. They had an awesome array of firepower at their disposal and they had the element of surprise. Would they need to use it?

If the visitors wanted to rumble, Matt and his fellow SEALs were ready to oblige. A well-coordinated SEAL attack was a simple action requiring the application of superior, concentrated firepower brought to bear on a well-defined area or kill zone. Surprise and violence of action resulted in success against greater numbers. They were ready.

SEALs had always been masters of the ambush. In the swamps and jungles of Vietnam, they refined the battle technique to a fine art, often employing demolition devices and claymore anti-personnel mines to increase their killing effectiveness. These lessons learned were passed down generation by generation. If it worked, don't fuck with it, as Chief Auger would say.

The troop's firepower was balanced across the patrol in a preplanned manner. Each SEAL was aware of exactly what to do if the shit hit the fan. In this particular form of choreographed attack, the riflemen were first responsible for individual targets. Once the adversary hit the ground, the riflemen would also sweep their weapons left to right.

From the start, Jorgy and his machine gun would sweep the kill zone, spreading the devastating linked 7.62 rounds left to right and back again. The effect of all the SEAL weapons used in this overlapping manner extended the width of the kill zone by five to ten yards on each side and ensured that no one caught in the middle could survive. Only Oby, with his scoped M-4, would continue to focus on individual targets until cease-fire was called. The combination of all these techniques was impressive to watch and deadly to experience.

Matt heard the crunching of boots as the military roving patrol on the road came closer and closer to their position. He realized he was going to have to defer to the judgment of his men because he couldn't actually see the patrol. If the group walked by harmlessly, so be it. If not, if just one Egyptian soldier paused or looked at the roadside in a funny way, Matt knew one of his guys would take the initiative and open up. Until then, all Matt could do was wait.

Chapter Twenty-Three

A few more minutes elapsed before Matt spotted movement. He could just barely see them. Their dark silhouettes were moving past Boone at a casual speed. Matt estimated the distance between the SEALs and the Egyptians to be no more than five yards.

In anticipation of a worst-case outcome, Matt applied pressure with his thumb on the M-4's fire selector switch. He realized that at this range he couldn't use the M203 grenade launcher mounted underneath the barrel of his rifle. His launcher was loaded with forty millimeter HE, or high-explosive rounds, great against men in the open, but useless this close.

Matt knew the chief and Doc were not carrying HE rounds but instead had special forty-millimeter loads similar to the buckshot used in conventional shotguns. The effect of these rounds on the human body was devastating. Each tiny pellet was the equivalent of a bullet. Fired at a distance of five yards, the cloud of subsonic lead would cut a man in half. Even a near miss would easily take off an arm or leg.

So far, Matt was sure he'd counted at least four men passing by their position. Without knowing what the enemy were doing, it felt like he was losing control of the situation. Matt tried to shift his weight in an effort to get a better view when suddenly all hell broke loose. BOOM! BOOM! BRAAAP! Matt recognized the crashing signature of a detonating claymore anti-personnel mine. He flinched as Jorgy's M-240B opened up right next to him. He hadn't realized Jorgy was so close.

Matt snapped out of it and took aim at a shape on the road. He fired two quick shots before the shape disappeared, then yelled to the other SEALs, "Shift your fire lower! Aim at the road!"

Men throughout the modern age of warfare have learned the hard way that shooting high at night was instinctive and also wrong. An emotional reaction based on nerves or adrenalin or both, it was also a complete waste of ammunition. People being shot at tend to hit the ground and stay flat. All the bullets in the world won't achieve anything unless they're aimed downward to where the targets were hiding after reacting to the initial volley of fire.

In Vietnam, the enemy had learned this lesson well, often escaping an attack by overwhelming but ineffective American firepower by staying low and beating a hasty retreat. As Matt repeatedly shouted the command, the SEALs red tracer fire dropped lower to create a tight impact area defined by the road in front of them. Matt observed that his men were sweeping their weapons effectively. The scene playing out before the frogmen was a wicked dance of light and sound. Although only fifteen seconds had elapsed since the SEALs attacked, it felt like hours.

Matt heard Chief Auger yelling through all the noise. "Cease fire! Cease fire!"

Matt realized the ambush was over before it started. In his first combat action as an officer, he'd given no commands and shot his rifle three times. It took only five seconds for the shooting to die out after Chief Auger's command to cease fire. As the last pop of a rifle echoed in the night, Matt stood up and barked out instructions.

"Set security! Search team, in!"

Wells immediately twisted around and faced away from the road watching the dunes and covering their backside. Boone jumped out of his ambush position and took up a firing position facing the direction where the Egyptians had come from.

Oby, as rear security, moved out onto the road and set up facing the opposite direction of Boone. Matt kept Jorgy close to him on the original firing line as Chief Auger, Doc, and Cruise moved out on a skirmish line to clear the kill zone.

"Fire in the hole!" Cruise popped a round into an Egyptian soldier lying on the road. His body was curled away from the approaching search team, possibly hiding a poised weapon or grenade. Doc acted as cover man for the search effort as Chief Auger and Cruise checked, one by one, each of the other bodies. The soldiers were scattered about the road like clumps of old rags.

Boone called out, "Thirty seconds!"

Boone's job during an ambush was to keep track of how much time had elapsed since the firefight broke out. Pursuit in the form of reinforcements would eventually react to the noise of combat. Boone needed to ensure the troop didn't stay in the kill zone too long. Chief Auger moved to Matt's side.

"Well, boss. The guys sure kicked ass! Not a scratch on any of us. And I've got a body count of twelve on the road!"

Matt stared at the dark shape next to him. Twelve? Twelve men dead in less than fifteen seconds of sound and fury? "Chief, are we that good or just lucky?"

"These men are pros, boss. They did their job! Luck didn't have a damn thing to do with it! We train the way we fight so the fighting comes naturally. That's why we're different."

Matt silently agreed with his chief's assessment. He wondered if Chief Auger ever got tired of babysitting officers. The chief was trying to get Matt's attention.

"Hey, LT. I think we should move these bodies off the road. The response force is likely to be in vehicles. They might miss the kill zone if we clean it up some."

Matt nodded. "If that's the right call let's make it happen. But do it fast, we still need to get to the airport on schedule."

"Roger that, sir!" Chief Auger moved up and down the line telling the troop the plan. Matt assisted in moving bodies and clearing up the debris of the fight while four of the troop kept a disciplined vigil at all four points of the compass. The SEALs cleaned up the kill zone as much as they could, moving bodies off the road and policing up loose Egyptian equipment.

Matt kneeled down and took out his red lens penlight. He studied a laminated, topographic map of the area. According to his calculations, they were still a good fifteen-minute tactical patrol away from the airport. If they moved faster, they'd make up some time—but the risk would be greater, especially now that the whole neighborhood knew they were there.

Matt moved aside the black wristband covering the luminous face of his Navy-issue dive watch. The SEALs were ten minutes behind schedule. Matt had a choice to make. Rush to the target and be in position to support the Sparrow Hawk reconnaissance objectives, or patrol properly and tactically, and by his reckoning arrive too late to provide timely intelligence data to the Ranger assault element coming in to hit the airport.

Matt looked around as the last of his men joined the defensive perimeter. The dark road appeared to be clear of any sign of the recent ambush. The dark pools of blood created by the dead were slowly soaking into the fine dirt covering the road. Matt slid toward Boone in the perimeter and waved for him to move closer. Doc edged closer to Matt.

"Sorry, LT. I had to open up on those guys. The fourth man from the front stepped off the road to take a piss and nearly stomped on my hand. Once he saw me, he panicked and I shot him before he could level his rifle at me."

Matt put his hand on Doc's shoulder. "You did the job. It was the right call. You know it, and I know it. The whole troop knows it. Don't give it another thought."

Doc nodded and stepped back.

"We need to get off this damn road, boss!" Boone whispered through clenched teeth. "I figure we're behind the power curve now. We need to move fast for ten minutes or so, then slow down and make a good final approach."

Matt thanked God that he had such great people to rely on. Boone had also been running the numbers. His idea had provided the team with a workable compromise for movement to the target. He nodded and pointed toward the airport. Boone angled off the road about twenty yards and moved out at a measured pace.

The rest of the SEALs filed in behind him. Matt looked back and saw Chief Auger pass the thumbs up signal, full headcount. He just needed to make it to dawn without fucking up, Matt thought to himself, for the tenth time since crossing the beach.

"Wells! Pass the word via the command net. TIC, troops in contact. All sierras are ok. We have twelve echoes KIA. Moving to the target now." Wells nodded and began making the call. SEALs were referred to as sierras, enemy personnel as echoes. When Wells finished the call, he gave Matt the thumbs up. Matt was pretty sure someone out there was reacting to the sounds of combat. Hopefully, the Rangers arrived before the Egyptians reinforced the airport.

Twenty-five Miles Offshore–Alexandria, Egypt

The young Army Rangers huddled together, checking and re-checking their individual equipment. The Air Force's CH-47 helicopter was not only a great parachute platform but was also an airframe designed to carry either cargo or troops into a hot combat landing zone. The helicopter also had other capabilities that went far beyond carrying men and supplies. It could jam enemy radar, sending a flood of deceptive electronic signals that simulated the radar signature of just about anything that flew.

Just one helicopter could make itself appear to enemy radar like a flight of B-52 bombers or a strike force of A-10 tank killers. The PAVLOWs also had sophisticated weapons systems. The highly trained crew controlled high technology targeting lasers linked to the weapons systems that could pinpoint stationary or moving targets on the ground, at night, and eliminate those targets with a number of deadly killing tools.

Six of the highly capable helicopters flew low over the water toward the Egyptian coastline. The flight of helicopters altered their course slightly at twenty miles out, setting a final heading for the airport at Alexandria. Once feet dry over the shoreline, the helicopters anticipated a short transit of one minute of flight time to the target site. Upon arrival, pre-designated aircraft would land and deliver the Ranger force while other PAVLOWs popped up to five hundred feet to establish a tight orbit around the airport ready to attack enemy reinforcements approaching the target or provide direct fire support for the Rangers.

The Rangers were heavily armed and equipped. Each man carried upwards of ninety-five pounds of bullets, guns, rockets, claymore mines, and communication equipment. Unlike their SEAL brothers, the Rangers were designed to perform as shock troops, to seize a target and then—if required—take the brunt of any enemy counterattack. They would typically hold on until relieved by a larger conventional force equipped with light mechanized capability, tanks, and dedicated air support.

In virtually every conflict since Vietnam the Rangers, Eighty-Second Airborne, Green Berets, and SEALs were employed on the ground well in advance of all other conventional forces. In Grenada, the Rangers jumped in from five hundred feet to seize a key Cuban-controlled airfield.

In Panama, during Operation Just Cause, they jumped in to claim a critical airfield in a failed attempt to find the rogue leader Noriega in the early hours of the invasion. In Operation Enduring Freedom, special forces went in early and led the Afghan warlords to victory over the Taliban, and in Operation Iraqi Freedom all the elite units were involved in pre-dawn raids against critical infrastructure and leadership targets.

Tonight's mission was a standard bread-and-butter situation and the Rangers were ready to lead the way. The Ranger officers and NCOs had planned the operation down to the very last detail. Every soldier knew his job. Every squad knew its assignment. The six helicopters would come in low—two or three feet over the airport tarmac. Once on the ground, the Rangers would pour out of the back of each helicopter, spreading out into a patrol formation resembling a large letter V.

These troop formations would advance across the target, spreading the formation outward as they moved to their assigned defensive positions. One group was responsible for seizing and controlling the critical airport entrance near the main road. They would occupy the control tower and establish landline communications.

Other groups would establish the east and west airport perimeter defense positions constructed and currently occupied by Egyptian military forces. The Rangers, like all special operations troops, expected that the intelligence estimates provided to them about the airport to be in error. The Rangers were ready to improvise, if necessary, to accomplish their mission.

At the very least, the information would be inaccurate by the time they arrived. The intelligence-types briefed the Rangers that only a few soldiers would be manning the defensive positions. They also said it was possible the airport would not be protected by regular Egyptian military forces. With the unrest going on throughout the country, it was highly likely most soldiers would have defected and returned to their homes to await the outcome.

Of course, there wasn't a single Ranger who believed that would be the case. Time and time again in their illustrious past, the Rangers had been sent in against light opposition. More often than not, they found instead heavy mechanized troops or troops well dug in and occupied by motivated soldiers who didn't realize that the Americans were supposed to win easily.

Chapter Twenty-Four

Ten nautical miles out, the aircrew commander, traveling in the lead helicopter, signaled the code word AJAX. AJAX was phase line three, indicating that the force was in Egyptian air space. This action was a violation of sovereign airspace and constituted an act of war by the United States.

While it may seem meaningless to outside observers, America has always tried to restrain itself by limiting its military operations to allow the State Department additional time to work its magic. However, having passed AJAX, the Rangers and the United States were fully committed.

The helicopters ripped through the night sky, spreading the formation slightly to make it more difficult for them to be hit by a single anti-aircraft weapon. The formation had thirty seconds before crossing the land-sea barrier and going feet dry. The PAVLOWs broke into two formations and dropped down to an altitude of thirty feet, skimming low over the water. All their active sensors were up and operating at one hundred percent, searching the coastline for active enemy coastal defense radars.

"CHARLESTON, CHARLESTON, CHARLESTON!" The lead commander passed the "feet dry" code word to the mission team. Each aircrew passed the code word on to the Rangers on their aircraft. In each helicopter, Ranger NCOs were passing the sixty-second to target standby alert to each soldier. Most of the Rangers had been ready to start fighting since leaving the NATO air base back in San Vito, Italy. A few checked themselves over one more time just to make their sergeant happy.

The leader of the flight detected a flash on the ground to his left. His night vision goggles were good, but it was hard to distinguish details on the ground up ahead, difficult to be sure of anything. He suddenly realized he couldn't activate his anti-missile flare system with the other helicopters in such close proximity. He began to warn everyone of a potential surface to air battery, but he never got the chance.

Washington, D.C.

In the Pentagon Situation Room, the duty officer watched as each of the code words flashed up on the screen in their proper order. He was aware that once the Rangers were in place and the airport secured, the rest of the invasion would continue on a larger scale. The airhead established in Alexandria by the Rangers would allow continuing heavy forces to flow in and land.

The heavier forces would bring their own light vehicle. This would allow them to spread out and seize vital strategic targets in Alexandria. The large open field adjacent to the airport could also be used as a drop zone, allowing the Eighty-Second Airborne to insert and add to the growing troop presence on the ground.

Within ten hours the United States would have seven thousand infantry troops on the ground with mechanized support, mobile artillery and a land-based, forward-operating site at the airport. Tactical air assets could also use the Alexandria airfield as a logistics staging area for follow-on support operations probing farther south toward Cairo.

An additional one thousand Marines would land within twenty-four hours near the same place the SEALs had crossed the beach, delivered by LCAC amphibious hovercraft. The most important element of their operational plan was almost complete.

The phone in the situation room buzzed loudly, startling the duty officer. He walked over and picked up the receiver. "Yes, sir. This is Major Johnson!"

"Hello, Major. This is General Fitzpatrick. I'm calling for the chairman. What's the latest status report on Sparrow Hawk?"

The duty officer's eyes scanned the brightly lit status board. "Sir, the last codeword flashed was CHARLESTON. That means feet dry for the Rangers insertion aircraft. They should be within sight of the airfield at Alexandria right now if not already disembarking. The next code word is DOGMA. Receipt of DOGMA means the Rangers have secured the airfield objective."

The major paused, waiting for the senior officer on the other end of the line to acknowledge his report. The general asked only one question. "So, as far as you know everything is going as planned for the SEALs?"

The duty officer replied immediately. "Well, general, I can assure you the code words from all pre-invasion operations have been received on schedule, including the SEALs at the airport. Sir, I suggest you give us a call back in about ten minutes. By then we should have hard information from all the operations currently underway."

The general mumbled a brief reply and hung up. After the call was completed, the major spotted the red light on another one of the phones as it started flashing. It was a silent phone and gave him a direct link to the commander of the Sixth Fleet in the Mediterranean. The duty officer picked up the phone, listened for a moment, and slowly put the receiver down. The caller had relayed a terrible message. Naval surveillance aircraft monitoring the Egyptian coastline had devastating news for the planners of Sparrow Hawk.

The Coastal Beach - Alexandria, Egypt

The Egyptian commander of the air defense unit lowered his night vision goggles, watching without the aid of technology as the last American helicopter drifted like a falling leaf into the sea. The explosions had sent shock waves rippling across the sand dunes. The men of the missile battery nearest him were cheering.

The ambush had been a gamble. Employing an old trick out of an outdated Soviet training manual, the young air defense officer had decided to concentrate all his surface-to-air missiles and anti-aircraft guns in a tight checkerboard pattern adjacent to the coastline an in a direct line to the airport. The Americans were predictable; in every incursion over the last twenty years they'd led by seizing the airfields and spread out from there. Bandar had foreseen this and directed the Air Force to set this trap.

He'd placed visual spotters along the beach with night vision goggles, binoculars, and hand-held radios. Their job was to watch the sky and let him know exactly when the American air assault force was about to cross the beach. Since the Americans relied exclusively on sensor systems to detect fire control radar emissions, he had all the active search systems turned off until the last second before firing. The American helicopter crews didn't know they were being targeted until it was too late to react.

The concealed Egyptians only needed to be patient. Once the spotters radioed the officer, he ordered the batteries to switch the tracking RADARs on and to begin firing. The attack hit the Americans at near point-blank range. Their helicopters were too close to each other to evade the concentrated ground fire and the saturation of the immediate air space with thirty missiles and thousands of rounds of bullets sealed their fate. The commander knew their success had been a lucky break. He also knew the Americans wouldn't make the same mistake twice.

Wells was working the encrypted UHF radio, attempting to establish communications with the lead PAVLOW so he could pass the next code word. Boone and Oby had left the team earlier to conduct an initial target observation leaving the troop fifty yards away from the target's chain-link perimeter fence.

They used special night vision scopes with a range that provided a detailed picture of the airport buildings, runways, and miscellaneous logistics equipment and vehicles. Boone and Oby returned after ten minutes with their assessment. The target was quiet. No military activity of any kind.

Upon hearing that, Matt directed Wells to make the code word call to the Ranger's insertion aircraft. SNOWBALL indicated a target environment free of immediate threats. It also meant the SEALs didn't need to sprint another fifty yards into the target to set up standoff sniper firing positions to support an opposed landing. If the target had been occupied by enemy forces, the SEALs would have passed FIREBALL—indicating the Ranger insertion would be opposed.

"SIERRA FIVE FIVE, this is X-RAY SEVEN, I have SNOWBALL, I say again I have SNOWBALL. Do you copy? Over." Wells listened intently.

The explosions surprised them all. Matt, Wells, and the rest of the troop hit the ground and went flat. Instinctively they crawled into a defensive circle, all weapons pointing outward. The sounds repeated and they were able to orient the direction of the noise. Matt saw what looked like a fiery meteor plunge straight into the ground. Several flashes and streaks of light erupted from the area of the beach and two more balls of fire plunged to earth.

"Holy Shit!" Chief Auger was suddenly kneeling next to Matt. "Those big streaks of light are SAMs. The little light streams are anti-aircraft artillery tracer rounds."

It took Matt a few seconds for the whole thing to register. The Rangers were under attack! He wasn't read in on the size of the force or the number or type of insertion aircraft being used to bring the Rangers to the target. He'd counted three fireballs for sure but he'd spent at least fifteen seconds flat on the ground so he couldn't be sure.

"If that was all of them, the brass is sure to send us the abort code word. No strike force meant no need for SEALs to stay on target."

Matt recognized Doc's voice in the dark. He realized his corpsman was probably right. "Wells!" The radioman slid over to Matt and waited for instructions. "Come up on the command net. Tell them the target is SNOWBALL. Then add there are multiple SAM and anti-aircraft artillery positions approximately six hundred yards east of our briefed BLS. Then tell them we saw at least three unknown aircraft downed by these ground units. Be ready for their response, they'll probably transmit the abort code word which is BLACKOUT."

Wells repeated the instructions back to Matt and after receiving an affirmative nod, keyed the handset to his satellite radio. He was communicating directly to the Navy airborne communications platform. "THUNDER, THUNDER, this is X-RAY SEVEN. I pass SNOWBALL, I say again SNOWBALL. How copy? Over."

The response was immediate. "X-RAY SEVEN this is THUNDER. Solid copy, SNOWBALL. Your status, over?" Wells passed the rest of the information on to the airborne platform and waited for a response. He waited for three minutes.

"X-RAY SEVEN this is THUNDER, roger all. Standby for new traffic."

Matt looked at Chief Auger. "Why not just pass the abort code word?"

The chief shrugged his shoulders in the dark. "Beats me, LT. My thought is there may be survivors. I'd hate to slink off somewhere and wait for a daytime extract without finding out how those guys ended up. It would be a big risk, of course. The Egyptians are probably looking, too."

Matt agreed with the chief's sentiments. Could he risk the lives of his troop to go on a rescue mission, unsanctioned and without any help from gunships or other fire support platforms? If he did do such a thing, he'd make sure they were all willing to make the attempt. He had no doubt that they would be.

The radio in Wells' hand burst to life. "X-RAY SEVEN this is THUNDER. New orders. New mission. Move into the target area and establish an overwatch position. Attempt to deny any reinforcement of the target using your standoff weapons. Continue situation reports every fifteen minutes on this frequency. Plan B is on its way. You will be provided a link up briefing via this net. Do you understand? Acknowledge."

Matt stared at Wells and Wells stared at Chief Auger. The rest of the troop were stunned as well. An eight-man recon team was being ordered to hold a commercial airport against the Egyptian military. The silence only lasted a few seconds.

"X-RAY SEVEN this is THUNDER. Did you copy my last?"

Matt nodded to Wells who placed the handset against his cheek. "THUNDER this is X-RAY SEVEN. Roger all. New mission understood. Will provide first report when position is established within the target facility. X-RAY SEVEN, out."

Matt needed to break the mood. "All right, you heard the man. We've had enough of a break. Boone, take us out of here and let's pick up the pace until we're really close to the boundary of the airport. SOPs guys. Rely on our SOPs and each other. If gets too crazy, we'll pull off target and let them know."

The chief was staring back toward the beach. "What about those Rangers?"

Chapter Twenty-Five

Headquarters–Commander, Sixth Fleet

Admiral Carden sat and stared at the situation report passed to his operations center by an airborne Navy reconnaissance aircraft orbiting at ten thousand feet off the coast of Egypt. On the wall nearby, a large operations status board displayed the exact position of every fleet asset and joint player in and around Egypt. It also showed the position of other allied and U.S. forces based in Italy and Spain, staged to support Operation Sparrow Hawk.

Shuffling the folders in front of him, Admiral Carden continued to psychologically absorb the gravity of the message. Within minutes, a second message came in providing a rough picture of what happened. This report was read to him by an aide. The entire Ranger strike force—along with the six helicopters carrying them to the Alexandria airport—was eliminated by a highly concentrated, and previously undetected, battery of Egyptian surface-to-air missiles and artillery.

A third intelligence flash report handed to him about the event hinted that the jihadists may have been guided by sources in Europe familiar with U.S. tactics and operational norms. It was even possible that advance knowledge of American military intentions and timetables were forwarded to the Egyptians.

The National Security Agency was reviewing its signals surveillance records to see if they could pinpoint the mode of communication used by whoever tipped off the enemy. If the theory was found to be reliable, they would trace the message back to the source and act accordingly. Admiral Carden hoped they were wrong. If a NATO member allowed this information to pass to the Egyptians, then most—if not all—of Operation Sparrow Hawk's planning details may be compromised.

The loss of the Rangers was a tragedy and it created a dilemma. They needed an airhead to flow troops and material into the theater of operations. Alexandria was perfect due to its proximity to the sea. With the Rangers out of the picture, the only available force on the ground was a small SEAL reconnaissance element. Still, the operational timetable required they act—and act fast.

A second robust assault force was spinning up in Italy and should be airborne in two hours at most. That put them on the airfield around first light. Could lightly armed SEALs hold that position for that long? Would it be insane to give them that order?

The airport at Alexandria would still have to be captured and held, one way or another, to ensure the success of Operation Sparrow Hawk. Admiral Carden looked up. His Chief of Staff cleared his throat, trying to gain the admiral's attention.

"Yes?"

"Well, sir," the Chief of Staff, a full Navy Captain, began, "I was thinking. You know, we do have forces in close proximity to that airport. The SEALs are due to check in within the next ten minutes. Even allowing for a little bit of slop in their schedule, their reconnaissance team should be on that target very soon. There just might be a chance these guys can take out the limited guard force and control the airport long enough for us to get some Marines or another company of Rangers on the ground."

The admiral squinted. "I've been pondering that option myself. Remind me how many SEALs we have on the ground at the airport?"

"Sir, there are only eight men in the reconnaissance team," the Chief of Staff reminded the admiral.

"Eight SEALs?" The admiral asked, not looking for confirmation. Just saying it out loud sounded crazy. But then again, according to the movies and books that were everywhere, SEALs were bred to like crazy.

"Sir, according to intelligence estimates this airport is very lightly patrolled and most of the troops likely to be stationed around the airfield are poorly trained draftees. More police personnel than hardcore infantry. Our boys believe that the Egyptian's most likely course of action would be to evacuate the airport at the first sign of trouble."

Admiral Carden looked up at the status board. "Tell that to those Rangers. Poorly trained draftees didn't shoot down those aircraft. That battery commander knew his stuff. Let's not underestimate our adversary again, understood?"

"Yes, sir!" The Navy Captain answered.

Two minutes passed. The Chief of Staff shifted his weight uneasily from foot to foot. The admiral finally broke the silence. "Draft an immediate message to the Chief of Naval Operations and forward a copy to the Pentagon. Tell them my recommendation is to employ the SEAL reconnaissance team currently in place at the Alexandria airport, to act as pathfinders for another assault group. When the SEALs call in, tell them to take up positions inside the airport facility without drawing too much attention to themselves.

The admiral paused for a moment then gave a second order. "Frank, I also want your operations guys to get hopping on a new action plan for a second assault group. I want the draft in my hands in thirty minutes. Consider the use of any and all forces not already committed to other missions. Also, have our tactics and operations people put together a suppression mission to take out those damn SAMs!"

"Yes, sir! I'll get on it immediately." The Chief of Staff turned on his heel and left.

Fifteen minutes later, the Sixth Fleet commander looked up as his Chief of Staff walked back into the situation room. "Sir, we have our reply from Washington."

"Yes?" said the admiral. "What did they say?"

The Chief of Staff answered. "I'm sorry sir, uh yes, they said yes. Yes, to everything, sir, yes to your whole concept. They said there's no time to argue with your proposed solution. And they don't have a plan in hand to try anything else. Washington concurred with modifying the SEALs original mission statement."

"Well, I'm glad to hear it since I gave that change of mission order a little over fifteen minutes ago. The SEALs should know the deal by now."

Admiral Carden looked down for a moment. To expect eight lightly-armed SEALs to occupy and control an airport was unrealistic. The tasking had been communicated in such a way as to give the young officer in command a clear idea of what was expected of him. They would have to do their best to prevent re-enforcement of the target by the Egyptians. The Chief of Staff interrupted the admiral's train of thought.

"Sir, one more thing. It's just my opinion but I think they were happy to put this all on you. The Rangers, and anything else that goes wrong on Sparrow Hawk. You'll be left holding the bag and maybe worse."

Admiral Carden looked up and sighed. "Frank, that's called command. Those poor bastards on the ground are about to be told to seize an airport because a much larger Ranger force couldn't get there to do the job! Instead of worrying about credit and blame, let's focus on putting the new plan together!"

"Yes, sir. I understand."

The admiral was a combat veteran himself. He knew the risks and he wasn't concerned about his career. The mission and the men were foremost in his mind but this was a new experience for his Chief of Staff. The admiral sighed. No, Frank didn't understand. Command was a unique privilege and failure was always a possibility. In the grand tradition of the United States Navy, the skipper went down with the ship. It would be no different if Sparrow Hawk was a mess. No, Frank didn't get it, but that's why Frank would retire a Captain.

The Airport – Alexandria Egypt

Matt hustled to catch up with Boone. He grabbed him by the shoulder strap of his ammo vest and gently directed the point man off farther away from the road. The entire team was sweating profusely. The pace Boone set wasn't crazy fast but with a hundred pounds of gear and weapons on each man, it was taking a toll. That was the way is was on most SEAL missions. They were freezing at high altitude or shivering after swimming for hours just to get feet dry and begin the mission. Then, once ashore, they experienced more extremes: heat, cold, radical terrain, swamps, or deserts. Each step on the way to the target broke them down bit by bit, challenging their capacity for handling pain and their level of mental commitment.

Boone had pushed them pretty hard, covering more ground than Matt would have thought possible since executing the hasty ambush. However, it was time to play it smart. Speed was not as important as stealth since they were within sight of the airport perimeter fence.

Matt whispered into Boone's ear, "We don't want to get stupid here. Let's slow it down and spread out. The airport is only twenty yards from here."

Boone didn't respond. He didn't need to say anything. He only nodded in acknowledgment of Matt's command.

Matt turned around and whispered his instructions to Jorgy, who turned and passed the word on down the line. Soon, the entire team knew what was going on. Matt spread his arms out and the team moved up online, increasing the gap in between each man to ten yards. Oby continued to swivel around to check their six o'clock—a slang term used by pilots for the vulnerable tail of their aircraft. A fighter swooping down on a pilot's six o'clock usually had a clear kill shot. Oby wasn't going to let that happen here.

Matt spotted a service gate to the airport off to the right and pointed in that direction. Bonne nodded and headed for that location. The SEALs could barely see each other as they moved online behind Boone through the brush. Matt glanced to his left and to his right to check their spacing.

His guys were on a straight line facing the airport and angling as they followed Boone's lead. Although they were spread out, the skirmish line-formation made the frogmen a more difficult target to ambush. The SEALs could hear firing and explosions far away in the city. Matt wasn't sure if that had anything to do with the American operation, or if the locals were only blowing off steam.

Matt guessed it wasn't the big American attack. Not yet. Matt knew that when the Americans began their action, all hell would really break loose. First, the gunships would move into their fire support orbits and start to pound critical targets. Air strikes and the helicopter gunships would execute strafing runs attempting to isolate and eliminate the Egyptian air and ground units before they could deploy. Then again, he mused, the Rangers were engaged before the appointed strike hour for Sparrow Hawk.

The firing could be another special operation unit in contact with the Egyptians. Matt said a little prayer for the Rangers and for whoever was out there in the night fighting for their lives. Then, he tossed in a hopeful note to spare his team.

The SEALs patrolled down along the fence line. The boundary had turned markedly to the south and his plan was to shadow the fence as far as the first hangar before breaching it and moving into the target. Matt stepped up behind Boone and pushed him forward a few yards. The rest of the patrol observed Matt's silent command. They responded by smoothly shifting from a skirmish line back into the familiar single-file patrol formation. After another five minutes of movement, Boone signaled to the others to form a defensive perimeter.

Sitting in their new perimeter, the R and S troop was twenty yards away from the first airport hangar. Matt could just about see the outline of the control tower from where they were without using night vision. That was close enough.

He knew the higher-ups would be pacing the floor of the operations center staring at the status board and demanding to know what happened to the little group of SEALs. He understood that and realized he really didn't care. The status report could wait. Matt needed to send Boone and Oby up ahead to have a look at the target area first.

The intelligence boys had assured the SEALs during pre-mission briefings that the target should be soft. That meant little to no formal military presence on-site, given it was a commercial and not a military facility. Boone and Oby's initial look-see revealed no threats but Matt wasn't going to blunder onto the runway with eight heavily armed Americans before knowing what lay just ahead of his team.

Chapter Twenty-Six

Matt hoped the intelligence and the initial recon were accurate, but the chances were just as good that the spooks were wrong. If the Egyptians took the time to prepare an anti-aircraft trap on the flight path from the sea to the airport, they might have had time to reinforce the airport and lay low, waiting to ambush the Americans when they came.

There was a growing concern in Matt's mind that this target may not be as soft as advertised and as a result, his troop might find themselves up to their asses in alligators. If that happened, he would be unable to stop and communicate anything to anybody. Matt made his decision. He sent Boone and Oby off for a quick look at the first hangar, and then directed Wells to send the on-target code word, CAMPER.

A few minutes went by and Matt began to get impatient. Wells seemed to be taking forever to get the message out. Matt decided to use the delay to check everybody's readiness. He spoke to the troop in a hushed whisper.

"Make sure you have your shit together. We have no idea who might be waiting for us on this target and I want everybody paying particular attention to their assigned fields of fire, don't focus forward. We are going to ease into this place. Boone and Oby cut a hole in the fence and we'll go through there when they get back from their look-see. Look around, move forward, and look around some more. Anticipate contact every step of the way. Is that clear?"

The enlisted SEALs nodded quietly. "Go ahead and check your gear as a buddy pair. One man on watch, while his buddy goes over his equipment, then switch." Matt stopped talking. It might be overkill but he was tired, and he was pretty sure the rest of the troop was, too. A heads-up chat seemed to make sense.

Matt hissed at Wells. “Are you finished with those comms yet? We need to start making tracks!” Wells leaned closer to Matt. Matt’s nervousness was evident. Chief Auger scooted across the perimeter and stopped next to his young officer.

“How’s it going, LT?” The voice was cheery, meant to convey a message to Matt. It might be time for Matt to get *his* shit together.

Matt heard the odd tone and realized immediately the reason for Chief Auger’s friendly visit. He was giving too many orders. Telling professionals to do things they would have already taken care of. His directives were actually sending them all the message that Matt didn’t trust them to do their jobs. Matt realized he’d slipped back into BUD/S mode. This was the big leagues. Truthfully, his team could accomplish this mission without his involvement.

Matt reached out in the dark and squeezed the chief’s shoulder. “Thanks, chief. I’m good to go.” His tone was also friendly and conveyed sincerity. Matt would be fine.

Just then Boone and Oby returned from their scouting patrol. Matt took them into the center of the defensive circle to hear their report. The chief was right to softly admonish him. Matt wondered where such men came from. The Navy had selected and trained the very best America had to offer and placed them in his care. Matt had to measure up and earn the right to lead them.

“What do you have?”

“Well, sir. There still isn’t any movement that we can see. A small private plane looked like it was getting ready to take off so that means someone is manning the control tower. A skeleton crew at this hour, I would assume."

Matt nodded. "Did you find a good place for us to set up?"

"That's a roger, sir. A big commercial hangar. Oby and I checked the inside. It was clear."

Matt thanked his point man. The SEALs stood up with Matt and followed Boone out of the perimeter, formed into a file formation once again. Boone cautiously walked toward the security fence surrounding the airport. He led the patrol to the left and then back to the right every fifteen yards, zig-zagging to the target. By moving this way Boone could view the target entry point at various angles. If anybody did spot them, they would have a tough time determining how many SEALs were approaching.

Matt had doubled the standard distance between each man. Being spread out amplified the effect of Boone's patrol pattern. He also didn't want them to bunch up going through the hole in the chain link fence. Matt hoped any Egyptian observation positions along that side of the target might be fooled into believing there were far more American troops heading in their direction than there were. This bit of misinformation could delay any counter-attack until the Egyptians felt they were sufficiently reinforced. By then, the SEALs would already be in position in the hangar.

It took four minutes to arrive at the large hole in the chain link fence. The mesh pattern of stood out clearly against the glow of Alexandria's city lights. Looking through his night vision scope, Matt could confirm that the immediate area was still clear of enemy personnel. But his view of the rest of the airfield was partially blocked by the metal aircraft hangars lining the runway.

Most of the structures were flimsy, consisting of corrugated tin sides and fiberglass roofing. Here and there, along the line of hangars, Matt could make out larger commercial buildings that probably held more significant aircraft. Structures made with cinder blocks, concrete, or lumber.

Far down the runway and to his right, he could just make out the control tower. A simple, unimposing building. It was constructed of simple brown bricks and stood four stories high. Light reflected off the tower's observation windows, but Matt couldn't tell if there was light emitting from inside the tower indicating it was manned and active.

According to their intelligence briefing, the airport could operate at night to support small to medium-sized private aircraft due to the presence of a radar-activated beacon at the end of the runway. The beacon was electronically activated by an aircraft on final approach and once activated, the runway lit up like a Christmas tree. So, it was likely at this late hour that there was no one in the tower at all.

No tower staff meant no support staff. The little armies of logistics people who were responsible for loading, unloading and refueling the larger commercial airplanes. All good so far.

The attack on the Rangers was foremost on Matt's mind. He felt in his gut that such a strategic location could not possibly go unguarded or unmanned, especially after the effort the Egyptians made to stop the air assault. His decision made, Matt tapped Boone on the shoulder. Oby stepped out of line and quickly joined Boone in the front of the file. The two men moved forward and stepped through the hole in the fence. Once through the fence, they turned right and kept moving, opening a twenty-yard gap between them and the rest of the troop.

Matt slipped through the hole and waited to cover the next man. Then, that man paused to cover the man behind him. Once the entire team was inside the fence line Matt gestured for Jorgy to come up alongside him. He wanted the machine gunner close at hand in case they were hit moving the short distance to the first commercial hanger. That way, he could maneuver Jorgy and orient him as needed if the shit hit the fan, directing the heavy fire to the right spot. The second squad of four SEALs stayed in a file formation behind him.

The main runway was approximately fourteen hundred yards long and at its narrowest point, closer to the ocean, it was only one hundred yards wide. As it stretched inland, other taxiways and small runways joined and intersected the main one causing the area of the airport to get wider and wider until finally, the width grew to just over three hundred yards near the control tower.

The majority of military aircraft, all training airplanes for new pilots, and a few of the smaller personal jets belonging to affluent Egyptians, were staged up near the wider southern end of the airport. These aircraft were staged both inside hangars and also outside the hangars on twenty-yard by twenty-yard concrete aprons. The aprons were connected with small taxiways leading out to the main runways.

Matt could see that a small plane trying to leave the airport would only require a few minutes to power up, turn onto the runway, and get airborne. Even the taxiways were long enough for a small plane to use, if it wanted to exit the airport in a hurry. If Matt was going to hold the airport for the next assault group, he'd have to find a way to keep any aircraft from departing. But that wasn't his biggest problem. His biggest problem was knowing what to do if the target became infested with enemy troops prior to the assault force's insertion.

Matt gave the signal to circle up in a perimeter next to the first hangar. A dim light bulb above the double door cast just enough light on the ground for Matt to show the troop his plan of action. He crouched down and sketched the outline of the airport in the dirt.

"Chief, come on over here for a second."

Chief Auger detached himself from the circle and moved closer, looking down at the shapes Matt had made on the ground. He watched as Matt's finger added to the general outline of the runway, making large squares to depict some of the commercial hangars at the southern end. Matt made an X on the southwestern point of the runway where the control tower was located.

"Okay, chief, here's how I see it. We have eight guys with only enough firepower to fight for a short period of time. So, it's obvious we can't get into any long, drawn-out firefights or the game will be over. I think we need to find a good observation position on the edge of the runway with our backs to an exit. Maybe cut a hole in the fence that runs behind the hangars so we can get everyone though fast just in case we have to make a run for it."

The chief was in agreement. "Sure, I see what you're getting at, sir. We can set up some basic security and get as much standoff weaponry in position as possible. I'm thinking the M-203s and rifles can handle basic area security. We can set up Oby with his fifty-caliber to deal with any armored vehicles that enter the area or any aircraft that try to take off. Do you think we should use Jorgy's heavy gun up front or hold it in reserve?"

"You've read my mind, chief. I'd like to hold off using the M-240B for any kind of basic reaction to movement on the airfield because we may need every round Jorgy has to cover our escape if and when were counterattacked by heavier forces. If we stay loose, keep good security, and pop anything that moves, we can give the Rangers, Marines, or whoever they send in, a fighting chance. What do you think?"

Chief Auger thought the plan over one more time. "It's not half bad, sir. It's basic, easy for our tired guys to understand, and it doesn't require spreading out all over the target or moving out into the open. If things got too hairy, we can just back up, move through the hole in the fence, and reposition closer to the northern end of the runway, or get the hell out of Dodge if they needed to haul ass. Yeah, I like it!"

"Good. Anything else I haven't thought of?" Matt asked.

"No, I think you nailed it. Not sure I'd pass this plan along to the higher-ups. They're probably sweating bullets right now wondering how the hell you're going to pull this off. The last thing we need is the brass micro-managing us. Give them only what they need to know, LT. Tell them we're in position to control movement and support the second assault force as it arrives, nothing else."

Matt nodded in agreement. "Got you, chief. If things really get out of control, we'll send the abort code word and get off the target. There's a chance we could still be of some assistance to the assault force with Oby's fifty-caliber. He can probably even engage targets from well outside the airport perimeter."

Chief Auger nodded. "That's right, basic SEAL tactics rely on the KISS principle, keep it simple and stupid. The guys will appreciate a straight forward approach." Chief Auger left Matt, working his way around the extended defensive circle, taking a moment to brief each of the enlisted SEALs one at a time.

Matt moved closer to Boone; he had his eye on one particular hangar approximately half way up the airfield.

"I want to move into that hangar," Matt said pointing. "The fifth one from here, the one with the large plane mover in front."

Matt gestured toward the structure ahead and Boone nodded, studying the hangar indicated. The big piece of equipment might come in handy. "LT, I think we should stay behind the hangars to patrol to the hangar instead of moving across the front of all these hangar doors. We can move in the shadows and heavy underbrush between the chain link fence and the corrugated steel structures. That will limit our exposure and remove the need to tactically clear every building on the way there. It's the best chance to get into position without being detected."

Matt agreed with his point man's assessment. "Good call, Boone. The chief 's almost finished briefing the rest of the guys. As soon as he's done, we'll get rolling."

A few seconds later Chief Auger crawled up to Matt and gave him a thumbs-up.

"All right," Matt said just loud enough for everyone to hear. "Let's do this!"

The SEALs stood up in an orderly fashion and followed Boone. The point man wove in and around the garbage strewn across the ground in the narrow space between the back of the hangars and the chain link fence. The shadows cast by the lights in the front of the hangars created an eerie atmosphere. Each SEAL stepped carefully, trying to avoid creating noise as they made their final approach. Boone and Oby cleared the gap between hangars before moving past the next one and so on. It took ten minutes for the SEALs to patrol to Matt's pre-selected commercial hangar.

Matt watched as Boone and Oby paused at the rear access door to the hangar. He placed the rest of the team nearby, poised for the takedown. The two lead men quietly checked the door, it wasn't locked. Boone counted to three and opened the door, sliding inside with Oby following close behind. The large commercial hangar was empty. Boone and Oby came out of the building and waved at Matt. The rest of the troop were cleared to enter the hangar. Matt gave the hand signal and the patrol moved up to and through the large double doors. This was their new home away from home.

Chapter Twenty-Seven

Matt walked into the structure with his rifle at the ready but pointed toward the cement floor. He saw his point element near the partially open hangar doors. The rest of the troop entered the dark open space behind him. Chief Auger pushed up to where Matt was standing while the rest of the SEALs took a moment to check out their new home. Oby and Boone lay down in the shadows near the front of the hangar, their attention focused on the watching the rest of the of the airport.

"You know, LT. By setting up a bit further back, in the corner of the hangar instead of the front, we could reduce our exposure to direct fire and limit the enemy's view of our team's position."

"I think you're right, chief. No sense letting them know how many of us there are. Besides, don't you snipers always set up away from windows and doors to mask your muzzle flash? Maybe that will work for us here, too."

"Cruise!" Matt whispered. "Take Doc and go back to the chain link fence behind this hangar. Cut a hole large enough for two or three people to get through at once. Then, set up just outside the back door. I need you to keep an eye on our six."

"Roger that, boss!" Cruise responded.

Cruise went to where the corpsman was sitting in the dark and motioned for him to follow. Matt watched the two enlisted SEALs walk quickly to the rear access door and clear the area immediately beyond the door before stepping out of the hangar. Matt waited until the two men were outside the hangar before he placed Jorgy in the southwest corner of the hangar. Matt would keep the machine gun out of the action until absolutely necessary.

The chief and Wells set up in the northeast corner, staying five yards back from the main entrance. They both had clear fields of fire in the direction of the most likely route of approach, the main feeder road coming into the control tower area to their south. Matt was satisfied with the placement of his men. He took up a position next to Wells.

"Make the status call. Keep it simple, we're in position midway down the runway on the east side, large commercial hangar. Tell them we'll mark with an infrared strobe when the second assault force is close."

"Roger that, LT." Wells broke out the satcom radio and made the call. Matt hoped it would be a one-way transmission. Chief Auger's words were worrisome. The last thing Matt and his team needed was orders on how to act tactically by desk-bound senior officers.

Wells gave Matt a thumbs up indicating the call was complete, message transmitted and received. Matt realized he'd been holding his breath and he let it out. He'd worried a non-special operations leader might order Matt and his small troop to seize and hold the airport tower. No special operations professional worth his salt would ever order them to do that, but then again, Matt had no idea who was sitting on the other side of these satcom conversations.

Matt glanced over at the chief and passed on a thumbs up. Matt next moved over to where Oby and Boone lay, three or four yards back from the large entrance to the hangar. The double doors were pushed open enough to allow a good field of vision but not so open that the inside of their hangar was visible. The thin sheet metal doors didn't offer cover from bullets, but it did provide concealment from prying eyes.

"How does it look out there?"

Boone rolled on his left side to make eye contact with his officer. "Pretty quiet. We both keep hearing what sounds like heavy trucks moving in the distance, but it doesn't seem to involve this place. Is everybody in position?"

Matt nodded. "Except you two. I'd like to get you outside, up high if possible. This hangar doesn't allow us to see very much. Assholes could be on us before we knew it."

Oby kept looking forward as he spoke. "LT, I saw a big ass metal box, a Dumpster or something. It's about seven or eight feet tall. It's just over there, north side of the hangar." Oby gestured with his head indicating the direction of the Dumpster. "If we get on top of that thing I can see up and down the length of the target."

Matt thought for a moment then eased himself forward toward the entrance until he could see the Dumpster. It was actually sitting only five feet away from the hangar they were sitting in. Matt looked around to see if there were any other possible firing positions available for Oby before he slid back.

"Okay. Nothing else out there and even if the roof of the hangar could hold both your body weight, and I doubt that, it would take too long to get your asses back down if we were hit and had to haul ass. Let's do a tactical radio check before you go out there. I'll let everyone know the plan."

Matt grabbed Jorgy and took up a position in the northeast corner of the hangar opposite the chief. He checked his watch—it was three forty-two in the morning. Nautical twilight was to occur at four fifty-seven. It would take another twenty minutes before the airport would be clearly visible. That left everyone an hour, plus or minus a few minutes, to get a second assault group into the airport. It didn't seem possible to Matt as he sat there in the dark.

"Head's up everybody! Boone and Oby are setting up on a Dumpster just outside and to the left of the main hangar door as you look out at the runway. I don't want any mistakes so acknowledge receipt."

Each SEAL, in turn, rogered up to the information.

"Cruise, everything quiet back there?" Even as Matt asked the question, he realized his gaffe. If everything wasn't kosher, he'd have been told so. Asking the question was a rookie error. His men knew their jobs.

"Cruise here. Nothing but big fucking rats. They're hungry but they aren't packing heat, so no tactical threat."

Matt smiled. "Roger that, thanks."

Matt watched them as they went outside the hangar. Boone helped Oby climb to the top of the large steel box then Oby reached down to grab all the gear and both men's weapons from Boone. Once everything was on the top, he assisted Boone as he climbed up the side of the metal box.

Matt knew that Boone's job in the sniper pair was to provide personal security for Oby while he worked. Boone's continuous scanning of the area would also help Oby find legitimate targets for extinction. Once the shooting began Boone would assist in reloading the big fifty-caliber rifle.

Matt peeked around the big hangar door and watched the two men until they were both securely on top. Then he looked back and surveyed his little kingdom. A two-man rear security element, a two-man sniper element, and Jorgy next to him in reserve with the machinegun and chief and Cruise across in the other corner.

He and Jorgy had a clear field of fire to the south, toward the control tower, and Chief Auger and Cruise had a good view looking north toward the Mediterranean. Yeah, Matt thought, guess this is about the best we can do. He'd relieved Wells of the secure UHF hand-held radio earlier. Should they be forced to engage the Egyptians, he'd interact with air support, freeing up Wells to fight.

Matt checked his watch. Dawn was coming fast. If someone didn't show up pretty soon Matt's troop would be easy to find and to attack. Only a few hours earlier he'd prayed repeatedly for an early sunrise. Ironically, the darkness was now his only ally.

Matt decided it was time to check connectivity with his airborne platform. He made contact on the first try. The strength of the signal meant the aircraft was very close, possibly just a mile or two off the coast. They didn't have any traffic for him. He didn't ask the key question, when? When was the assault force expected to hit the airport? He was done sounding like a rookie on the radio. When they knew, they would pass it on to the SEALs on the ground.

0355 Hours, Office of the Commander–Sixth Fleet

Frank was pleased with his work. The final arrangements for the strike package were in place. F-18 Hornet strike aircraft from the Teddy Roosevelt battle group were assigned to swoop in low over the water, directed and supported by a host of specialty units.

A combination of Air Force AWACs aircraft, and airborne communications, command, and control or "A, triple C" aircraft, were moving into position right now to monitor the entire operation. Add to that a flight of ground attack F-15 eagles on standby in Italy.

These battle-tested airframes were capable of multiple strike sorties at night and in all weather conditions. All together fifteen strike aircraft supported by seven mission support planes. The entire strike package was fed by KC-130 air-to-air refuel tankers and controlled by the Teddy Roosevelt battle group commander.

The sophisticated aircraft and Navy ships deployed in the eastern Mediterranean since the very start of Operation Sparrow Hawk had collected and then shared the SAM fire control radar emissions from the earlier disastrous Ranger insertion mission.

The mix of collected enemy transmissions were painstakingly organized and deciphered by American technology experts. The Egyptian radar and communications transmissions were identified by equipment type. Their capabilities and limitations were now understood. They were also able to pinpoint the exact location of the emissions on the ground.

Using this collected information, especially the presence of small unit radio activity near the ambush site, Navy F-18's would take out the specific area where the Egyptian SAMs were operating. One of the key weapons being used by the strike force was a clever development in air-to-ground munitions referred to as cluster munitions. These large bombs were dropped at altitude and upon reaching a predetermined height above the target they dispersed thousands of smaller bomblets.

The bomblets dispersed in a wide cloud of death and destruction, detonating over an area the size of two basketball courts. Upon contact with the ground, the explosives detonated, spraying a deadly pattern of shrapnel with devastating effect.

After the initial strikes, other high-explosive cluster munitions would be dropped in a checkerboard pattern around the area. The purpose of the bomblets was to destroy material and disable equipment. Once the SAM site was defeated, a signal would be sent releasing the second Ranger assault force orbiting in their insertion helicopters at a control point four miles off the Egyptian coast.

Just prior to the SAM suppression strike, the "A, triple C" boys would advance the Rangers incrementally by phase lines, closer and closer to the Egyptian land mass. The idea was to coordinate the SAM strike with the Ranger insertion with a minimum separation in time from one event to the next. Everyone involved was aware that time was critical to the survival of eight Navy SEALs attempting to control the airport.

The second assault force was a beefed-up version of the first one. A flight of CH-47 helicopters containing soldiers from the eighty-second airborne would follow the PAVLOWs carrying the Rangers. The Ranger's mission was once again to deploy throughout the airport and secure the facility. The Army's elite paratroopers were an airborne reserve should the Rangers need help once on the ground.

Army air traffic control personnel would also accompany the Rangers. They were critical to getting the airport up and running to support the main U.S. evacuation effort. Once the Rangers were in control, the airborne troops would land and set up heavier defensive positions.

The paratroopers would also push the perimeter out beyond the airport boundaries to control the major choke points and roadways leading to the critical air hub. Then, the last phase would begin with sorties of C-130 Hercules cargo aircraft, flying in, depositing hundreds more airborne infantry, and heavier armored transport vehicles.

If all went well, within thirty minutes a total of eight hundred elite American troops would be on the ground controlling the airport and surrounding area. The continuous flow of large-scale forces could then begin in earnest.

The Chief of Staff picked up the new strike plan and left his office bound for the situation room. The admiral will be very happy he thought, and I won't be in the doghouse anymore!

Chapter Twenty-Eight

Bandar's Headquarters

Bandar sat with his legs crossed, quietly reading the Koran. He believed in the old ways, the desert ways. He also believed that a true Muslim should devote time each day to the study of Allah. He'd found the prophet's teachings were appropriate for all aspects of life, even in modern times.

Alas, in modern day Egypt, people did as little as possible to observe the book's wisdom. They'd adopted the ways of the west; greed and the pursuit of material wealth above all things. No loyalty to family, to friends, or to their community. That was why Egypt was so easy to manipulate politically, from within or without. In his new Egypt, things would be different. Bandar's solitude was abruptly shattered when the door flew open with a loud bang!

"Enlightened one!" a disheveled Egyptian Army officer, obviously roused from a deep sleep, stood in the doorway. "The infidels are here!"

Bandar calmly peered at the frenzied man. He slowly closed his Koran, making sure the soldier saw he'd interrupted Bandar's time of prayer. "Stop your babbling and tell me what you know to be true."

The man lowered his head. "I will try, Enlightened One." He took a moment to regain his composure. "Sir, we've just received a communication. It arrived minutes ago that one of our roving military patrols was wiped out near the Alexandria airport at two forty this morning."

Bandar was aware it was now ten minutes after four. "Why am I only hearing about this now?"

Bandar watched as the officer reacted to his stern tone, melting a bit. "I needed to confirm the report. When I received that confirmation, I immediately headed over here to tell you, then…"

Bandar was getting frustrated with the simpleton's shattered demeanor. He couldn't have officers running around acting defeated.

"Then, what?"

"Sir, I was informed that apparently, only a few minutes after the patrol was ambushed our air defense batteries near the coastline reported shooting down several American helicopters. It's believed by the Air Force that these aircraft were traveling to the Alexandria airport!"

Bandar waited patiently as the Egyptian officer breathlessly ended his speech and lowered his eyes. Bandar set the holy book aside on a small but ornate X-shaped table and stood up.

He smoothed out the wrinkles in his robe then walked casually over to a large map of northern Egypt displayed prominently on the opposite wall. The Alexandria airport was a commercial facility, not a military target. Why would the Americans waste their time there, of all places? Could the officer in charge of the missile battery be wrong in his conclusion? Bandar looked toward the south on the map. Cairo should be their focal point. Not Alexandria.

Just then, another officer—this time from the Air Force—barged into the room.

Bandar did not waste time acknowledging the man as the new arrival started to repeat the same report submitted by the Army officer. Bandar raised his hand gently and the man stopped in mid-sentence. He continued to ponder the tactical situation. There was something here he couldn't see. Something that his intuition told him was very important.

The ambushed Egyptian patrol had been fairly large. Bandar estimated that it would have taken at least twenty enemy troops to eliminate a patrol of that size. But an even more important question was, why would an enemy force of that size be on that particular road?

What advantage would the Americans gain by seizing a commercial airport? Putting the ambush and the destroyed helicopters in context, it was obvious the Americans were focused on the airport or something valuable near the airport. Could the Americans be trying to cut off access to the airport? Maybe an attempt to prevent Bandar's escape? Or was this only the first move in a much larger military operation?

Bandar's eyes roamed over the map focusing his attention on the area in and around the city of Alexandria. His eyes eventually moved back to the dark black line representing the airport on the map. Helicopters just offshore?

Bandar froze suddenly. Alexandria has a port! The Americans needed the port of Alexandria for their amphibious ships! It all fell into place. The airport would serve as a critical early re-supply hub. It would also provide the Americans with a way to exercise their airpower across all of northern Egypt.

If the American Marines, embarked on ships, came to Egypt they could use the expansive port facilities in Alexandria to offload personnel, supplies and armored vehicles. After the Marines were on the ground, they could spring board from the port to the interior of the country.

This American strategy had the double effect of cutting off the supply of food and essential materials that flowed south to Cairo and the rest of the country via the large Mediterranean port city.

Without the flow of foreign commerce through Alexandria's harbor and airport, Cairo would know hunger very quickly. Bandar stepped back from the map. An invasion, a full-scale effort to prevent him from controlling Egypt. If the Americans thought the airport was the key, then he must stop them!

The Egyptian fighters and main force armor units were dispersed inland to avoid U.S. pre-emptive strikes from the carrier battle group positioned offshore in the Mediterranean. If he could thwart the American plan to establish a foothold at the airport, he might buy enough time to move his army and air force assets closer to the coast. Raising the cost of an American incursion.

If he was successful defending the airport, the Americans could still try to use helicopters elsewhere. However, Bandar knew the enemy's helicopters were much too small to bring in enough troops to make a big impact.

Denying the airport would set back the American time table, giving his recently enlightened high command enough breathing room to mount a vigorous defense. Bandar turned and brushed past the two officers standing by the door. He barked out orders as he cleared the doorway.

"Have my personal vehicle ready for immediate departure!" Bandar twisted back around looking for his personal aide.

The man was scrambling to put his shoes on.

"Make sure there's a truck with at least twenty troops ready to accompany me to the airport. We leave in ten minutes! Radio ahead to the airport. If anyone is there place them on alert. Inform them I will be arriving within the hour!"

As he left the building, Bandar bent down and picked up his AK-47 automatic rifle from beside the door. Slinging it across his back, he walked to his Jeep feeling confident Allah had shown him the way to victory against the Americans.

0415 Hours the Airport–Alexandria

The SEALs had forty-two minutes before the first light of dawn peeked over the horizon. After that, the sunlight would increase faster and faster for twenty minutes until the airport was bathed in light. Forty-two minutes for a second assault group to arrive unscathed, seize the target area, and secure the airport for the follow-on missions supporting Operation Sparrow Hawk.

Matt peered out from his vantage point relying on a small night vision scope which gave him greater range than the goggles. He studied the target's layout, starting at the northern end and then shifting his gaze farther and farther south along the line of hangars on the opposite side of the main runway until he arrived at last at the control tower. Everything seemed quiet.

Once in a while, they heard dogs barking and an occasional angry voice shouting in Arabic. The airport was surrounded on three sides by homes and small businesses. Matt realized everybody would be waking up soon to take advantage of the early, and much cooler, part of the day to get things done.

At four thirty, Oby's voice punched Matt's eardrums. "Hey, LT. We have movement to the south."

Matt's first reaction was to pull the earbud out and wince. "Oby! Turn down the volume on your radio. You just blew my ear wax out through the other side of my head!"

Oby didn't respond immediately and when he did his voice was muted. "Sorry about that boss, we have movement up by the tower. A small pickup truck just offloaded six or seven men. All armed."

Matt crawled five feet out of the hangar and put his scope's cross hairs on the tower. He could see the flashlights and just make out the bed of the truck sticking out behind the tower. "Roger that, Oby. Let me know if they deploy anywhere else other than the tower."

"Check," Oby replied. He was calm and poised, in stark contrast to Matt's racing heart.

The second Oby's report had come through, Matt had started sweating. Gone was the cool demeanor and relaxed state he'd been feeling since the ambush. Was it always going to feel like this? Were the other men in the troop feeling the same stress?

Matt felt the new information changed things. He contacted the airborne communications platform and relayed Oby's observation.

After a brief pause, the voice on the other end—high above the Mediterranean Sea—acknowledged and told Matt the second assault force was inbound. He also told him he'd hear the preemptive attack on the coastal anti-aircraft battery so assume wheels on deck at the airport no more than five minutes after the fire suppression mission ended.

More time passed without incident. Then at four forty-three Matt thought he saw movement in some of the buildings that had offices. These were located on the opposite side of the airport, across from the control tower. Looking at his watch, Matt realized that they'd soon lose the cover of darkness. He began to call Oby but the sniper called him first.

"Hey boss, this is Oby. I've got a column of light vehicles moving along the road near the entrance to the airfield. It's hard to tell, but there may be as many as three or four of them. Some are carrying troops and one may be a command vehicle. Okay, wait just a sec, now they're slowing down and pulling into the parking lot behind the control tower!"

"Roger, what about the movement on the other side of the runway, in and around those offices?" Matt asked.

"Okay, I see them now. I was preoccupied with ranging those assholes in the trucks in case I needed to take a shot. There are ten, make it fifteen armed men milling about. It looks like more are arriving from the area directly behind those aviation offices. There must be a gate back there or something. That puts the total on target at fifty to sixty soldiers."

Matt listened then checked his watch again. It was now officially the beginning of sunrise. The assault force needed to arrive in the next ten to fifteen minutes or they'd be taking this target in daylight. "Oby, you keep looking at the north end, tell Boone to sweep everything else. I don't want us to get jumped by a close threat because we're focused too far out, understood?"

"Roger all. Out." Matt could see the two SEALs up on the container from his position. They were exposed and vulnerable. At some point, the Egyptians would notice and concentrate fire on that weak defensive location. He watched as Oby twisted slightly, bringing his fifty-caliber sniper rifle around and into position, setting his M-4 rifle aside. That shorter-range weapon was retired for the time being.

"All set?" Oby asked his shooting partner.

"I'm good to go." Boone replied.

Matt turned his attention away from his sniper team. He heard more military vehicles in the distance. It didn't mean they were hostile or that they were heading to the airport, but if they were… He sensed movement to his right in the hangar. Chief Auger kneeled down next to him. "Hey boss, sounds like we are about to have a lot more company."

Matt nodded and continued scanning the far side of the commercial facility. The early morning glow was beginning to interfere with his night vision scope, so he decided to switch to binoculars.

"That's right, chief," Matt replied. "Adding a few more truckloads to Oby's estimates so far, we're looking at close to one hundred troops deploying at the northern end. I need to keep the boys in the sky updated. I sure hope they are bringing enough guys to do this job."

Chief Auger sat quietly using his own set of binoculars to watch the area around the control tower while Matt called in the update on the UHF encrypted radio. Once finished with the call, Matt turned his attention to the more experienced SEAL kneeling next to him.

"We can't fight off a hundred guys, chief. If we can withdraw on our terms, get back to the far northern tip of the fence line and set Oby up with the fifty cal, we could still help the assault group. Maybe keep a few heads down long enough to allow them time to unass the helos and deploy on the ground."

Chief Auger stopped looking around and listened to Matt before answering. "Well, whatever happens, we can only do what we can do. If it isn't enough, so be it. We'll need to get the hell out of here before we take too many casualties. There aren't enough of us to fight and drag wounded men through the hole in the fence then back down to your secondary firing point. The end of that fence is several hundred yards from here."

Matt looked at his assistant troop commander and smiled. "Don't worry, chief, I don't believe in being a hero! If you're good with that plan, pass it around and I'll tell Oby and Boone. We'll all have to be ready to move on my command. I'll need your help in making sure every man makes it through that hole in the fence. Full headcount."

"Roger that, sir! Full headcount. I'd better get moving, this hangar isn't going to give us much protection—it's already getting light enough in here to see our guys in the shadows."

Matt watched his chief leave. "You get all that Jorgy?" Matt nudged the machine gunner with his toe.

"Yes, sir! We kick ass until it's time to stop kicking ass. Exit this place through the hole in the fence, full headcount, then head north to the end of the runway fence. Set up again and help the guys flying in. Simple as shit, sir."

Matt smiled then patted Jorgy on this leg. "Sounded like a better plan when you said it."

No heroes, Matt thought. Isn't that ironic! The whole reason he became a SEAL was to become a hero. The thought of his father earning glory in combat, going through the same stressful experience he was facing, hadn't entered Matt's mind until then.

In a strange way, Matt felt a new kinship with his father, but only so far. Arthur Barrett had led men in combat. But one distinction was worth noting. While the old man walked away wearing the big blue, many of the men under his command didn't walk away at all. Matt had no intention of emulating his old man on that score.

Out there it was just you and your men, no staff officers, no instructors, and no bullshit grading systems. Matt realized during the readiness exercise in the Bahamas that it didn't matter how you made it happen, mission accomplishment was the responsibility of the officer in command. So, what if higher authority didn't like the way you accomplished your mission? Tough shit. The only opinions that really mattered when it came right down to it, were those of the men who served with you on target.

Chapter Twenty-Nine

Control Tower–Alexandria Airport

Bandar walked away from his Jeep with a purposeful stride. "Where is the company commander?" he shouted. "I want him now!"

A young officer nearby reacted, scrambling to catch up with Bandar. He caught up just as his leader entered the tower facility.

Bandar stopped. "Do not step all over me you fool! What is the status here?"

The Army Captain calmed himself. "Enlighted one, we have one hundred soldiers here on the grounds. They are holding the northern section of the airport."

Bandar waited for more, but the captain ended his report. "Why are you here? Do you think the Americans are going to drive up the same street as I did and park out front? Are you aware of the great victory we scored earlier this morning?"

"Yes, yes, our coastal battery destroyed several American helicopters, a great victory, I agree!"

Bandar would remember this man. His mind was weak and his willingness to grovel rather than lead indicated he'd do whatever it took to stay alive, align with any party to preserve his precious status as an Army officer.

"Listen closely. I want you to send out patrols, twenty men each, down both sides of the airport. The Americans always come from the sea. They use their Navy to defeat their enemies. We need to get heavy weapons deployed to the northern end of the runway. The Americans will not quit. They will come at us again and we must be ready!"

The officer mumbled his understanding, saluted and ran.

Bandar walked briskly through the open foyer, turned to the right and entered the first-floor office belonging to the airport supervisor where he had been informed a large map of the airport's layout could be found. He found what he was looking for and stood a moment absorbing the information, the position of each hangar, the area to the north between the facility and the beach.

As he pondered the display, another officer entered the room. The man's name was Colonel Samir and he was the commander of the Alexandria military district. The colonel waited patiently until Bandar acknowledged his presence.

"Here and here!" Bandar said, stabbing his index finger at the wall map. "I want your forces to aggressively patrol behind the commercial hangars. I sent a foolish young captain out to rally his men and get patrols moving down the airport toward the north. Call him on the radio, let him know you are here and in command. Tell him to have his men follow the fence line instead of walking the runway and tell him to report anything out of the ordinary—and I mean anything."

The colonel stepped forward and studied the map for a minute. "We need heavy weapons to stop a helicopter assault," he opined, stating the obvious. "I have communicated with the coastal anti-aircraft battery commander and he's requested a replenishment of missiles and ammunition for the guns. He will receive this in the next twenty minutes. He will be the first line of defense. If the Americans get past that line they will be flying at a very low level, landing on the airport, too low for missiles. I will need MANPAD surface-to-air weapons to be effective."

Bandar listened but as he did so he became angry with the senior officer's nonchalance. "Why are you standing here lecturing me? Go do what needs to be done."

The colonel didn't appear to be intimidated by the jihadist. "Sir, I cannot get access to the Russian SA-7s, you have ordered the Air Force Commander to control the inventory, I believe so no one can use these weapons against our own military."

Bandar vaguely remembered this order. He'd tried to avert one threat only to hamstring his ability to deal with another threat. "Colonel, get me a communications connection with the head of the Air Force. I'll get you those SA-7s!"

Four of his personal bodyguards moved around with Bandar as he completed his inspection of the control tower area. He knew it was the Americans and the British who had trained most of the Egyptian military including the soldiers deployed at the airport.

Of course, the infidels never considered that their students would be fighting them someday. Since the time of the peace accords between Egypt and Israel, Egypt had been treated like a puppet of the western governments. It was time to change that arrangement.

Hangar Position – Alexandria Airport

Matt's earpiece crackled to life again. "Hey boss, it's Oby. It looks like there are two groups, each about fifteen guys. They're leaving the tower."

"What do you think they're up to?" Matt asked. His brain was spinning up and the fatigue that he'd felt only moments ago was mysteriously gone.

"Wait one." Oby looked through his scope while Boone scanned the broader landscape with his binoculars.

"Boss, they're military patrols. Looks like one is heading our way down the west side and the second patrol is setting up to move down the east side."

Matt listened intently. The noises were carrying across the open space, drifting from the tower area to the SEALs.

Chief Auger stood up and went over to Matt. "What's up? Sounds like a party setting up somewhere to the south."

Matt nodded. "Oby and Boone have one hundred troops on target so far. About thirty guys split into two patrols and they're heading down both sides of the airport, moving north."

Chief Auger raised his small set of binoculars to his face. "I don't see anyone moving across the way. Are you sure that…wait, I see them!"

Matt raised his binoculars and tried to look where his chief was looking. "Yep, those bastards are patrolling *behind* the hangars!"

Chief Auger grunted. "They're staying between the perimeter fence and the back side of the buildings. I'd better give Wells and Doc a heads up. They're about to have company!"

Matt watched his chief head for the back of the hangar. Chief Auger wanted to look at the situation for himself. Matt watched him for a second then keyed the UHF radio.

"THUNDER, this is X-RAY SEVEN. SITREP 0516. Infantry on target, one hundred to two hundred. Patrols consisting of fifteen to twenty men moving south to north along the perimeter fence. Be advised we are still in original position and will stay here until directed to move or enemy contact forces us to move. Over."

The voice boomed through the handheld radio forcing Matt to muffle the sound, pushing the radio into his chest. "X-RAY SEVEN, this is THUNDER. Understood. Big players inbound and estimate you position in fifteen minutes. THUNDER, out."

"You think we'll still be here in fifteen minutes?" Jorgy had listened to the conversations and was using his binoculars to watch the progress of the patrol across the runway.

Matt shrugged. "Beats me. This is a better position to keep eyes on things for the guys flying in. Better firing position, too. Hate to get pushed north to the fence, won't be able to see shit from over there.

Jorgy kept his eyes on the patrol. "Just a thought, sir. But when someone tells SEALs they're going to relieve them it rarely goes according to schedule. Too early, or too late, but never on time. Probably time to put a ground panel out in front of the hangar. The predators will see hot bodies and assume we're bad guys, simple airstrike and poof, no more team guys."

Matt liked the idea. He fumbled around his shirt and then checked the cargo pockets on his pants until he found what he was looking for. The bright orange panel was five feet long by four feet wide. Its fluorescent orange color was easy to spot from the air and more importantly, it marked a friendly U.S. position on the ground. Satellites, predators, everybody looking down on the target would instantly know where the SEALs were set up. He should've thought of it himself.

"Fucking great idea, Jorgy. You haven't said a word all night and when you do open your mouth its brilliant!"

Jorgy snorted. "Basic shit, LT. You've been too busy thinking about everything. Me, I have only one task here, lead on heads."

Matt couldn't help but chuckle. Jorgy was always quiet around the workplace, but the guys had stories. Stories about the wild side of Jorgy once he started drinking. Nothing mean spirited or criminal, just a complete personality transformation. Jorgy was a party animal.

Chief Auger sat in the tall grass next to Wells and Doc. They were tired and his visit was a welcome diversion from the boredom. The space between the hangar and the fence was approximately fifteen feet wide. Not much room but an advantage to the SEALs. The chief told the two men about the patrol moving their way.

A superior force wouldn't be able to bring all their guns online and they couldn't flank to the left, the fence blocked that maneuver. That meant a savvy patrol leader would split his patrol, sending half to the right and around the hangar to hit the SEALs from behind. Not a good thing.

"Can't fight here, chief," Wells stated the obvious.

"Can't bluff them either." Added Doc. "This big ass hole will be enough to bring every goy they have down here."

Chief Auger hadn't thought about the hole in the fence. He'd been ready to pull the two men into the hangar, setting up inside and hoping the patrol would pass by them without issues. Doc's insight killed that plan.

"You guys are going to have to stay here and watch for a minute or two. I'll go brief Barrett and see what he wants to do."

"You think this guy is the real deal, chief?" Wells was curious and mildly concerned at the same time. The LT was brand new. He had a good personality, treated the enlisted guys, okay, but none of that mattered in a stand-up fight. It was a question they'd all been asking themselves ever since the ambush.

Chief Auger knew the answer. In his gut he'd felt good about the young officer from the beginning. Stable, smart, but humble. Humble enough to ask good questions. Professional enough to allow the enlisted SEALs to do their job without interference.

"Yeah, he's the real deal. I'm glad he's the guy in charge, too. We could've drawn worse, much worse."

At the front entrance to the hangar, Matt calculated the amount of time it would take for the patrols to reach the northern tip of the facility. Small arms fire shouldn't deter an assault landing, depending on the aircraft types used to insert the troops, there should be sufficient onboard firepower to suppress whatever the Egyptian military patrols threw at them.

If they deployed heavy weapons all that went out of the window. Then, the odds would swing in favor of the enemy. Matt decided then and there that his SEALs wouldn't let that happen.

The radio crackled to life. "Hey LT, those guys are getting awful close. We have a plan?" Boone's voice was calm.

Matt thought before answering. "Yeah, the chief went back to brief Wells and Doc. I estimate the patrol on our side is no more than four or five minutes from contact. Wait one and the plan."

Matt's mind was churning. Five minutes. Do we take out the patrol or do we try to evade them? Do we engage the patrol at a distance, or do we wait until they get in close and personal? Matt's thoughts were interrupted by Chief Auger arriving at his side.

"Anything new up here?"

Matt shook his head. "No, but I figure we have less than five minutes before those goons show up behind the hangar…"

"And spot the big ass hole in their fence."

"And spot the big ass hole in their fence, exactly," Matt replied. "Any ideas, chief?"

Chief Auger laid out the plan he, Wells, and Doc had discussed. It would require Jorgy and the Chief to move pretty soon to set up in the gap between the hangars. If the patrol stood their ground, Wells and Doc would take them out. If they split and tried to flank to the right, talking the path between the hangars, the Chief and Jorgy would finish them.

Matt liked the plan. "Simple and smart. I'm good with it. I'll pull Cruise over here with me. Once the shooting starts there's bound to be a reaction force heading our way from the tower. Oby can handle knocking it out with his fifty but after that, it will be all point targets, every one of them heading straight at us."

Chief Auger understood. "Don't worry, LT. I'll get Jorgy back online once we take out the patrol on our side. He and I can help Oby and Boone work over whoever has the balls to come to us and play."

Matt couldn't see a flaw in the logic. "Okay, enough jabbering. Go, and take Jorgy with you!"

Chief Auger tapped Jorgy on the foot and the machine gunner stood up, following his chief out through the hangar entrance.

"LT!" Wells' voice surprised Matt with its urgent tone.

"Roger, what's up?"

"Sir, we have a crowd moving toward us at a leisurely walk. Not in a formation exactly, just filling the space with their bodies, kind of like a double file but sloppy."

"Distance?"

"These guys are two hangars away. Estimate contact in two minutes. We clear to open up back here?"

Matt couldn't micromanage what was about to happen. There were too many moving parts and he still needed to figure out how to protect the inbound aircraft. "Wells, you guys hit them when you're ready, break. Chief, you hearing all this?"

"All good, boss. We'll take it from here."

"Roger, good hunting guys." Matt had about ninety seconds until the whole country found out the Americans were at the airport.

Chapter Thirty

BOOM! The loud report of Oby's fifty caliber rifle shook the hangar. Matt knew Oby would've called him on the radio if he'd had time. Matt could now hear Boone's M-4 opening up, also.

"Sir, somehow the guys across the way spotted us here in the hangar. They set up in a firing line."

Matt didn't fault Oby. He was smart enough to know the call and he had a scope. The sniper could read lips at this range if needed. "No issues, Boone. You guys pay attention to them."

Wells came over the radio, his voice hissing as he tried to whisper. "What the hell's going on up there?"

Matt started to respond but his answer was suddenly drowned out by the sound of a double explosion. Wells and Doc had cranked off the two claymores they'd set up for security behind the hangar.

Matt and the rest of the SEALs then heard the distinctive sound of SEALs rocking and rolling. The empty hangar was amplifying everything, but Matt was sure their position was more than compromised. It was now somebody's job on the other side to rapidly plan a counterattack against him. He only had a few minutes.

Boone stopped shooting and again tried to provide an update to what was happening out in front of the hangar. "Heads up, guys! Straight across the main runway, the hangar on the right, the blue one. Check out the small office on the right side. There are five or six riflemen on the ground. Oby hit one of them and they hit the deck. They're on the southern side of the hangar back in the shadows!"

Just then the firing from behind their hangar abruptly ended. "LT!" Wells' voice was excited.

"Claymores took out half these guys back here. Doc and I dropped a few more and the rest hightailed it to the south. Probably headed back to the tower."

Matt rogered up. "Understood. You guys stay in position and report if they come back with any reinforcements. Don't engage unless you don't have a choice. I may want to pull you in here instead of fight. Break, break. Chief, you copy all that?"

"Roger, sir! Jorgy and I are turning around to face the assholes across the runway. You want me to keep quiet or hit'em?"

Matt peered across the runway. The sun was breaking, and the target area was getting brighter by the minute. Oby's fifty caliber rifle was overkill, shooting individuals wasn't his highest and best use. "Go ahead and have Jorgy dust 'em up a bit. I want these people to know we have some heavy firepower."

"Roger that, sir. Auger out."

They all heard the deep-throated roar of the M-240B when opened up on the Egyptians. The big gun ripped up the rifle squad on the far side of the runway. The soldiers didn't have cover and instead of getting up and running they simply froze, staying in place. The weapon's 7.62 NATO round was designed to travel eleven hundred yards. Jorgy was tearing the enemy apart from only a football field away.

Boone helped to pick off the few men who attempted to crawl away. Matt didn't need the radios anymore; the silence was shattered forever. "CEASE FIRE!"

Matt stayed on his belly and crawled to where Jorgy and Chief Auger were laying. He directed Cruise to follow him. The chief wasn't shooting. He instead was focusing his attention toward the tower. When Matt slid up next to him, he handed him his binoculars.

"LT, look to the north. I think I saw more intense vehicle movement. They're getting ready to do something."

Matt grabbed the binoculars and peered at the spot the chief had indicated.

There were more Egyptian troops between the hangars firing at the SEALs.

Matt nodded. "You're right. They are getting ready to move a bunch of people somewhere."

"Any word on the assault? It's going to get a lot worse for us. We've been lucky so far. Now they know where we are, they won't be so passive the next time."

Matt realized he hadn't communicated a SITREP in over ten minutes. He was sure the eyes in the sky were aware that the shit had hit the fan just by observing the amount of tracer fire and explosions. "I need to call and find out. If they don't get here in the next few minutes we're going to move north. This hangar is about to become a bullet trap."

Matt slid the binoculars over to his chief and then reached over grabbing Cruise by the leg.

"What's up, LT?"

"I want you to fire your 40MM grenade launcher at those vehicles near the tower. Let's see if a few high explosive rounds give them a reason to stay away from us."

Cruise didn't need to reply. He nodded then smoothly jacked the antipersonnel cannister round out of the M-203 grenade launcher. Then he pulled a HE round from his vest and loaded it into the tube. Cruise took careful aim and adjusted the angle of his weapon a bit higher. The control tower was right on the edge of the grenade's effective range.

BLOOP! The forty-millimeter round shot from the black tube under his M-4 and traveled in a high lazy arch. It rose for a second or two before tilting down toward earth, accelerating and heading right for the truck on the right side of the tall building.

The HE round landed squarely in the middle of an enemy squad waiting to load into a truck. A loud CRUMP echoed across the airfield. Cruise quickly pulled the empty canister out and reloaded another HE round. The second round fired by Cruise was in the air. He again scored a direct hit, this time hitting the truck and starting a secondary explosion caused by the stored fuel.

Cruise looked at Matt to see if the officer had any more guidance. Matt winked at Cruise then checked his watch. "That's enough for right now. We need to conserve that HE ammo. We may need it later." Cruise reloaded the M-203 and relaxed.

Matt pulled out the UHF radio and thought about what to say. "THUNDER, this is X-RAY SEVEN. SITREP, time is 0527. In contact. Enemy vehicles hit near tower but more arriving. No evidence of heavy weapons yet. We can stay in position for another five minutes, over."

Matt waited. There was no response for what seemed like forever. The entire airport was revealed in the late-breaking dawn. A column of smoke rose high into the air over the control tower. It was a beacon to every armed Egyptian. The radio surprised him.

"X-RAY SEVEN, this is THUNDER. Understood. The show will begin no later than 0531. Hold your position as long as possible. Continue reporting. We are putting an AC-130 over the target in two minutes. They will check in with you on this net. Confirm."

Matt responded, confirming his understanding of the message. The chief, Jorgy, and Cruise were all close enough to have heard the exchange. "Oby, Boone, Wells, Doc. The assault force is three minutes out. Remember we'll hear the fire suppression strike on the coastal battery first. That means we will be one to two minutes away from the lead helicopters landing on the airfield. Everybody got that?"

Each SEAL acknowledged Matt's radio call in succession. He looked up at the brightening morning sky. Was he going to get off this target without losing anyone? All his thoughts of personal glory and professional recognition associated with combat operations were a distant memory. For the last four hours his only goal, the only sign of success, was to get his troop home alive.

Matt fingered the smoke grenade secured to his vest to confirm its presence. When the time came, he would toss the grenade out on the concrete parking area in front of their hangar. It should provide sufficient smoke to screen their withdrawal through the back of the hangar. Matt's UHF radio came alive.

"X-RAY SEVEN, this is CONDOR TWO TWO. Checking in over your position at two thousand five hundred feet. Any updates on your situation? Over."

Matt snatched the radio from its pouch. "Roger, this is X-RAY SEVEN. We're solid at this time. Can you see the bad guys on target, over?"

"This is CONDOR TWO TWO, that's affirmative. You have quite a party building up at the control tower. The estimate is two hundred. We see more vehicles coming your way on the main avenue leading to the target. At least two of them appear to be light armored patrol vehicles each with a main gun. We also see ten to fifteen contacts moving behind the hangar directly across from your position."

Matt glanced across the runway. He couldn't see the newcomers, but he was sure they were aware of what happened to the first patrol. These guys wouldn't be so sloppy. He needed to direct fire from the gunship, but his men needed to know the score first.

"Chief! Pass the word we have a gunship in orbit at two thousand five hundred feet. They have close to two hundred troops in the open near the tower, reinforcements inbound on the main avenue of approach to the airport, there's a couple of light armored vehicles in that convoy. The biggest threat to us is the new patrol hiding behind the hanger straight across from here." Matt pointed to the hangar and the chief nodded.

"Got it! You want Wells and Doc up here with us?"

Matt considered it but decided against the idea. If they had to run, the egress point behind the hangar was preferable to moving in the open across the front of the hangars. "No, keep that door open, chief. If the shit hits the fan we go through the hole in the fence, turn hard right, and head to the sea."

Chief Auger gave Matt a thumbs up and proceeded to tell Jorgy and Cruise the story. He had them briefed and facing the new threat across the runway, before getting on the tactical radio to bring the rest of the troop up to date.

Matt saw things were in good hands. Time to see what the big gun in the sky could do to help them. The Air Force Special Operations Wing had an arsenal of combat airframes. The AC-130 was a C-130 cargo plane, refitted with advanced avionics, computer-guided firing systems, infrared and daytime cameras for target surveillance, and weapons.

Lots of weapons. The concept of a fixed-wing gunship went back to the early days in Vietnam. In each succeeding war, the concept grew, evolved. New airframes and new technology. The airborne weapons system was capable of hitting a man or a building, with bullets, grenades, or artillery rounds.

"CONDOR TWO TWO, this is X-RAY SEVEN. Do I have the authority to direct your fire? Over?"

There was a pause and Matt's heart sank. It was nice to have the surveillance tracking all the bad guys on target, but Matt would like to have a way to deal with those threats decisively, without exposing his small team to a bloody fight.

"X-RAY SEVEN. We have confirmed you are the ground force commander until the Rangers are on deck. We are all yours."

Matt's jaw dropped. Ground force commander? Holy shit! There were precise few seconds remaining before the Rangers arrived. At least now he knew who was making the second assault attempt. What was the best use of this asset? He decided to take out the convoy first then the large gathering by the tower. That left the group straight across from their position for his guys to handle. That was manageable.

"CONDOR TWO TWO, this is X-RAY SEVEN. Fire mission. Primary target: destroy reinforcement column. Secondary target: destroy troops in the open next to the tower. Acknowledge, over."

Matt had never made a live fire mission call to an AC-130 gunship before. He was already regretting his choice of words. They would know there was a rookie on the ground telling them what to do.

"X-RAY SEVEN. Understood. Breaking to the south to engage convoy. Then we'll come back and resume orbit. The party at the tower will be dealt with at that time. Good luck down there. Be advised fire suppression mission will engage the coastal battery in sixty seconds. CONDOR TWO TWO, out."

Chapter Thirty-One

Bandar and his handpicked team drove their four-wheel drive vehicle to the northern tip of the airport on the dirt utility road that paralleled the facility to the east. Once they arrived at the end of the fence line they turned left and drove to the western side of the airport. Bandar directed the small three-truck convoy to stop once the closest hangar blocked the American's view.

He planned to approach the enemy on foot. Once close enough to attack, he would swing his soldiers out onto the runway like a door slamming shut on the American's position. The other soldiers deployed across from the invaders had served their purpose. A diversion to occupy the Americans. They had performed their part well.

Matt's voice came over the tactical radio. "The air strike is less than one minute out. Expect the assault force within two to three minutes after that. I want everyone to keep their heads on a swivel. We won't have the AC-130 back over target for a few minutes so stay sharp!"

Chief Auger's voice broke in. "LT, you have any problem with me hitting the hangar, the one those assholes are hiding behind? I've been carrying this LAAW rocket on my back forever."

Matt didn't like the idea of shooting blind or destroying property needlessly, but the chief's suggestion made tactical sense. The other option was to cede the initiative to the enemy and then react. He made his decision. "Go for it, Chief. Break, break. Standby guys, we're putting a LAAW round into the hangar where the Egyptians are hiding."

The explosion shook the hangar and Matt realized he'd never heard the weapon fired without hearing protection. The chief's shot was dead on target. The round flew through the open front of the hangar and then detonated upon impact with the back wall of the building. The LAAW was designed to kill light vehicles but it could be used to clear rooms, bunkers, and as a deterrent noise maker. If the soldiers were still back there, he mused, they were either cut up from building shrapnel or stunned and scared.

A fire started in the hangar from the explosion and from the appearance of the dark plume of smoke, the chief may have hit fuel or oil with his rocket. Nearby, Chief Auger discarded the green rocket tube and looked over at Matt, a big smile on his face. "I doubt those suckers will hang around after that!"

"I'm sure that shook them up a bit!" Matt replied.

Oby called in. "By the way boss, there's more company arriving near the tower. I thought those flyboys were dealing with that problem."

Matt looked at his watch. Where was the air strike? The gunship was taking its sweet time killing that convoy. He needed them back there, helping them deal with the small army forming at the tower. Just then he heard a series of dull thuds in rapid succession.

"It that the air strike, sir?" Wells felt blind in his position by the fence.

"No, that's the gunship taking out the reinforcement convoy. Those were 105 howitzer rounds. I counted five or six."

"I counted six," Boone piped up.

The sounds of multiple explosions that rocked the airport prevented Matt from responding to Boone's comment. They were definitely close and coming from the north. "That's it, everybody! They're taking out the anti-aircraft batteries. Rangers on deck in two to three minutes."

Matt felt his fatigue wash away. They'd accomplished the mission!

Suddenly, a torrent of lead slammed into the hangar walls and ricocheted off the concrete all around Matt.

Jorgy screamed, "I'm hit!"

Chief Auger jumped into action when he heard the scream. He was almost on top of Jorgy when he grunted and flipped into the air, twisting grotesquely in mid-flight. His body landed in a crumpled pile next to Jorgy.

Cruise was pointing and shouting frantically. He was pointing north.

Bandar wasn't a soldier, far from it, but he was keenly aware of his value as a leader. Without his presence, he had no doubt the young men formed around him would have run as soon as the American air strike began. They had little stomach for a fight, but they didn't want to lose face in from of him. They were also afraid of his power.

His men had lined up alongside the building two away from the Americans' position. They'd stayed low and the diversion, however costly, had distracted the two men on the garbage dumpster. Both Americans were still facing south when Bandar gave the order to attack.

As one, the fifteen hand-picked fighters stood up and swung out in a line until they'd formed a skirmish line facing south. They started jogging and waited as long as possible before firing. Bandar was stunned at how close they were able to get before the first American spotted them.

The initial volley was effective, the Americans were caught by surprise and they were not returning fire immediately. It might be easier than he'd hoped. He retained a few bodyguards but had stayed in place when the soldiers advanced. The air strike was an issue. He attempted to raise the battery commander directly by cell phone but there was no response.

Bandar called the tower and after connecting with the colonel it was confirmed there were no survivors. He thought for a few seconds then barked an order to a specialist in his temporary bodyguard. A man trained in using a specific weapon they'd brought with them, just in case.

The man ran north, back to the trucks, to retrieve a Russian made SA-7 surface-to-air missile system. The second attempt to take the airport was close at hand. Bandar could make things uncomfortable for the Americans if he could get the man-packed missile system in position and ready to fire. Bandar made another call to the tower.

A bullet had passed through Jorgy's right hand and shattered his weapon's pistol grip. He pivoted to align toward the north and shifted his good hand to what was left of the firing mechanism and opened fire. Cruise fired frantically at first and then settled down to deliver his shots more methodically, more accurately at the soldiers advancing in a line only thirty yards away.

Matt swiveled when he heard Jorgy scream out and as he turned, he opened up on the men advancing toward them. Boone and Oby were in the middle of the firefight. Boone rolled back and began pumping rounds into the advancing Egyptian soldiers. Oby kept watching the tower.

"Oh, shit guys!" Oby's voice shouted the warning and he fired the fifty a second later. Three trucks were racing down the runway at sixty miles an hour. One took Oby's first round in the windshield but kept coming. The sniper's second round was lower, taking out the engine and causing the truck to seize up and twist. At sixty miles an hour, the vehicle left contact with the ground and began to roll, flinging bodies out of the back as it danced across the concrete runway.

Cruise saw Oby shoot south and he immediately rolled onto his back. The remaining two trucks screeched to a stop twenty yards away and troops began pouring out of them. Cruise pumped five rounds into the surprised soldier, unfortunately, as a fast runner he was the first to die.

"Doc!" Matt screamed without thinking to use his radio. "The chief has taken a direct hit in the chest. Get your ass up here!"

Matt walked backward, still firing at the troops to the north, the survivors of this attack were on the ground and crawling toward the closest hangar. For a few seconds, the SEALs had fire superiority. When he lay down next to Chief Auger, the SEAL was making a loud gurgling noise. Matt stared at the growing pool of blood on the hangar floor under the chief's body.

Doc burst through the rear door and rounded the main hangar door just in time to shoot an Egyptian near the trucks drawing a bead on Matt. He dove to the ground near the chief and grabbed the man's combat vest. He started dragging and sliding the chief back toward the rear of the building. It was always a bad idea to treat a man in the middle of a live firefight.

Matt crawled up online with Cruise and started picking targets.

Doc got the chief all the way to the back door where Wells helped pull them both out of the line of fire.

Matt wanted to help the chief, but he knew Doc could take care of it. If they stayed there much longer, Matt realized, his team would be cut to ribbons. The troop leader glanced at his watch for the tenth time. It was 0545, where the fuck were the Rangers?

As if on cue, Matt heard the sound of an Apache helicopter gunship as it screamed overhead at one hundred feet, belching death in the form of twenty-millimeter electric cannons directed at the tower and the infantry assembled there.

"Boss!" Wells' voice cut through all the noise in Matt's ear. "Boss, throw the damn smoke!"

Matt rolled on his side and struggled for a moment to dislodge the smoke grenade attached to his vest. Matt looked north and saw a second apache heading in for a gun run. Matt pulled the pin, gauged the wind, and then tossed the grenade.

The spoon separated from the grenade with a loud pop! Green smoke began to pour out of the beer can-sized signaling device, the smoke drifting east. Jorgy was still keeping the Egyptians to the north occupied. He and Boone were able to force the remaining soldiers to abandon their attack and seek the shelter of a nearby tin building.

Bandar was screaming at his men to pull back. The stupid farm boys had executed poorly. After seizing the initiative they'd been mowed down by the Americans. Only a few had been able to crawl toward the nearest hangar and out of the withering return fire.

The Apaches meant the main assault was happening at that moment. The second attack from the tower was still in doubt. One truck down but the soldiers were still fighting. He couldn't see the full picture. He suddenly spotted a plume of green smoke, lazily drifting across the runway. Where was that missile launcher?

Bandar was beginning to have second thoughts about staying. Maybe it was best to leave this place before it was too late. A gasping sound behind him caused him to spin around and draw his personal sidearm. The weapons specialist was sweating profusely, he stood there just behind the corner of the building, the SA-7 in his hand.

"Hey, boss!" Matt could hear the alarm in Oby's voice.

He'd taken a minute to wrap Jorgy's hand. It wasn't pretty but it helped stop the bleeding.

"Go ahead!" Matt answered.

"LT, I've got two fifty-caliber rounds left. With the cavalry here blasting everything in sight I'm going to break the big gun down and help you guys fight the short fight. I don't think Boone and I can do much good up here anymore. Request permission to join you guys."

Matt thought about the request for a moment. It definitely was time to circle the wagons and get off the target. "Sure thing, Oby!" Matt agreed. "Stay low in case we have to engage those assholes to the north again. We're mustered up at the southeast corner, outside the hangar."

Boone and Oby ran around the hangar wall just as a blast of twenty-millimeter cannon rounds shredded the Egyptians deployed near the two trucks. The AC-130 was back. The Apaches had broken off their gun runs and turned over air support to the Air Force.

Oby and Boone threw themselves flat as a PAVLOW screamed by directly overhead. Boone popped a second green smoke and rolled it onto the taxiway, Matt's first grenade was petering out. Matt saw the second grenade ignite. It was time to get the hell off the main target.

Matt stood up and at a crouch started to run toward Boone and Oby. He'd changed his mind. He wanted them to head straight back to the back of the hangar to muster up with Wells, Doc, and the chief.

He saw the young officer fall from Oby's first shot then watched as his sniper killed the last Egyptian soldier foolish enough to stick around. He'd only taken a few steps when he was suddenly hit by a sledgehammer in the right leg. Matt struggled to regain his feet. Oby's voice on the radio cut through the chaos. "I see them! Rangers on the ground, Rangers on the ground! First bird on deck!"

Chapter Thirty-Two

Bandar watched as the first large helicopter landed, deploying the Americans from the rear of the aircraft. There were a lot of men. “Are you ready yet?” he shouted at the soldier fumbling with the missile launcher.

His plan was to drop the second helicopter and then escape this mess. He’d accomplished all he could at this location. If the Americans were here in force, he’d have to organize the resistance until the Americans, bled white by the jihadist warriors, put their tail between their legs and went home.

Matt fell down again. He could see the large wedge-shaped formation of Rangers spreading out over the northern end of the airport. The American helicopters were coming in, all in a line to deploy hundreds more of the elite Rangers.

Bandar watched as a second helicopter landed near the northern tip of the airport. The only way out was to the west but that took him perilously close to the American reconnaissance team. The firing from the Americans in the hangar had died off completely, possibly indicating the small unit had moved or succumbed to multiple attacks. Bandar gathered the four bodyguards closer and gave them their new instructions.

“Sir, I’m ready.” The Russian surface to air missile system was up at last.

Bandar stopped in mid-sentence. “Excellent! I want you to take out the very next helicopter that arrives. They’ve landed troops in the south and in the north, so they’ll be landing in the middle of the airport next. Do you understand?”

"Yes, sir!" The man was shaking.

Bandar almost took the weapon from him but no one else knew how to use the advanced weapon.

Behind the SEAL's hangar Doc was working frantically to save Chief Auger's life. Wells had already used the SATCOM radio to alert THUNDER that the SEALs had a critically wounded man requiring a CASEVAC unit. Doc overheard Boone call over the tactical net to tell Wells that the LT was hit.

Boone and Oby crossed the last five yards of open space and threw themselves down next to Matt. The hangar was flooding with light from the sun rising higher and higher. "Hang in there, LT!" Boone shouted as he started treating Matt's ugly thigh wound. The SEALs were formed in a horseshoe to cover all directions. Matt was lying in the middle.

"What's the picture out there?" Matt asked through clenched teeth.

Oby looked around. "The first Rangers to land are taking the control tower. The second lift landed near the northern fence line. I assume the next aircraft will start landing and deploying more men in the middle of the runway."

Matt pointed back toward the hangar that had been home for the night. "Let's get our asses back to the rest of the guys near the hole in the fence. Fall back in two groups. Cruise, me, and Jorgy go first. Oby, Boone, I want you to cover our movement. Pay attention to the north. I don't think we nailed everyone in the group that attacked us from that direction. With the Rangers moving this way they may squirt and head right into us."

"You got it, LT!" Oby responded. "Well, you heard the man! Grab him and get the hell out of here!"

Cruise lifted Matt to his feet, then helped Jorgy. Once on his feet, Jorgy was mobile enough. The three SEALs shuffled and moved into the hangar. Cruise shouted out to Wells to let him know they were receiving company. They pushed through the rear door and collapsed to form a circle. It was clear to the newcomers from the color of his face that Chief Auger was in big trouble.

Matt turned his head to look at his second in command. The gurgling sound coming out of his mouth gave Matt a sinking feeling. The SEAL chief was struggling for his life. He'd been hit in the lung and that wasn't good. Doc knew his stuff, but out there he wouldn't be able to do much for a collapsed lung. Matt rose up on his elbows to get a final head count. "Okay, Wells, call Oby and Boone, tell them to get their asses back here and join us."

Bandar could hear firefights all around them as the Rangers began cleaning out the Egyptians one position at a time. At least some of the soldiers were fighting back, he thought to himself. His plan was simple. He would move west, sticking tightly to the back of the hangars.

Once clear of the airport he would return to Cairo and organize the Egyptian military counterattack. The Americans may have secured an airport, but conquering Egypt was another thing altogether. This land had swallowed up invading armies for centuries. This was only a minor setback. The men who died here today would be avenged!

The sound of a C-130 cargo plane making its approach filled the air. Bandar turned and stared in disbelief. Not a helicopter carrying forty men but a cargo plane. He turned to the weapons specialist and pointed to the plane. "Now, you idiot! NOW!"

Bandar watched as the soldier stepped a few feet away to clear his back-blast area and raised the weapon to his shoulder. This would be much easier than training, Bandar mused. The target was so close his man couldn't miss. He saw the soldier begin to apply pressure to the firing mechanism.

Boone yelled, then pointed, but didn't wait for Oby to orient himself. He dropped to one knee and let the air in his lungs halfway out and then held his breath. The trigger eased back slowly, be surprised, be surprised, Boone kept saying to himself. He'd only have time for one shot.

The sound of Boone's rifle firing was the last sound the weapons specialist ever heard. Boone's round took him in the right side of the head, a misty spray of pink blood erupted from the opposite side of his head as he shuddered and then sank to the ground.

Oby had acquired the target and was ready to fire if Boone had missed. He watched the kill through the high-powered scope mounted on his M-4 rifle. His laser Aimpoint was switched on and he began to control his breathing.

Bandar watched the surface to air weapon clatter to the ground. The C-130 cargo plane was only a few feet off the runway, it was now or never. Bandar took three quick steps forward and began to pick up the weapon. The soldier to his left tried frantically to get his master's attention. Stuttering incoherently, interrupting his thoughts.

"What? What red dot, you imbecile?" The sergeant was pointing at Bandar's forehead, but the jihadist leader couldn't appreciate the warning.

Oby squeezed the trigger of his suppressed M-4 carbine and saw with satisfaction that his aim had once again been true. The loud man picking up the surface to air weapon flipped violently backward and then laid still, a small hole in his forehead oozing blood. Just another dead asshole, Oby thought. Maybe the others will disperse now. He put the laser on the weapons missile tube and fired two rounds into the weapon to disable it. The rest of the Egyptians ran away.

Bandar couldn't hear the sound of his men throwing their weapons down. He didn't see the plane land or see the Rangers spreading out toward his men. The bodyguards were tearing off their uniforms and running in terror from the approaching Americans. Bandar's eyes were frozen open, staring blankly at the dawn sky.

Oby stood over Matt trying to tell him something about a great headshot. Matt couldn't focus. He knew that he'd lost a lot of blood and he was beginning to drift in and out. His fatigued mind began to wander, back to a time when only one thing mattered in life. Capturing the love and respect of a rugged old Marine. Matt could still hear Oby chattering, but it seemed like he was a million miles away. He passed out.

When Matt woke up, he couldn't shake the mental fog. There seemed to be new faces around him, people he didn't know. Army medics were working on the Chief and attending to Matt's swollen leg.

A Ranger squad was deployed around the SEAL's hangar. The SDV troop had moved into the hangar to get out of the blazing Egyptian sun and to give the medics more room to work. Matt shot back into full consciousness when the medic started the IV in his arm. The medics had stabilized Chief Auger for the flight back to the carrier, placing a tube into his collapsed lung and inflating it sufficiently enough for him to breathe. Doc saw Matt looking over at the chief. He leaned over Matt.

"He's going to make it, LT! The chief's going to pull through!"

"Jorgy? How's his hand? Anyone else hit?"

Doc placed his hand on the officer's shoulder. "Jorgy's fine. The bullet went straight through, no major damage. You and chief are it, everyone else is tired but all in one piece, thanks to you, sir."

The Ranger sergeant barked out a few words and the Rangers went into motion. The Rangers lifted Matt and Chief Auger up and transported them to the edge of the runway.

The CASEVAC helicopter was only minutes away. To Matt's right, Chief Auger had just regained consciousness. The medic told the chief he had lost a lot of blood, but he'd be okay. As the sound of the fast-approaching helicopter began to build, Matt looked over at the chief and yelled.

"Well chief, we did it!"

Chief Auger looked over at Matt and shook his head slightly. "No boss, you did it! You're bringing all our guys home." Chief Auger reached out to Matt, gripping his hand.

"Anytime, anywhere, LT!"

"Anytime, anywhere, chief!" Matt responded in kind before passing out. "Anytime, anywhere…"

Made in the USA
Columbia, SC
02 October 2021

46566055R00174